Praise for *Last Bus to Coffeeville*

'exceptionally good… the characters and plot are fantastic
and I really couldn't praise it enough'
– *Bookseller*

'I found myself laughing out loud with the characters.
I really enjoyed this story'
– Jane Brown, *Book Depository*

'A wonderful cast of eccentric people in the best tradition
of old-time American writers like Capote and Keillor.
I was enthralled throughout and recommend it to
anyone who wants a feel-good read'
– *New Books Magazine*

'There is heartbreak… black humour… and the charm
of *The Unlikely Pilgrimage of Harold Fry*'
– *Daily Mail*

'A fascinating and poignant novel'
– *Woman's World*

'… the shimmering humour and life values Henderson explores
are certainly something you wouldn't want to miss'
– *The Star Online*

'A funny road trip story… but this brave debut novel also tackles
sensitive issues and does so in a confident manner'
– *We Love This Book*

'Deftly handled with an offbeat humour and a
of worldly compassion'
– *Sunday Sport*

'J. Paul Henderson is someone to watch out f
– *The Bookbag*

THE LAST OF THE BOWMANS

J. Paul Henderson

NO EXIT PRESS

First published in 2016 by No Exit Press,
an imprint of Oldcastle Books Ltd,
PO Box 394, Harpenden,
Herts, AL5 1XJ, UK

noexit.co.uk
@noexitpress

ISBN
978-1-84344-277-6 (Print)
978-1-84344-278-3 (Epub)
978-1-84344-279-0 (Kindle)
978-1-84344-280-6 (Pdf)

2 4 6 8 10 9 7 5 3 1

Typeset by Avocet Typeset, Somerton, Somerset
in 11.5pt Minion Pro
Printed in Denmark by Nørhaven, Viborg

For the Uncle Franks of this world

ACKNOWLEDGEMENTS

Opening credits: Jimmy Two-Crowns, John, Keshini, Mike, Poh Eng, Rich (literally), Sheila, Steve, Steven, Trevor and Val.
Exiting credits: Claire, Clare and Ion.

16 JUNE 2012

Lyle Bowman was an old man with a sweet tooth, though which of his twelve remaining teeth the adage referred to is unknown.

He was in the downstairs hallway, painting an area of scuffed skirting board, when the day's sugar craving hit. Immediately he walked to the kitchen and placed his paintbrush in a jar of white spirit, wiped his hands on a damp cloth and pulled on his jacket. What he needed, he decided, was a Cadbury's Double Decker.

He was about to leave the house when he remembered the sachet of antibiotics he'd dissolved in water that morning and forgotten to drink. (His dentist, Mr Blum, had insisted on him completing a three-day course of the drug before extracting yet another of his teeth that had loosened in the gum.)

'Teeth!' Lyle sighed, and downed the liquid in one.

He was prepared for the unpleasantness of the taste, but was surprised by the heat of the liquid as it passed down his throat. He grimaced, the same way he did after swallowing a tablespoonful of cod liver oil, and reached in his pocket for a peppermint.

'Blooming dentists!' Lyle sighed.

Lyle locked the front door behind him and walked up the garden path. He saw Mrs Turton standing at the next-door window and waved to her. She waved back and smiled. He fumbled with the catch on the wrought-iron gate and set off for the local shops.

Lyle Bowman had never once in his life been drunk and was therefore incapable of recognising the tell-tale signs of inebriation. A glass of sherry on Christmas Day, and the occasional half pint of beer during the year, had made for a lifetime consumption of probably no more than 250 units. Consequently, he placed the feeling of light-headedness – and his increasingly unsteady gait – at the feet of the magnolia paint fumes he'd been breathing, and reminded himself to open the window when he returned home.

He entered the shop and made his way uncertainly to the shelves where the confectionery was displayed. Eventually, he found the Double Decker he was looking for and took it to the check-out. There, he faffed in his trouser pocket for a pound coin and, at last, placed it on the counter.

'That's 72p,' the assistant said.

'72p?' Lyle slurred. 'They're only 57p across the road. That makes your price…' He struggled to calculate the exact price difference, and was reduced to ending his sentence on a less emphatic note – 'a lot more expensive.'

'I just work here, mate, I don't set the prices,' the assistant shrugged. 'Now do you want the Double Decker or don't you?'

'I don't!' Lyle said, a little more aggressively than he usually spoke to people. 'I'm taking my business across the road.'

It was a bad decision.

Rather than walk to the zebra crossing, Lyle took the more direct route – or, at least, it would have been more direct if he hadn't traversed it diagonally – and crossed the road at a bend where motorists and pedestrians were blind to each other.

It was here that Lyle Bowman made his fateful acquaintance with a bus.

A small crowd gathered and stood around his unmoving body, keeping him company while the ambulance arrived.

'I think he's trying to say something,' one of the bystanders said.

A man in his twenties knelt down by Lyle's side.

'Double Decker,' Lyle sighed softly.

'No, it was a single-decker,' the young man replied helpfully. 'One of those small buses.'

Lyle Bowman died in the ambulance on his way to hospital. He was eighty-three years old.

1

Bamboo

Three weeks later, Lyle Bowman was lying in a bamboo coffin at the front of a small crematory chapel. It was unusual for him to be the centre of such attention.

Although the summer was at its height, a low pressure system had moved in from the west and the day of the funeral was one of grey skies and rain. Barometric gloom shook hands with atmospheric gloom and, to Mrs Turton's way of thinking, made for the perfect funeral. She turned to her son Barry, who was sitting next to her.

'I think God's sad that Mr Bowman's dead,' she whispered. 'The raindrops are His tears.'

Barry, who was as credulous as his mother, nodded in agreement. He looked at his watch. 'I'm supposed to pick Diane up from the hairdresser's at twelve,' he whispered back. 'Shouldn't the service have started by now?'

The same thought was running through The Reverend Tinkler's mind. Conscious that mourners for the next funeral would soon be arriving, and aware of the crematorium's reputation for gridlock, he approached Lyle's eldest son, who was sitting with his wife and young daughter.

'I'm sorry, Billy, but I think we need to start.'

Billy looked flustered and turned again to the rear door.

'Face it, Billy, he's not coming,' his wife said sharply. 'He never made an effort to see your father while he was alive, so why on earth do you think he's going to make an effort now?'

'But he promised, Jean,' Billy replied. 'He said he'd be here.'

'Go ahead and start,' Jean told The Reverend. 'I don't want the service to end before Katy's had a chance to sing her song.'

Billy reluctantly nodded his acquiescence and The Reverend Tinkler walked to the podium. He stood there silently for a moment and surveyed the congregation, wondered if so few people would gather for his own funeral when the time came. Even though a modest man by nature, he was still hoping for more than twelve.

Unaware of The Reverend's private reflections, the small congregation returned his gaze expectantly, no one more so than Lyle's younger brother Frank, who was wrestling with the volume control of his hearing-aid.

'Turn it down, Uncle Frank,' Billy whispered. 'It's whistling.'

'What's he saying then?' Uncle Frank replied. 'I can't hear a damn word!'

'He's not saying anything,' Billy explained.

'Why not? You paid the man, didn't you?'

'Of course I did – and keep your voice down: you're shouting.'

'Well, what's he doing then? Holding out for more money?'

'He's just gathering his thoughts. Look – he's about to start.'

As if on cue, The Reverend Tinkler coughed gently and welcomed the gathered few. They were there, he said, not to mourn the passing of Lyle Bowman but to celebrate his life, and suggested they start by singing 'O Happy Home' – though just the first and last verses, as time was now short.

On hearing the name Lyle Bowman, two of the congregation rose from their seats and headed for the exit, explaining to the persons nearest to them that they were at the wrong funeral.

(It was fortunate for Lyle, The Reverend Tinkler reflected, that no quorum was required for such occasions.)

Billy, who had presumed the couple to have been his distant cousins, Beryl and Kenneth, turned to Uncle Frank and queried their absence.

'They've been dead for six years,' Uncle Frank answered matter-of-factly. 'They drowned on holiday.'

'Well, I never,' Billy said, and passed on the news to Jean.

The ten remaining members of the congregation went ahead and sang the hymn, and at its conclusion The Reverend Tinkler read a passage from the Bible. He then closed the Book and took some index cards from the inside pocket of his jacket.

He'd lost count of the funerals he'd conducted over the years, barely remembered the names of the deceased he'd eulogised, and only ever recalled the number of six-by-four cards each life had warranted. Although, on occasion, a departed loved one had called for fifteen such cards, the average was nearer six, and Lyle's life had been reduced to two: one which spoke of the man Lyle was, and the other – importantly – of the man Lyle wasn't.

The Reverend Tinkler had never met Lyle Bowman and had therefore relied heavily on Billy's disjointed and elliptical memories of his father for the basis of his address. To ensure that a retelling of Lyle's life would run for more than three minutes, however, he'd been forced to add stock phrases and throw in a philosophy of life based on personal experience. Even so, and despite several redrafts, he was aware that this wasn't one of his finer encomiums, and was still troubled by some of the segueing.

'People come and people go in a person's life,' The Reverend Tinkler intoned. 'Some leave memories that bring a smile to our faces long after their lives have ended, while others simply haunt our subconscious like an uninvited guest.'

This latter classification included his ex-wife Joan who, despite holding a senior position in the Blood Transfusion Unit, had run off with a Jehovah's Witness.

'Lyle Bowman belongs to the former category,' The Reverend smiled. 'He was a good man, a quiet man; a man who sighed a lot and a man who kept himself to himself. He didn't live life on the grand scale, and neither did he strive to do so.'

And neither, in fact, did The Reverend Tinkler. A constant source of friction between him and his ex-wife had been his lack of ambition; while Joan had aspired to be the wife of a rural bishop, he'd been more than happy to remain the vicar of a small parish in a northern industrial city.

'Lyle was born here, grew up here and lived his entire life here,' The Reverend continued.

'He didn't like cats.

'A bright child, he gained a place at the local grammar school and, on leaving, bought a parrot and went to work for a local firm of accountants. Though no one blamed the parrot, shortly after its purchase Lyle developed a painful form of rheumatoid arthritis and was confined to bed for long periods. Unable to work on a regular basis, the firm of accountants he'd only recently joined terminated his contract – something, I'm glad to say, that wouldn't happen in this day and age.

'Two years later, however – and once the condition had eased – Lyle found work as a packer in the dress department of a ladies' mantle manufacturing company, and remained there for the next fifty years. At the time of his retirement, he was not only managing the coat department but was also a director of the company.

'After the parrot died, Lyle gave the cage to the Salvation Army.

'Lyle Bowman will be remembered by some as a particular man, a man who placed as much emphasis on the correct usage of the gerund as he did to wearing a collar and tie or polishing his shoes. Above all, he will be remembered as a family man – a loving husband, father, grandfather and brother – and nothing in life is more pleasing to God than a loving family man.'

This too had been a source of contention between The Reverend and his ex-wife. Although they'd never actually discussed the subject of children before marrying, he'd naturally assumed that, in due course, they would have a family, and was therefore shocked when Joan had refused point blank to bear him either sons or daughters. Shortly thereafter, she'd also refused to submit to any of his sexual advances, and The Reverend Tinkler was left a reluctant celibate with the beginnings of carpal tunnel syndrome in his right wrist.

'Lyle married late in life to a young woman who accidentally spilt custard over his brown supervisor's coat. It was a marriage made in Heaven, or as Lyle used to joke, in the staff canteen.'

There was a ripple of polite laughter – in truth, rather less than The Reverend had hoped for – and he paused for only a moment.

'Mary proved a loving wife,' he continued, 'and the happiest years of Lyle's life were spent in her company. They enjoyed Old-Time dancing, going to performances of Gilbert & Sullivan operas and listening to the music of Jim Reeves.

'Mary didn't like cats either.

'Sadly, Mary's death was untimely, and it was left to Lyle to raise their two sons – Billy, who's sitting here at the front with his wife Jean and daughter Katy; and Gregory, who, unfortunately, can't be with us today.'

'How come he didn't mention me by name?' Uncle Frank asked Billy.

Billy was in no fit state to reply and ignored the question. Tears welled from his eyes and his body shook silently. The minister noticed Billy's upset and immediately his own spirits rose. With one card to go, it was obvious that things were going well.

'I mentioned earlier that Lyle lived his life on the small scale,' The Reverend Tinkler continued. 'That his death was splashed over the front page of the local newspaper is therefore a matter of some irony. Some of you might remember reading the editorial that questioned the nature of a society that abandoned its old people to the margins and left them there to die of loneliness or, in Lyle's case, turpentine poisoning.

'Billy has asked me to set the record straight. Lyle Bowman was not an alcoholic – and certainly hadn't been drinking turpentine on the day of his death. He had, in fact, been drinking white spirit, but more to the point had done so accidentally. Lyle Bowman was no toper.

'Lyle had in fact been painting the house before his death and, after mistakenly placing his brush in a glass of liquid antibiotics, had inadvertently drunk the jar of white spirit. It was a mix-up that caused not only his death but – as his brother Frank wryly noted – also ruined a good paintbrush.'

'Now he mentions me, the daft bugger!' Uncle Frank grumbled. 'I didn't want that made public.'

'It goes without saying that Lyle would be with us today if he'd used the zebra crossing that morning. And it's also more than likely he'd still be here if he'd crossed the road directly, instead of diagonally.

'I don't know why,' The Reverend Tinkler mused, 'but old people tend to cross roads at an angle rather than taking the shortest route – and this is a recipe for disaster. If Lyle's death is to have any meaning then we, as his friends, have to learn from it and signal its lesson to others.

'Now, can anyone tell me what that lesson is?'

'Don't get old,' Uncle Frank chuntered.

'I was rather thinking of something else, Frank,' The Reverend Tinkler smiled.

'That we should never cross roads diagonally,' Mrs Turton said primly.

'Bull's eye, Mrs Turton! Well done!' The Reverend said, and slowly repeated her words. 'Never. Cross roads. Diagonally.'

Uncle Frank glanced at Mrs Turton and scowled.

The Reverend Tinkler fell silent for a moment and looked at the congregation meaningfully. He then returned the two index cards to his pocket and announced that Katy Bowman was going to sing her grandfather's favourite song.

Katy jumped to her feet and stepped out to face the congregation. Jean nodded to The Reverend Tinkler and the minister pressed a button – evidently the wrong one, as the bamboo coffin containing Lyle's body started to move in the direction of the oven. The Reverend quickly reversed its progress and then pressed the button he'd originally intended. Music started to play and Katy to sing: *Oh baby, baby...*

Katy not only sang the words but danced to the music, sashaying suggestively from side to side and occasionally foraying up the central aisle.

'I didn't know Mr Bowman was a Britney Spears fan,' Barry Turton whispered to his mother.

'Neither did I, Barry,' Mrs Turton said disapprovingly. 'I think it's more likely that this is one of Katy's favourite songs. That girl is such a show off!'

The same thought was running through The Reverend Tinkler's mind. He'd had no idea that this was the song Katy had chosen to perform. He'd been expecting something more along the lines of 'Grandad', a song made famous when he and Joan were still a couple and the subject of children not yet broached. He was consequently relieved when Katy sang *Hit me baby one more time* for the last time.

Katy returned to her seat frowning. 'There was no applause, Mummy. No one clapped.'

Jean explained that it wasn't the custom for people to

applaud in churches or crematoria, but assured her daughter that she'd sung the song beautifully. Once they returned home, she told Katy, they'd add her performance at the crematorium to her CV and give it a glowing review.

The congregation bowed its head and The Reverend Tinkler led the mourners through a series of uneventful prayers. He then invited them to spend a brief moment remembering Lyle in ways more particular to themselves, and the chapel duly fell silent. No sooner had this period of quiet reflection commenced, however, than it was rudely interrupted by a loud squelching noise.

Katy was the first to turn and see the man. He was tall and suntanned, with long blonde hair swept back from his eyes and wearing Bermuda shorts, a Hawaiian shirt and flip-flops. She nudged her father. 'What's that surfer man doing here?'

Billy turned and smiled. 'That's your Uncle Greg, Katy. I told you he'd be here!'

It was the first time the two brothers had seen each other in seven years.

Beech

The Beech Hotel was located five miles from the crematorium, close to the moors. Although the establishment had six bedrooms, the last overnight guest had paid his bill more than three years ago and the hotel now made its living from weekend carveries and catering private functions. A banner hung from the outside wall advising people to *Book Early for Christmas*. The month was July.

Just after midday on this cold and rainy summer's day, five cars crunched over the gravel of the Beech Hotel's forecourt and came to a halt close to the entrance. Although the management had been asked to provide food for eighteen, in the event only eleven people climbed out of the cars: Billy, Jean and Katy Bowman, accompanied by Jean's widowed mother, Betty Halliwell; Greg Bowman and Uncle Frank; Mrs Turton and Lyle's oldest surviving friend, Syd Butterfield; Ian and Margaret Collard, neighbours of Mrs Turton, but no longer on speaking terms with her; and The Reverend Tinkler.

While Billy went to speak with the manager, Greg made his way to the bar and ordered drinks for the mourners. He shivered. It was as cold inside the hotel as it was outside and, judging from the clunking noises coming from the radiators, it was clear that the heating had only just been turned on. He now regretted not wearing warmer clothes for the journey, but how was he to have known that the plane would suffer technical difficulties and make a forced landing in Iceland?

And there, he surmised, was the probable location of his suitcase.

Uncle Frank sidled up to him and tapped him on the forearm. 'You look half-starved daft, lad,' he said. 'Buy yourself a brandy – that'll warm you up. What are you getting me?'

'Half a bitter – that's what you usually drink, isn't it?'

'It is, but today I'm drinking a pint,' Uncle Frank replied. 'I've just said goodbye to my brother.'

Greg turned to the small man and smiled. 'It's good to see you again, Uncle Frank.'

Uncle Frank noticed a glint when Greg turned to him and studied his nephew carefully. 'What in God's name is that thing in your ear – a ring?'

'It's a diamond stud,' Greg replied. 'Cyndi bought it for me.'

'Hell's bells, Greg. I never figured you for a big girl's blouse!'

Greg laughed. 'Everyone's wearing them these days, Uncle Frank. Even cowboys.'

'Not real cowboys,' Uncle Frank sneered. 'All the real cowboys are dead.'

'We can discuss that later,' Greg said. 'In the meantime, can you take this tray of drinks to Jean's table: white wine for her and her mother, a pint for Billy, orange juices for Mrs Turton and Katy, and a dry sherry for The Reverend Tinkler.'

Uncle Frank went off with the tray and the barman placed more drinks on the counter.

'It was lager you asked for, wasn't it?' Greg called to Syd Butterfield.

Syd came over to join him. 'Please, Greg. Ask him to put a splash of lime in it, will you?'

Syd was in his late seventies, as much hair growing from his ears and nostrils as there was from the top of his head. He was a tall man – taller than Greg – but had a thin frame and a stoop that made him appear smaller. He'd met Lyle at a refuse dump nearly twenty years earlier, and it was there that they'd struck up a friendship.

Lyle had been struggling to lift an old television set from the boot of his car when Syd – who had just off-loaded eight bags of leylandii clippings – had offered his help. In the ensuing conversation it had become apparent that the two men had much in common: neither could understand why council employees – whose employment, after all, was dependent on the taxes they paid – were allowed to sit around smoking cigarettes and drinking mugs of tea when patrons of the dump were visibly in need of their help; and both, it turned out, had a keen interest in the music of Gilbert & Sullivan. Syd had even joined the local G&S Society and still appeared in amateur productions.

'I read your first book,' Syd said to Greg. 'It was an impressive piece of research. Who'd have thought the US government would drop bombs on its own people – even though they were miners? I bet Arthur Scargill didn't know that or he'd have milked it for all it was worth. Your dad and me weren't happy when the miners in this country went on strike, but we never for a moment thought that the government should drop bombs on them!'

He paused for a moment, sipping the pint that had been placed in front of him, and then pronounced it perfect.

'Your dad liked the book too, but he thought you weren't using the gerund properly. I've never understood the rule myself so I can't comment, but it certainly didn't spoil the writing for me. Very fluid. Of course, your dad believed that the only writer who ever did grasp the gerund was Charles Dickens, but I can't say I've read any of his books – not since I left school, anyway. They're too depressing for my liking, and when you've lost your wife to cancer they're not the kind of books you want to read.'

Greg was nodding in agreement when Billy interrupted the two men. 'Sorry to cut in, Syd, but can I have a quick word with Greg?'

'No problem, Billy,' Syd said. 'I'll go and sit with the Collards. No one seems to be talking to them.'

Billy waited while Syd left with his pint and then lowered his voice. 'When it comes to the meal, Greg, can you take charge of one table and I'll take charge of the other? Obviously, I'd have liked the two of us to sit together on a day like today, but I'm afraid it's not going to be possible…' He looked around the room to make sure no one could overhear him and then continued.

'Mrs Turton and the Collards haven't spoken to each other for five years, and Mrs Turton says she's not prepared to sit with them. And Jean's mother can't stand to be in the same room as Uncle Frank never mind sit at the same table. I think the safest thing is for me to have Jean, her mother, Katy, Mrs Turton and The Reverend Tinkler on my table, and for you to have Uncle Frank, Syd and the Collards on yours. That way it doesn't look like we're ignoring anyone. Is this okay with you?'

'Sure,' Greg said. 'Do I need to start rounding people up?'

'Not yet,' Billy replied. 'We've got another ten minutes before they start serving the tomato soup.'

The mourners, apart from Uncle Frank and The Reverend Tinkler, had already split into the aforementioned groups of their own accord, and Greg went to sit with Syd and the Collards.

'Margaret and I are very sorry about your dad, Greg,' Ian Collard told him. 'He was a real gentleman, one of the old school. We always said that, didn't we, Margaret? Always said it was a pity more people weren't like Mr Bowman. And your mother, she was a lovely lady too – such a beautiful smile.'

Greg thanked them and took a sip of brandy.

'You've learnt some fancy ways in America, haven't you?' Margaret said, indicating the brandy.

'I'm not sure about that, Margaret. I'm just trying to get warm.'

'If you don't mind me asking you, Greg: why are you dressed like that?' Ian asked.

'My suitcase went missing,' Greg answered. 'The plane I was on developed a fault and had to be diverted to Iceland. They put everyone on a flight to Shannon and then on another one to Heathrow, and in the confusion some of the luggage went missing. That's why I was late for the funeral. What did I miss, by the way? I haven't had a chance to catch up with Billy.'

'Well, Katy sang a lovely song…' Margaret started to say.

'I don't think your dad would have liked it, Greg,' Syd said, shaking his head. 'It was one of those pop songs, and your dad hated pop songs. The girl would have done better singing something from *The Pirates of Penzance* or *The Mikado*. That would have been more to your dad's liking.'

'I think you're right, Syd,' Ian said. 'If Mr Bowman was anything, he was a man of the old school. His radio was always tuned to either Radio 3 or Radio 4.'

'And why the hell did they put him in a bamboo coffin?' Syd asked. 'I'm not sure your dad would have liked that. It's not as if he was an environmentalist or anything.'

'I have to agree with you there, Syd,' Ian said. 'Mr Bowman was a traditionalist.'

'The Reverend Tinkler spoke well, though,' Margaret Collard said. 'I thought he really brought your father to life.'

'He did,' Syd agreed, 'but what was all that stuff about cats and parrots? I never once heard Lyle mention either. Do you know anything about this, Greg?'

'I know my mother didn't like cats, but I can't remember my father passing comment one way or another. As for parrots, I think that's a question we'll have to ask my uncle.'

Uncle Frank was standing in the corner of the lounge talking animatedly with The Reverend Tinkler. The conversation had started innocently enough, but had then taken an unexpected turn.

'So, Frank,' the minister had started by saying, 'I gather you're the confirmed bachelor of the family.'

'It's not by choice, if that's what you're thinking, Reverend. By the way, what's your first name? Can I call you by that?'

'Of course you can, Frank – it's Bill.'

'Okay, Bill, going back to what we were saying. I'm a bachelor, yes; but I'm not a bachelor by choice. My hat's always been in the ring, it's just that no woman's ever bothered to bend down and pick it up. I don't think women find me all that attractive if you want to know the truth. Jean's mother refers to me as a goblin – did you know that?'

'No, I didn't, but I'm sure she means it as a term of endearment.'

'When was the last time you ever heard goblin used as a term of endearment?' Uncle Frank snorted. 'What love letter has ever started with the words *my dear goblin*?'

The Reverend Tinkler pretended to give the question some thought.

'I'll make it simple for you, Bill: if you were a woman, would *you* ask me out?'

'That's a difficult one, Frank,' The Reverend Tinkler said. 'A bit too hypothetical.'

'Okay then, what if you were a shirt-lifter: one of those blokes who find other men attractive. Would you ask me out then?'

The Reverend Tinkler placed a finger between his dog collar and neck and breathed deeply. Why, he wondered, had he ever started this conversation? All he'd been trying to do was be polite and engage in some light-hearted banter, and now he was being forced into an explanation of the church's position on homosexuality which, to his way of thinking, appeared to change every second month of the year. It was at times like this that he wished he'd entered the priesthood. If nothing else, the Catholic Church had certainty.

Fortunately, he was spared from having to give an exposition on the church's current thinking by Greg, who arrived to tell them it was time to take their seats for lunch.

'I'll sit with you, Bill,' Uncle Frank said.

'The Reverend Tinkler's sitting with Billy and Jean,' Greg explained. 'You're with me.'

'But I want to ask Bill about Noah's Ark,' Uncle Frank protested.

'You can ask him later,' Greg said. 'There are a number of us here who want to ask you about parrots!'

He then guided his uncle to the table where the Collards and Syd Butterfield were already sitting.

It was a seating arrangement of in-crowds and out-crowds, and it was no surprise to Greg that he'd been placed on the latter table. He wondered for a moment if Billy had purposely exaggerated the disagreements in the room and that the real problem still rested with them – that this was the true reason they were sitting at different tables. There was, after all, no cause to believe that the silence of the last seven years had changed anything.

'What were you talking to Uncle Frank about?' Jean asked The Reverend Tinkler.

'Nothing in particular,' The Reverend replied nonchalantly. 'He's quite a character, isn't he?'

'That's one way of describing him,' Betty Halliwell chuntered.

'Barry sends his apologies for not being here, Billy, but he had to pick Diane up from the hairdresser's,' Mrs Turton said. 'He wondered about bringing her, but in the end decided against it. They're both on diets, you see, and I'm afraid Diane doesn't have much willpower.'

Barry and his wife had been fat for as long as Billy could remember, and he was intrigued to know why they were now dieting.

'Diane needs a new hip,' Mrs Turton explained, 'and the doctors say she has to lose weight before they operate. Barry's just doing the diet to give her moral support.' She turned to The Reverend Tinkler and clarified her statement. 'Barry's naturally big boned,' she said.

'That's one way of describing him,' Betty Halliwell thought.

Mrs Turton then turned to Katy. 'That was a beautiful song you sang at the service, dear. How long were you practising it?'

'About three months,' Katy said. 'I was good, wasn't I?'

Betty Halliwell put an arm around her granddaughter and kissed her on the cheek. 'You were wonderful, darling. One day you're going to be a star.'

'I know,' Katy said. 'And Mummy says I have to look beyond television.'

'First things first,' Billy advised. 'First you have to do well at school and then go to university. If things don't work out, you'll need a good education to fall back on.'

Katy looked at her father open-mouthed. 'I'm not going to fail, Daddy! Failure's not an option – is it, Mummy?'

(Failure was always an option, Billy thought. Mindless repetition of a mantra learned at performance school couldn't change that. The sooner his daughter came to terms with the idea, the better.)

'No it's not!' Jean said. 'Just because Daddy sells books for a living doesn't mean that you can't do something with your life.'

Billy ignored the comment: he'd heard it all before.

The Reverend Tinkler dipped a toe into the silence. 'It was an interesting idea to place Lyle in a bamboo coffin,' he said. 'What made you think of that?'

'That was my idea,' Jean said. 'I did it for the planet, Reverend, and I'm hoping that other people will follow my example. It's no secret that the earth's resources are finite, and it's the duty of my generation to conserve them for future generations. I don't want Katy growing up in a world without trees, and while mahogany – and probably oak now – are endangered species, bamboo is plentiful.'

'It's also cheap,' Billy added, 'and the difference between what we'd have paid for a traditional casket and what we paid for the bamboo casket is going towards a photocopier for Katy's performance school. The principal's agreed to put a plaque in memory of my father on the wall next to it.'

'That's very laudable,' The Reverend Tinkler said admiringly. 'It's a pity more people don't take recycling as seriously as you do.'

'That bamboo wasn't recycled, Reverend Tinkler. It was brand new!' Jean said firmly. 'Besides, Billy and I don't recycle. We believe that's the job of local government. We pay enough council tax as it is and we don't see it as our responsibility to wash out cans and sort rubbish into containers.'

'I don't recycle either,' Mrs Turton confessed. 'I've heard they lump all the refuse together anyway – sorted and unsorted – and Barry says there are enough mountains of paper and plastic in the world already. To my way of thinking, it's more important that we stamp out littering. If we can do that, then Barry says the crime rate will fall automatically. He's always said that the basis of any ordered society is clean streets.'

'I completely agree with you there, Mrs Turton,' Betty Halliwell said. 'I get too depressed for words when I drive through the city now – paper blowing all over the place and broken bottles and cans on the pavements and in the gutters. It's like visiting a Third World country. I'm just glad Henry isn't here to see it.'

'Barry says we're not even a Third World country these days. He says that when the asylum seekers came to this city, the average standard of living actually went up.'

Betty Halliwell shook her head in despair.

The Reverend Tinkler now regretted starting this conversation too. How, he wondered, had a simple question about bamboo coffins led to this?

'Was Henry your husband?' he asked Betty, determined to steer the conversation into less troubled waters.

'He was,' Betty Halliwell replied. 'And if you ever had anything wrong with your feet, then Henry was the man to go to. He was the best chiropodist for miles around.'

Billy squirmed uneasily, moved his feet from under the table to under his chair and wiped a bead of sweat from his forehead.

'Are you alright, Daddy?' Katy asked.

'Yes, I'm fine thanks, love. I'm just missing your granddad.'

'I can't believe there were so few people at the funeral,' Betty Halliwell said. 'When we buried Henry there were well over 150 in the church. Didn't your father have many friends?'

'Not many,' Billy replied. 'He was never much of a socialiser – especially after my mother died – and most of his friends are already dead. To tell you the truth, I don't think he ever expected more than six people at his funeral, so I think he'd have been happy with eleven.'

'Actually there were twelve people,' The Reverend Tinkler said. 'A young woman came into the chapel during the singing of the first hymn and slipped out just after the blessing.'

'I wonder who that was,' Billy said.

'Well, for most of the time, Billy, there *were* only eleven of us,' Jean said. 'Your brother only made it in time for the final hymn and the committal. You'd have thought he might have made more of an effort – and at least worn a suit!'

'I've already explained this to you, Jean. Greg had problems with his flights and his suitcase has gone missing. He didn't turn up late on purpose.'

Jean looked unconvinced, but said no more.

A waitress gathered the empty soup bowls and told the mourners to help themselves to the cold buffet.

Mrs Turton noticed the Collards standing at the buffet table, no doubt in her mind they were filling their plates with all the prawn mayonnaise sandwiches and leaving the cheese and hams for everyone else. She leaned across to Betty Halliwell and whispered that the Collards were common people who would no doubt take all the chocolate biscuits as well.

Betty, too, was holding back from visiting the table: Uncle Frank was loitering there and she had no desire to be dragged into conversation with him. When, eventually, she saw him leave, his plate piled high with sandwiches, she raised herself from the chair and took her own plate to the buffet. She'd only just started making her selection when Uncle Frank – having forgotten to take any sausage rolls – suddenly reappeared.

'Hello, Betty,' he said.

'Hello, Frank,' she replied cautiously.

There was then a prolonged silence while Uncle Frank thought of a follow-up question.

'What did you have for your tea yesterday?' he asked eventually.

'I don't have tea, Frank. I eat dinner,' she said somewhat curtly.

Uncle Frank was unsurprised by her condescension, but it still annoyed him. 'Well what did you eat for your dinner then – tripe?'

He knew this jibe would sting. Betty hated to be reminded of her past; hated the fact that it had been the sale of entrails that had allowed her to attend boarding school and mix with the class of person she now did.

'I had lamb chops if you must know, with some broccoli and dauphinoise potatoes,' she said, resolved to stay calm.

'Very tasty,' Uncle Frank said, smacking his lips. 'Not bad for a girl who grew up eating offal.'

Cypress

Coffee was served in the lounge.

Mrs Turton waited while the others filed from the dining room and then placed the last of the custard creams in her coat pocket. If anyone saw her, she would tell them she was sending them to India. It was well known in church circles that she knitted scarves for the orphans of that country, so she had no doubts that her story would be accepted at face value. She was, however, coming to the belief that charity should start closer to home these days.

Greg was sitting with Uncle Frank when Katy approached him.

'If you're my uncle, why haven't I seen you before?' she asked.

'I live in another country, Katy,' Greg said. 'America.'

'Do you know any film stars?'

'Fortunately not,' Greg replied. 'I teach in a university and we don't get many film stars turning up for class.'

'I'm going to be a film star when I grow up,' Katy said. 'I'm going to be famous and earn lots of money.'

'Good for you! If you do become rich, I might well ask you for a loan. Is that okay?'

'Do you want some money now, Uncle Greg?' Katy asked, opening her purse and making a brief study of its contents. 'I can lend you three pounds, but I'll want it back before you leave.'

Greg laughed out loud and Jean looked in their direction.

'Katy darling, I need to see you for a minute,' she said. 'Can you come here, please?' There was no *need*, there was no *minute*: Jean was simply reluctant for her daughter to form any sort of connection with Greg.

'You and me, Greg, we'll die of disease and old age,' Uncle Frank said to his nephew after Katy left. 'That little girl is going to die of encouragement – you mark my words.'

A waitress placed coffee on the table, but Uncle Frank waved his cup away and said he was going to have a whisky instead – it wasn't every day he said goodbye to his brother.

The import of Lyle's death had yet to take effect on the old man. It would come, he knew, in the weeks ahead, the months that followed and stay with him for the rest of his days. His brother had been his only friend, the one person in life to have ever looked out for him. There was no one to rely on now but himself, and from experience, Uncle Frank knew how hit-or-miss an affair this could be.

'I'm the last one standing, Greg,' he said thoughtfully. 'First Eric, then Irene and now Lyle. It's me that's in the firing line now. Mine will be the next funeral you go to.'

'You've a few good years left in you yet, Uncle Frank.'

'To tell you the truth, Greg, I always thought I'd die before your dad. I'm four years younger than him, but I've always looked older. Hell, the last time he came with me for a hospital appointment the nurses thought he was my son. That tickled him, that did.'

'Let me get you that whisky, Uncle Frank,' Greg said.

'I'll get it myself,' Uncle Frank said. 'I'm not completely useless yet.'

Greg poured himself a coffee and Billy joined him.

'I think it's gone well, don't you?' Billy asked.

'Yes I do, and thanks for organising everything. I'm afraid I haven't been much use so far, but I'll stay and help get the house sorted.'

'That would be great, Greg, and needless to say you'll stay with us while you're here. Jean's already made up the spare room.'

'You're sure that's no trouble – Jean's okay with it?'

'Jean's fine about it,' Billy lied. 'It's about time we caught up with each other. I still can't believe we fell out over something so stupid.'

Greg nodded. 'What the hell were we thinking?'

Billy didn't answer the question – which struck him as being rhetorical anyway – and started to explain the arrangements for getting people home. 'Syd's going to give Mrs Turton a lift back; the Collards and The Reverend Tinkler came in their own cars, so they're okay; and I'll take our family. Can you drop Uncle Frank off and then drive out to our house?'

'Sure,' Greg said, 'but remind me again how I get there, will you? I know I turn right at the crossroads and drive over the bridge, but then what?'

'Keep going straight until you get to the T-junction. Turn right there and go to the top of the hill. Our house is the last one on the left. You can phone if you have any problems.'

'My mobile's in the suitcase but I should be able to find it all right. Everything comes back eventually.'

'How true that statement was,' Billy thought, but instead said: 'I'll just go and settle up with the manager.'

The Reverend Tinkler had wandered away from the others and was staring at a painting on the wall at the far end of the room. It was a portrait of a woman and he was struck by its similarity to his ex-wife Joan. For an instant, he wished she was there with him; there to support and guide him through the pitfalls of conversation. He heard someone call his name and turned to see Uncle Frank fast approaching.

An approach by Frank Bowman was never for the faint-hearted. The man's enigmatic smile and determined step made it difficult for a person to know if it was his intention to engage in polite conversation or a fistfight. It was understandable why Betty Halliwell referred to him as a goblin, the Reverend Tinkler contemplated – even if her description was a tad on the harsh side. Frank Bowman, he decided, was more reminiscent of Mr Punch, as in Punch and Judy. Or was that Richard and Judy?

'Bill, I'm glad I've caught you. Ever since the government turned off my television set I've been reading the Bible, and this story about Noah's Ark has been bothering me. Before we get into it though, what the hell's gopher wood when it's at home?'

'The wood they built the Ark from?'

Frank nodded.

'No one's too sure, Frank. It's only ever mentioned in the Bible once, but the common presumption is that it's cypress.'

'That clears that up then, but there's a lot more that isn't clear. Let me give you the basics.

'By my calculation it starts raining on 17 May and doesn't stop for five months. The Ark comes to rest on Mount Ararat on 17 October, but it isn't until 27 May of the following year that the flood completely disappears. So, from beginning to end, we're talking about a year.'

The Reverend Tinkler nodded in agreement. So far, so good. He was on firm ground when it came to discussions of The Bible. He knew from recent experience, however, that firm ground around Frank Bowman could easily turn to quicksand.

'I can appreciate the length of the flood, Bill, but it's the size of the Ark that bothers me – I don't think it was big enough. I converted the cubits into imperial measurements and its proportions were approximately 440' long, 73' wide and 44' high. It had three decks, but the most floor space it could have had – and this is being generous – is 10,000 square yards, and that's little more than the size of a rugby league pitch. And into that space you've got to cram seven pairs of every clean animal, one pair of every unclean animal and seven pairs of every bird. And you couldn't have had all these animals wandering about on the decks willy-nilly or there'd have been all kinds of mayhem. You'd have had to separate them, corral them somehow, and that would have reduced the space even further. And on top of that, you'd have had to use some of the space to store a year's worth of food for the animals – and that's presuming none of them were meat eaters.

'The logistics just don't stack up, Bill. These animals would have been taking a dump every day of their lives, and you've only got eight people to clean up the mess and throw it overboard before the Ark starts to sink. That would be a full time job for ten times their number. Noah and his boys must have been worn to a frazzle by the time they got off the boat – and another thing. How did they manage to clean out all the cages without being attacked by some of the animals?

'And it's not so much what was mentioned, as what wasn't mentioned.'

The Reverend Tinkler swallowed hard and again placed his finger between the dog collar and his neck.

'First of all, there's no mention of insects,' Uncle Frank continued. 'How did insects manage to survive if they weren't allowed onboard? Spiders can't swim and neither can worms and butterflies. By rights, they should have been wiped out.

'Secondly, what about kangaroos and elephants and animals like that which didn't even live in the Holy Land? How did they survive?

'And thirdly, how did three men and their wives manage to populate the world after they climbed out of the Ark knackered as fish. I know Noah was 600 when the rains started and that people lived longer in those days, but even so, it's a lot to ask of three men, isn't it – and even more to ask of their wives.

'So what's the situation, Bill? Is the Bible lying to us or what? I thought the Bible was supposed to tell the truth.'

'Oh my goodness!' The Reverend Tinkler said looking at his watch. 'I was supposed to make a hospital visit ten minutes ago. Let me think about this and get back to you, Frank. I'm pretty sure we should look upon the story as an allegory rather than a gospel truth, but let's discuss this at a later time. Poor Mrs Hodges will be wondering where I've got to.'

The Reverend Tinkler made a hurried retreat, said his goodbyes to Billy, Greg and the other mourners and stepped out into the rain. How refreshing a summer's downpour could be after a conversation with Frank Bowman!

He shouldn't, however, have lied about visiting Mrs Hodges in the hospital. She'd died two years ago and, from memory, had warranted nine index cards.

2

Plastic

Greg stopped the car by the gate to Uncle Frank's house and cut the engine. The garden, he noticed, was as immaculate as ever: bushes neatly trimmed, flowerbeds meticulously weeded and the lawn mown short and edged with precision.

'Are you coming in?' his uncle asked.

'I'd better not, Uncle Frank. Billy and Jean are expecting me.'

'How are things with you and Billy?'

'We've broken the ice, I suppose, swept the past under the carpet like we've always done, but there's still a hill to climb. We'll get there eventually.'

'You should have got there while your Dad was alive.'

'We know that, Uncle Frank. It's the first thing we said to each other. Anyway, we're talking now and that's the main thing. I don't think Jean's talking to me, though.'

'That's because she doesn't like you. Just like that mother of hers doesn't like me. I wish to God it was her funeral we'd been to and not your dad's.'

Greg laughed. 'I'll tell Betty that if I get stuck for conversation.'

'You can tell her what you damn well like. It's no skin off my nose.'

Uncle Frank paused for a moment, and when he spoke again his voice was more plaintive: 'You'll come and see me while you're here, won't you, lad?'

'Of course I will. Once I get settled, I'll give you a call. We can drive out into the country, if you like.'

'As long as it's not to The Dales,' Uncle Frank replied. 'I'm sick to bloody death of The Dales.'

He then took Greg's hand and pressed it gently. 'I'm sorry about your dad, Greg. I know he meant a lot to you.'

Without further ado, the old man climbed out of the car and walked to the side door. Greg waited while his uncle stepped inside the house, and then made a careful U-turn.

He drove slowly at first, looking from one side of the road to the other for the familiar landmarks of his youth. He was pleased to see the Brown Cow still there, but the cobbler's and bank were gone – as was the barber's shop where a man called Cyril had simultaneously cut hair and dropped cigarette ash on the heads of his customers. The dental practice, however, where Mr Blum had extracted most of his father's teeth, and the Methodist chapel attended by Mrs Turton and Barry were still in business.

About two miles from the city centre the landscape changed dramatically and Greg found himself driving through an area of blight he no longer recognised: abandoned mills and run-down businesses; rows of unloved terraced houses and burnt-out buildings; boarded-up pubs and second-hand shops; take-away restaurants and pawn shops; and churches now repurposed as warehouses selling cheap carpet and vinyl flooring.

He stopped at a crossroads near the old Plaza cinema – now a ramshackle DIY store – and then carried on down the hill and past the city's sprawling university. The central road layout had changed since he'd last driven there and for a time he lost his bearings, first heading one way and then another before catching sight of the signs he was looking for.

As the worst of the city disappeared into his rear-view mirror and the sky cleared, Greg's nascent depression lifted and he began to feel better about life – until, that is, he remembered he was driving to Billy's house, and then it returned.

It was at Spinney Cottage that the two brothers had fallen out.

On the day of the argument Billy had been painting the outside of the house. He had, in fact, just applied the final coat of black gloss when Greg arrived, and was standing at the back of the garden admiring his handiwork. (Greg was home from America and had arranged to go for a drink with Billy that evening, as much to escape his father's company as to enjoy his brother's.)

Greg walked to where Billy was standing, glanced cursorily at the paintwork, and then asked what the drainpipes had done to piss him off.

Billy was genuinely perplexed by the question. 'Why do you think the drainpipes have upset me?'

'You haven't painted them,' Greg replied.

'You don't have to paint drainpipes. They're tinted black when they're manufactured to save you the trouble. Besides, even if you did paint them, the paint would only peel off.'

'Why's that?' Greg asked.

'Because plastic expands and contracts with the weather. I'd have thought you'd have known that.'

'The drainpipes are turning grey,' Greg persisted. 'The tint's fading.'

'Nonsense. It can't be. It's not a superficial tint – the whole pipe's impregnated with the dye.'

There followed a period of toing and froing, Greg arguing one point of view and Billy the other, their voices rising and the exchanges becoming more heated and personal. Jean came out of the house to see what the commotion was and, uncharacteristically, took Billy's side – simply because it was the opposing side to Greg's.

'What do you know about British drainpipes, anyway?' she demanded. 'You don't even live in this country!'

It was at this point that Greg grabbed a Stanley knife from Billy's open toolbox and cut the drainpipe deep enough for a grey centre to appear.

'Now do you believe me?' he said. 'There's no way that pipe's been impregnated with dye.'

'Flipping heck, Greg! I'll have to buy another drainpipe now.'

'Nonsense,' Greg said. 'Just stick a piece of electrical tape over the cut and paint the pipe black – like you're supposed to!'

'You'll have to pay for a new drainpipe *and* the cost of its installation,' Jean told Greg.

'For God's sake, Jean! Why do you always have to be such a fucking arsehole?'

'I think you'd better leave,' Jean said. 'Billy, tell him to leave. I'm not having him talk to me like that, especially now that I'm pregnant. I might have a miscarriage.'

'I think you'd better do as Jean says, Greg,' Billy said, more than a trace of anger in his voice. 'You always have to know best, don't you? Always have to take things a step too far.'

Greg had said nothing, simply replaced the Stanley knife in his brother's toolbox and left.

That was seven years ago.

The brothers had exchanged Christmas and birthday cards over the intervening period but, until Billy called with news of their father's death, had never once spoken. Effectively, they were estranged. The rights and wrongs of painting plastic drainpipes had never been the issue between them, only a battle ground. The argument had been symptomatic of something else, something deeper – though just what that something was, Greg had no real idea.

It was his brother's final words that had stayed with him over the years: *You always have to know best, don't you? Always have to take things a step too far.* He didn't understand the implied resentment of the first statement, but the explicit truth of the second he did. It could only have referred to his behaviour at their wedding.

Even he had to admit that it hadn't been his finest hour.

Greg had known Jean long before Billy met her: they were the same age and had gone to the same independent school. Jean was there by dint of her father's wealth and old boy connections, while Greg had sat the entrance exam – the same exam Billy had failed four years earlier – and passed well enough to win one of six scholarships.

Although in the same year, Greg and Jean had been placed in different streams and were never in the same classes. They both, however, belonged to social groups that ran into each other at weekend parties or in city centre clubs where licensing laws were lax and fake IDs went unquestioned. Even so, the likelihood was that Jean would have remained just a face in the crowd if Greg hadn't been pressed by a friend to ask if she'd go out with him.

It was the ungraciousness of Jean's reply that registered with Greg: 'I'd rather die!' she'd said. 'Look at him! He's got nostrils big enough to park cars in. It would be like going out with a double garage!'

At first, Greg wondered if it was just the awkwardness of the moment that had caused Jean to make such a boorish statement, and that her response was no more than a flustered reaction to an unexpected question. By the time he left school, however, he'd decided that it wasn't: it appeared that Jean was insensitive and uncaring to all people she had no use for.

Consequently, the day Billy introduced her as his fiancée, Greg was genuinely alarmed.

Billy and Jean had met at a charity gala. The event had been organised to raise funds for cancer research, and the accountancy firm where Billy worked had sponsored three tables. The firm had invited several of their more important clients and one of them was Henry Halliwell, the owner of a large chiropody practice.

Henry was accompanied by his wife and daughter, and Billy had been seated next to Jean. Fortunately – as far as their future together was concerned – Billy had no idea that Henry was a chiropodist and, when he did find out, it was too late. When Henry died two years after they married, Billy had to confess that he was more relieved than sad.

Though neither would have admitted to this, at the time of their meeting, both Billy and Jean were actively looking for spouses. Whenever they met new people of the opposite sex, each would mentally launch a profile page of their ideal partner and place either ticks or crosses in the appropriate boxes. That night, all appropriate boxes were ticked.

Billy, Jean decided, was a reasonably handsome man with no noticeable physical deformities. He was an accountant with prospects – or at least a trainee accountant with prospects – and wanted children. More importantly, he also struck her as being malleable: any marriage to Billy, she determined, would be a marriage on her terms.

Jean, Billy decided, was an attractive, almost beautiful girl, and he would have happily settled for less. She wanted children, came from a good family and displayed a distinct humanitarian spirit. He was touched by how willing she'd been to sacrifice her Saturday night for the benefit of others less fortunate than herself, and mentioned this.

Jean dismissed his idea that her attendance at the gala was an act of selflessness. 'Cancer affects us all, Billy – not just poor people,' she told him. 'It's affected me!'

'I'm… I'm so sorry to hear that,' Billy stammered, unsure if she herself or a close family member had suffered from the disease. 'Would you like to talk about it?'

Jean drained the contents of her wine glass and Billy prepared himself for the worst.

'I read an article in *Reader's Digest*, Billy,' Jean said, her voice faltering. 'It was about a young woman in her twenties – *my age* – who died of the disease. It was the most moving and upsetting story I'd ever read and I cried for days afterwards. Mummy became quite concerned about me.'

Jean then refilled her wine glass and cut herself a large piece of cheese.

It wasn't quite the story Billy had been expecting, but he was again struck by the sensitivity Jean exuded. Mentally, he placed another tick in her humanitarian box. What a stroke of good fortune it was to have been seated next to her!

'My own mother died of a thrombosis,' he said.

'I'm very sorry to hear that, Billy, but let's face it: she didn't die from cancer, did she?'

Billy nodded thoughtfully, but held on to his belief that one premature death was no sadder than another – whatever the cause.

After the meal had finished and the speeches delivered, Billy plucked up his courage.

'I know you might not think it appropriate, Jean – considering the sad circumstances of the evening and everything – but I wonder if you'd care to dance?'

'I thought you'd never ask!' Jean said.

And for the next year the dance continued.

Jean's insistence that they delay full sexual relations until their relationship was more defined – an insistence, Greg later told his brother, that had never been made to boys at school

– probably spurred Billy's proposal of marriage, as Jean had fully expected it would.

One cold November night, Billy slipped from the park bench they were sitting on and bent down on one knee, inadvertently placing it in a puddle. 'Jean,' he said, 'would you do me the honour of marrying me and making me the happiest man in the world?'

Jean immediately accepted and six months later they were married. It appeared, however, that Jean had stopped listening after the words *marry me*, for Billy never became the happiest man in the world.

It was on their wedding day that Greg burned his bridges with Jean and soured an increasingly distant relationship with Billy. His outburst might have been construed by the generous as the concern of one brother for another or as a misguided expression of love, but even Greg had to admit that it was more likely the effects of the magic mushrooms he'd ingested that day.

Greg had been given no responsibilities for the wedding other than to show up, which for Greg, at that time of his life, was responsibility enough. Billy had asked his friend Bob Prickett to be best man, and all appointed ushers were similarly friends. Greg had no disagreement with this. He didn't like weddings at the best of times, and the lack of any official role would allow him to slip away from the nuptials and meet up with friends in the Brown Cow. Indeed, his only reason for taking the hallucinogenic was to make the day pass more interestingly until that event could happen.

The mushrooms had been given to him by the same large-nostrilled friend Jean had earlier dismissed. Under his direction Greg first froze and then boiled the fungi – to rid them of as many toxins as possible, the friend had explained – and then, to kill the taste, mixed the residue with dandelion and burdock cordial. Greg had tripped on psilocybin before, and on both occasions his experiences had been happy ones. There was, therefore, no reason for him to believe that the hallucinations on the day of his brother's wedding would be any different – and certainly the day had started well enough.

After drinking a small glass of the dandelion and burdock mixture, he took a leisurely bath, dressed in his suit and went downstairs, where his father and Billy were discussing the day's arrangements in the lounge. He sat down at the breakfast table, buttered a slice of toast and then, while spreading marmalade over it, was suddenly overcome by the sparkling and bejewelled properties of the preserve. Reality, he sensed, was in the process of discarding its threadbare clothes and changing into something a little more alluring.

He chewed the toast slowly, savoured its flavour and sensed its texture, wondered if scorched bread had ever tasted better. He drank the most flavoursome cup of coffee he'd ever drunk, and then went to the bathroom to clean his teeth; he heard every deafening brush stroke, felt every bubble of toothpaste explode in his mouth. He went downstairs again and walked into the garden, stared at the trunk of a cherry tree for five minutes and then studied the grass. The world – as Louis Armstrong was proclaiming from the kitchen radio – was indeed wonderful. Why, he puzzled, was Billy about to spoil it by marrying Jean?

'Come on, Greg. We haven't got all day, lad,' his father prompted.

The ride in the back of the wedding limousine was a 3D journey through Wonderland, and the inside of St Christopher's Church was no less spellbinding. Greg was transfixed by the carved woodwork and rich ornamentation, the twinkling colours of the stained glass windows and the spidery intricacies of the plaster cracks. He watched as the words in his hymn book bounced to the music, and smiled when a small frog ate all the punctuation marks. Louis

Armstrong's words again came to mind: the world was indeed wonderful.

And then, all of a sudden, it became anything but!

Without warning the euphoria dissipated, and a terrible feeling of dread washed over him. His visions darkened, and he entered a strange world of nightmare. The church was no longer a church, but a dank and threatening cave. His brother was now an oscillating crow, and the vicar the grimmest of Grim Reapers. No mutation was more marked or alarming, however, than the change he saw in Jean. Her bridal gown had turned black and raggedy, and the mesh of her veil writhed with trapped and fetid bugs; her face was leprous, eyeless, and two large fangs protruded from her mouth. Blood dripped from them, trickled down her chin and pooled on the floor, until she and Billy – now losing his feathers and looking more like a plucked turkey – were standing in a small lake of red haemic liquid.

It was unfortunate that the vicar – still masquerading as the Grim Reaper – chose this moment to ask if anyone knew of any reason why Jean and Billy shouldn't be joined together in holy matrimony. Greg did, and felt compelled to share his knowledge.

'I DO!' he shouted. 'JEAN'S A VAMPIRE!'

The congregation turned to Greg. His outcry had been heartfelt and his expression, they noted, was equally sincere. Unsurprisingly, they next turned to Jean and scrutinised her for any telltale traces of vampirism, only returning their attention to Greg after he'd started to hyperventilate. They then watched as the groom's brother toppled sideward and cracked his head on the hard edge of the wooden pew.

The ceremony was halted while his father and two ushers carried Greg concussed to the choir vestry and laid him on the floor. Fortunately, before anyone had time to call for an ambulance – which, in turn, would have brought the police

– Greg's eyes opened and his breathing slowly returned to normal. He looked at his father and his father looked at him. The love between them was palpable, the moment special.

And then, Greg spoke... and the special moment passed.

'You've got wings growing out of your shoulder blades, Dad. I think you might be an angel.'

'Good God in Heaven, Greg!' Lyle replied. 'You've been at those damned drugs again, haven't you?'

The wedding continued without Greg, who remained in the choir vestry contemplating a chair leg. Jean became Billy's wife and, reluctantly, Greg's sister-in-law. It was generally agreed, however, that Greg's strange outburst had marred the day, and Jean for one never forgave him.

The only person to disagree with prevailing opinion was Uncle Frank. To his way of thinking, Billy's marriage to Jean had been one of the best days out he'd ever had.

Bricks

Jean and Billy lived in a small town in the Wharfe Valley, fifteen miles from where Billy and Greg had grown up. The distance was short, but the world there entirely different.

It had been Betty's idea for her daughter and son-in-law to move into the family house after Henry died. Although she'd quickly come to the conclusion that the house was too big for one person, she'd been unwilling to either sell or move to a smaller property. The obvious solution, she decided, was to invite Billy and Jean to share the house with her. It would be a win-win situation for them all: the arrangement would allow her daughter and son-in-law to move out of their dingy semi-detached house, while allowing her to remain in Spinney Cottage.

It wasn't so much the lifetime of memories that tied Betty to the Tudorbethan house, as the actual bricks and mortar.

In a town renowned for its exclusivity, the Halliwell house stood in grounds of more than two acres in one of its most select areas. It was a house and address most people would have killed for and was, for Betty, the visible affirmation of her standing in life – a concrete testimony to the distance she'd placed between her past and present lives.

As long as she remained in Spinney Cottage she would forever be Mrs Betty Halliwell, the wife – now widow – of a successful professional man and respected magistrate. Never again would she be mistaken for Betty Stott, the awkward girl who'd stood behind her parents' counter on a small wooden box and wrapped portions of thick seam and honeycomb tripe for shabbily-dressed customers, most of whom had been half-deaf from working in the textile mills. It was the image of their hands, however, hands she tried never to touch, that remained with her and occasionally brought nightmares: gnarled hands, liver-spotted hands and hands with missing fingers. (Although Betty never developed full-blown cheirophobia, the odds were always stacked in favour of her marrying a man who specialised in feet rather than hands.)

When Betty introduced the idea of living together, Jean had jumped at the idea. Billy, however, had been less sure, and silently doubted the wisdom of any arrangement that would leave them indebted to Jean's mother and susceptible to her interference. Betty, however, had foreseen and prepared for such reservations. She had, she told them, no intention of interfering in their lives any more than she already did, and certainly didn't want them interfering in hers. What she proposed was to convert a part of the house into a self-contained granny flat with its own entrance, and transfer the ownership of Spinney Cottage to Billy and Jean. There were, however, certain stipulations: they could never sell the house while she was alive and, similarly, they could never turn her out of the flat against her will.

'But what if Billy and I get divorced?' Jean had teased her mother. 'What if Billy runs off with a floozy?'

'Like that's going to happen,' Billy had laughed.

'Our family doesn't believe in divorce, Jean, and neither I'm sure does Billy,' Betty had replied flatly.

Billy and Jean's house sold quickly – 'I told you pebble dash was a winner,' Billy had said to his wife – but it had taken longer than expected for the necessary alterations to be made to Spinney Cottage, and there was an overlap of some two months when the three of them lived together under the same roof.

Against all odds, Billy found that he liked his mother-in-law's constant company, and was appreciative of the times when she did interfere in their lives, as nine times out of ten it was with him that she sided. When, after its completion, Betty disappeared into the granny flat and was thereafter seen only rarely, Billy actually missed her.

'You're sure you won't come in for a coffee, Betty?' Billy asked, after they'd returned from the funeral.

'I won't, thank you, Billy. Alan Titchmarsh is interviewing Joan Collins this afternoon and I'm hoping she's going to share her beauty secrets with him.'

'She wears wigs, Granny,' Katy said.

'I'm sure you're wrong, dear,' Betty replied. 'And I don't for a moment believe those people who say she's had plastic surgery, either. I think she's just one of those rare women who've been gifted with good bone structure.'

'I'm getting plastic surgery when I grow up, aren't I, Mummy?'

'It's just an option to bear in mind, dear,' Jean smiled.

Billy turned to look at his wife despairingly. 'What on earth are you doing putting ideas like that in her head, Jean? She's seven, for goodness sake. Give her a chance to grow up!'

Jean was just about to say something in defence of her long-term strategy for Katy's future success when Betty butted in. 'Billy's right, Jean. Katy's beautiful as she is, and she'll grow up to be a beautiful young woman without any need for surgery. It's not as if she looks like Uncle Frank, is it?'

A beautiful little girl, yes, Jean thought. And no, fortunately for her she didn't look anything like Uncle Frank. But – and this is what worried her – Katy already had the makings of Auntie Irene's hair. (Auntie Irene was the late sister of Uncle Frank. Although God had given her the body of an athlete, He appeared to have lost interest in her creation by the time He got to her hair and had left it looking frail and lacking in confidence.)

'What time are you expecting me tonight?' Betty asked.

'Come for seven and we'll eat at eight, Mummy. I've made a lasagne.'

'You're not killing the fatted calf for the prodigal son, then?' Betty asked.

'No, mince meat will do for Greg,' Jean replied. 'Come on, Katy. Let's get you out of those clothes.'

'I'll get some wine from the cellar,' Billy said.

Billy made his way to the top of the garden and walked down a short flight of stone steps to the door of a wine cellar dug into the hillside by workmen employed by Henry Halliwell more than thirty years ago. It was the ideal storage place: the temperature was steady, the room dark and the wine safe from vibration. He pulled a selection of bottles from the racks and placed them in a wooden box, and then carried the box to a nearby shed.

The shed was Billy's refuge from the world, from Jean and from his daughter's incessant tap dancing. It was a place where he could be alone with his thoughts and, if lucky, smoke a furtive cigarette without being caught.

Billy had only recently started smoking and no-one knew anything of this except him and the newsagent who sold him the odd packet of ten. His secret, he knew, was safe with Mr Brownlow, as the shopkeeper lived in a town some seven miles distant and had no idea who Billy was.

The game of stealth was new to Billy, and he was still unsure of its rules and uncomfortable with deception. Indeed, the fact that he now smoked cigarettes was a consequence of his failure to master the game's finer points in the first place, and this was another thing he kept from Jean.

Billy retrieved the packet from behind a false log and lit a cigarette. He breathed the smoke deep into his lungs and exhaled slowly. His father, he knew, would have been disappointed to know he was smoking. He wondered if Greg still smoked and, if so, whether the tobacco he rolled these days was legal or illegal.

The impending arrival of his brother made him anxious. He often thought it was easier to meet a stranger than it was a family member, a person you weren't expected to have feelings for rather than someone you were. Billy didn't doubt that he loved his brother, but did wonder why there was such a distance between them. It wasn't so much the coolness, however, as the occasional feeling of unexplained bitterness he felt towards Greg that concerned him most, and so far the therapist he'd been ordered to see hadn't come up with anything to explain this. (That Billy was seeing a therapist was also something he kept from Jean.)

He was about to light another cigarette when he heard the sound of a car making its way up the drive. He quickly replaced the cigarette in its packet, made a mental note of the number remaining and sprayed his mouth with breath freshener. He locked the shed door behind him, picked up the box of wine bottles and walked down to the house.

'You got here all right, then,' Billy called out to Greg, when he saw his brother climb out of the car. 'Do you need a hand with anything?'

'This is the sum total of my belongings,' Greg replied, holding up a small plastic bag containing a miniature tube of toothpaste and toothbrush the airline had given him, and a bottle of duty-free whisky he'd bought at the airport. 'I know this is asking a lot, Billy, but do you have any clothes I can wear until my suitcase arrives?'

'Sure I do. Let me take this wine into the kitchen and then I'll show you to your room and sort something out.'

Greg held the door open for Billy and then followed him into the house.

'You got plenty of white wine, didn't you?' Jean asked. 'Not just red?'

'Three bottles,' Billy replied. 'That's more than enough for you and your mother.' He then turned to Greg a little uncertainly. 'It is red wine you drink, isn't it?'

Greg nodded.

'I don't drink red wine,' Jean said, turning to face Greg. 'The enamel on my teeth's porous, so if I drink red wine my teeth turn purple. You might not believe this, Greg, but someone once accused me of being a vampire. It's all a bit hazy now, but I think I was in church at the time getting married to your brother. Anyway, because some people think there's no smoke without fire, I have to avoid drinking anything that might give the impression I've been sucking blood from a person's neck. It's a pity really, because I used to really like red wine.'

How long, Greg wondered, was Jean going to hold this grudge? How many times was he supposed to apologise and not have his apology accepted? If it had been just the two of them in the kitchen and he didn't have to stay in the house overnight, he would have simply laughed it off or told Jean to go fuck herself. Instead, he mumbled his usual excuses for one more time, despaired of his youthful craziness yet again, and then – for the first time – mentioned the name of a new toothpaste intended to protect teeth from acid erosion.

As far as he was concerned, this new information now settled his debt.

Judging from the smile on his face, Billy appeared to have enjoyed the exchange between his wife and brother. The smile, however, quickly disappeared when Katy came cart-wheeling into the room barefooted.

'Katy! How many times have I told you *not* to do that in the house? And where are your shoes?' Billy added, his voice becoming slightly desperate in tone. 'How many times have I told you not to walk around the house barefoot? Go and put your socks and slippers on, will you? Now!' he shouted, when he saw Katy preparing to do another side flip.

'Don't have a cow, Daddy,' Katy said. 'Uncle Greg hasn't seen me do a cartwheel before, and I can't do them wearing slippers.'

'Your Uncle Greg didn't come all this way just to see you do cartwheels, Katy,' Billy said. 'He came to say goodbye to his father – your granddad. On a day like this, you should be showing more respect. Now, for the last time – go and put some shoes on!'

Katy pulled a face and left the room. Jean told Billy there'd been no cause for him to talk to Katy like that, and even Greg looked discomforted by Billy's outburst. Exhausted, Billy slumped into a chair. His breathing was laboured and small beads of perspiration formed on his top lip.

'You okay?' Greg asked.

'Yes, it's just the day: you know, saying goodbye to Dad and everything. I'll go and apologise to Katy once I've shown you to your room and got you some clothes. Let's do that now, shall we?'

Greg picked up his small plastic bag and made to follow Billy. Before he left the kitchen, he turned to Jean and thanked her for letting him stay with them.

'Don't thank me, Greg – thank your brother. He's the only

reason you're staying with us. When will you be leaving, by the way?'

'In a day or two – no more than that,' Greg replied. 'I'll move into Dad's house once my suitcase arrives.'

The evening meal passed without event, but for the most part conversation was polite and uninspiring. It was left to Betty Halliwell to inject the only controversy of the evening, and wisely, the debate she introduced revolved around the lives of others rather than their own.

She complained that Joan Collins' appearance on *The Alan Titchmarsh Show* that afternoon had been a complete waste of time, and wondered what a gardener was doing interviewing famous people in the first place.

'Poor Joan,' Betty said. 'She travels all this way to share her thoughts with us and ends up being interviewed by a gardener. It's like Dame Judi Dench going to America and being interviewed by a pool attendant!

'"*I've got rid of the moss and dead leaves, Ms Collins,*" Betty mimicked. "*I wonder if you could tell me about your film career before I start planting the turnips*".'

'Honestly, I ask you! How disrespectful is that? And they had her sharing a couch with a cake decorator and a plate spinner of all people. Why on earth would they think she had anything in common with them?'

(Katy made a mental note never to be interviewed by Alan Titchmarsh when she was famous, and then asked for another bowl of ice-cream.)

'They should have had Michael Parkinson talking to her,' Betty continued. 'At least he's trained as a journalist, and it's not as if he has anything better to do with himself these days. The only time I see him on television now is when he's advertising insurance policies for the over fifties. You'd think he'd have more self-respect, wouldn't you? He can't have any need for the money, and why on earth would he expect anybody to take out a policy just because they get a free Parker pen?

'I'll give Michael one thing, though: at least he faces the camera when he talks to you and looks you in the eyes. I hate those advertisements where people look off to one side and try to hoodwink you into thinking they're real people instead of actors. I don't know where those television people get their ideas from, or how stupid they think we are... you're not putting Katy forward for any adverts, are you, Jean? You'd look well if she got typecast as the face of some pet food or a toilet roll.'

'I haven't done so yet, Mummy, but we're keeping our options open. I think we have to... no, Katy, no more! You've had enough ice-cream, and it's time you were getting ready for bed. Anyone like a coffee – it's only instant, I'm afraid.'

No one did. Greg and Billy said they'd stick to wine, and Betty said there was a detective show she wanted to watch on television: one about a Scandinavian policeman who developed a different medical condition every episode.

'They're all life-threatening, too,' she said. 'Every blessed one of them. I'll be surprised if he's not dead by the end of the series, and if he isn't, then someone should tell him to cheer up a bit. It's not as if we don't get rain and snow in this country!'

Betty kissed Jean, Katy and Billy goodnight and then made a point of shaking Greg's hand. 'It's not as if we're close or anything, is it, Greg?' she said, by way of explanation.

'To say they're regular churchgoers, Jean and her mother don't go in much for forgiveness, do they?' Greg said to Billy, once they were alone in the kitchen.

'Betty's too old to change her ways, Greg, but I've got a lot of time for her. She'd never accept the comparison, but I think she's the Halliwell equivalent of Uncle Frank. And Jean will come round eventually. To tell you the truth, I think she's secretly pleased you're staying with us.'

'You reckon?' Greg said. 'She gave me the impression she wasn't. Anyway, how about a whisky? We can toast Dad while we're waiting for Jean.'

'That's a champion idea,' Billy said, and then turned thoughtful. 'I wish Dad could have been with us tonight, don't you? The three of us sitting round the table again. He'd have liked that. And Jean would have let him sit at the head of the table. That's where he always sat when he came for meals.'

'Jean used to give him pride of place?' Greg asked, surprised by the idea. 'It doesn't sound like her.'

'Well, no, it's not, really. It's just that she didn't like looking at his teeth when she was eating.'

Greg smiled. 'His teeth were the talking point when he came to visit me in Texas. Everyone liked Dad, but they couldn't get over the state of his teeth. His choppers confirmed every prejudiced idea they had about British dentistry. I tried telling them that Dad's teeth weren't the norm for the country, but they didn't want to listen. I bet they're still talking about him.'

'You know the story of his teeth, don't you?' Billy asked.

'I didn't know there was a story. I just presumed they were a victim of all the junk he used to eat.'

'There's much more to it than that, Greg. It was his first dentist who caused the problems. He didn't believe in anaesthetic and used an old treadle drill; hollowed out Dad's teeth so much when he was filling them that he weakened their walls. That's why they started to crumble when he got older. And then the dentist committed suicide…

'He was Scottish,' Billy added – as if somehow this piece of information made the man's action more understandable.

'Anyway, after that, Dad developed an aversion to dentists, and it was years before he started seeing Mr Blum. The damage had been done by then though, and all Mr Blum could do was extract any problem teeth. What Dad should have done was get dentures, but he wouldn't brook the idea. He thought false teeth were for cissies.'

'How much did you see of Dad?' Greg asked. 'Did he come to Spinney Cottage much?'

'He did before the accident, but after he stopped driving I'd have to go over and collect him and then drive him back again after the meal. It got a bit much, really. I wanted him to stay over the nights he came, but he always refused; always said he preferred sleeping in his own bed at night.

'We took him out for drives, of course, and visited him with Katy, but Jean never liked going to his house. She always thought there was too much dust there and was never too sure how clean the cups were. I used to call in by myself though, every week if possible and usually on my way home from work. I'd do odd jobs he needed doing and go through any correspondence he couldn't read because the print was too small. I liked those visits the best, just the two of us spending time together, drinking coffee and putting the world to rights. It's odd to think I won't see him again – that neither of us will. It must be worse for you… not having seen him for so long. I'm sorry you didn't get to spend more time with him, Greg.'

'We talked on the phone a lot,' Greg said. 'Well, once a week anyway, and always on a Sunday. I can't say we ever had much to say to each other though. Not that I don't miss Dad, but I think you had a lot more in common with him than I did… anyway, how about that toast?'

'Yes, let's do that. Why don't you go through to the lounge and pour us a couple of glasses, and once I've finished rinsing the plates and stacking the dishwasher I'll join you there.'

When Jean came into the lounge, Billy was showing Greg the awards he'd been presented for either hitting target or being voted salesperson of the year: small pieces of glass in the shape of globes, pyramids and books. None had his name engraved on them, only *Award Winner* and the year the bauble was presented. Despite the lack of any personal touch to indicate the award hadn't been stolen from another person – 'it's a multinational company,' Billy explained – they had, nevertheless, been given pride of place on the mantelpiece and stood either side of a carriage clock – a wedding present from the firm of accountants Billy no longer worked for.

It had been his father's idea that he apply for a position in accountancy after the woollen manufacturing firm he'd worked for had closed down. The world, his father had argued, would always need accountants, and a professional qualification would shield him from the insecurities of economic life and allow him to pick and choose jobs. At least, that was the theory.

In practice, Billy's career as an accountant never left the runway, forever grounded there by his inability to understand more than one of the six ways to provide for depreciation. He took the first stage examinations three times, and each time failed. It became obvious to both him and the firm – though not to Jean – that he would be better off looking for another profession. Eventually he alighted on the idea of a career in sales, and went to work for a publishing company.

Jean had been unable to hide her disappointment at Billy's choice of vocation, and had in fact gone out of her way to tell him just *how* disappointed she was. She'd married him, she said, on the firm understanding that he was going to be an accountant – a professional man like her father – and not a common salesman, or commercial traveller as she sometimes referred to his position.

'I'm sure Greg doesn't want to see those,' Jean said dismissively. 'I'm surprised you even want them on display.'

'Jean believes that selling is a base occupation and that I

should be doing something else,' Billy said. 'Personally I quite enjoy it.'

'Your own grandparents sold things for a living, didn't they?' Greg asked, careful to omit any mention of the word tripe.

'People *came to them* to buy things,' Jean said, equally careful not to mention the word tripe. 'There's a difference. They didn't knock on someone's door and hawk their wares.'

Billy poured Jean a glass of wine while Greg decided to try another tack which, if successful, might prompt Jean to question her assumption that selling was a tawdry occupation.

'Some people say that Jesus Christ was the greatest salesman to have ever lived. How do you feel about that, Jean?' he asked.

'Am I missing something here, Greg, or is this just one of your stupid comments? Are you trying to tell me that Billy's the Son of God or something because, if you are, it's a detail that appears to have slipped his mind? Certainly he's never mentioned it to me.'

'There were times growing up when I thought he was the Son of God,' Greg laughed.

'Well he's not! And he's been selling books for more than *three* years!'

Billy glanced at Greg, as if to warn him not to push things further. Greg, however, either didn't notice or chose to ignore his brother's warning.

'The point I'm trying to make, Jean, is this: what purpose would Jesus' death have served if no one had bothered to sell Christianity to the world? In fact, what would be the point of anyone making anything if no one's prepared to sell it? Do you think your father just set up practice and waited for someone to hobble through his door – that *he* didn't sell his service?'

Jean poured more wine into her glass and glared at Billy.

'There's nothing wrong with selling,' Greg continued. 'And

there's certainly nothing unseemly about what Billy does for a living. Publishers' reps visit me all the time and I know how difficult their job is. They have to know the basics of every academic discipline they publish in, the details of every book they promote and the details of every competing book. They have to know who teaches what, who recommends what and what changes are taking place in the curriculum. And, if that isn't enough, they have to stand in front of entire departments and demonstrate how their textbooks can be delivered online.'

Billy listened carefully as Greg explained his job to Jean. Worryingly, his brother appeared to know more about academic calling than he did – he didn't do half the things Greg said he did.

Greg topped up his glass and pressed on: 'Higher Education's in a state of flux, Jean. Everything about it's changing. Hell, I work in the sector and even I don't know what's going on. Billy probably knows more than I do. What I'm saying is that Billy's job isn't nearly as straightforward as you might think it is. It's a lot more complicated than taking care of someone's feet. Feet don't change – they've been the same for thousands of years – and once a chiropodist's learned the basics and got his certificate, all he has to do for the rest of his life is join fucking dots together.'

Billy noticed the growing number of red blotches on Jean's neck – never a good sign – and was about to change the subject when Greg mentioned the dreaded 'T' word.

'And another thing, Jean,' Greg smiled, 'Billy's doing a lot more with his life than just standing around in a shop memorising the only two facts known to mankind about tripe.'

A starting pistol sounded in Billy's head. 'That reminds me, Jean,' he interjected. 'I have to go to Denmark on Monday.'

Cake

By the time Greg made it down for breakfast the next day, it was well after two in the afternoon. He'd slept well, remarkably well considering the jetlag and amount of whisky he'd drunk the previous evening. He found Katy and Billy sitting at the dining room table, Katy drawing in a sketchpad and Billy making notes in a Filofax. Jean had gone shopping with a friend.

'Hi, Uncle Greg,' Katy said. 'Mummy said you and Daddy got drunk last night and made fools of yourselves. She's mad with you, isn't she, Daddy?'

'No more than usual,' Billy smiled. 'And besides, your uncle and I didn't get drunk. We drank a toast to Granddad, but we didn't get drunk.'

'Shall I sing the song I sang for Granddad again?' Katy asked. 'Uncle Greg didn't hear it.'

'Not for the moment, sweetheart,' Billy replied. 'I have a headache, and I suspect your Uncle Greg might have the same one.'

'Maybe you could sing it to me when I get back,' Greg said. 'I was thinking of taking a walk into town and clearing the cobwebs. Get some money while I'm at it.'

'I'll go with you,' Katy said. 'I can sing the song while we're walking. That's okay, isn't it, Daddy?'

'It's okay with me if it's okay with your uncle.'

It was.

'I'd go with you myself,' Billy said, 'but I have some work to do here.'

'Denmark?' Greg asked.

'Denmark?' Billy puzzled before the penny dropped. 'Oh yes, of course, Denmark.'

Spinney Cottage was situated at the top of a steep wooded hill about a mile from the town's centre. Summer had returned to the valley and the day's skies were bright and the sun warm. Katy skipped down the drive singing her Britney Spears song and Greg whistled along in accompaniment.

'You're sure that was my Dad's favourite song? It seems a bit modern for him. He used to hate my music. Every album, every CD I bought, he told me I was wasting my money.'

'I'm sure,' Katy said. 'I only sang it for him once, but he said it was the nicest song he'd ever heard.' (Fortunately for Katy, Syd Butterfield wasn't on hand to disagree.)

Cars were parked on either side of the road by the bridge, and here Katy took hold of Greg's hand. The town had always been a default setting for anyone wanting to go to the country and not get mud on their shoes, and over recent years it had become increasingly popular with tourists.

They stopped for a while at the centre of the bridge and looked down at the fast moving, iron-coloured river.

'Does water get hurt when it hits rocks and drops down waterfalls and gets smashed into little pieces?' Katy asked.

Greg had to think for a moment. 'No, it's a fluid. We'd get hurt because we're a solid, but water just rolls with the punches. It doesn't feel a thing.'

Satisfied with the answer, Katy decided to ask her uncle another question. 'There's a sign on the moors that says there are slow sheep on the road. Why do they put slow sheep on the road and not fast ones?'

Greg thought for a longer moment. 'There aren't any fast sheep,' he said eventually. 'I think the sign's just warning people to drive slowly because there are sheep in the area. They should have put a comma or an exclamation mark after the word slow, like: *Slow! Sheep on the Road.*'

He decided to introduce some conversation of his own: it was easier talking with a hangover than answering questions with one. 'I used to come here when I was small. Your Daddy and I used to ride out here with our parents on a red bus. We'd sit down there on the bank and have picnics – eat homemade sandwiches and cakes my mother made.'

'Mummy says you're a wanker,' Katy said, interrupting Greg. 'What's a wanker?'

'It's someone you care about deeply,' Greg fabricated, somewhat taken aback by the comment. 'Someone who's polite and helpful.'

He paused for a moment and then asked Katy if Jean had made this comment to her.

'No, I heard her telling Daddy.'

'And what did your Daddy say?'

'*Keep your voice down, Jean: he might hear you,*' Katy said, in an imitation of a loud whispering voice.

Greg laughed.

'Are those cobwebs still in your head, Uncle Greg?' Katy asked.

'They've just about gone thanks, but I could do with some coffee. How about we drop by The Tearoom?'

Katy screamed with delight, clapped her hands together excitedly and started to recite the names of The Tearoom's famous delicacies: curd tarts, fat rascals, vanilla slices, fruit meringues, cream hearts, coffee and walnut cakes.

They strolled from the bridge to the parish church, crossed the road and headed up the wide main street to a cash machine where Greg withdrew money. With Katy tugging at his hand, they quickened their pace and walked towards a Victorian parade of shops on an adjoining street.

There was a small queue inside The Tearoom and a wait of some ten minutes before Greg and Katy were eventually shown to a small window table overlooking the rear car park. Greg glanced around the room and noticed that the ambience had changed little since his first visit there more than twenty years ago. The piano was gone, but otherwise everything was the same: the cane chairs and leather banquettes, the marquetry and mirrors, and the eclectic array of teapots that lined the walls.

A young girl wearing a Victorian server's uniform of white blouse, black skirt and long white apron brought menus and introduced herself as Emily. Greg ordered a glass of lemonade for Katy and a large cafetiere of Nepal Snow River coffee for himself. He toyed with the idea of eating an all-day breakfast but decided against it, and watched with amusement as Katy asked the waitress to tell her, and then retell her, the names of every cake and pastry on the three-tiered trolley. After much oohing and aahing, his niece chose a small Genoese sponge cake covered in red marzipan.

'Are you married, Uncle Greg?' Katy asked, after she'd finished the cake. 'Do you have any children or pets?'

'No,' Greg replied. 'I have a girlfriend. Her name's Cyndi and she has two children – a boy and a girl.'

'Sindy like the doll?'

'No, it's spelt differently. It starts with a C rather than an S, and the *i* and the *y* are swapped around.'

Katy looked at him confused, and Greg wondered why he'd made the explanation so complicated.

'She was hoping to come with me but the doctor advised her against it,' he added.

'Doesn't the doctor like you?'

Now it was Greg's turn to look puzzled. 'I'm not sure he's even met me,' he said.

'What's wrong with her then?' Katy persisted. 'Is she sick or something?'

'No, it's nothing like that,' Greg reassured her. 'She's just had some surgery and the doctor thought it would be best if the stitches healed before she flew anywhere.'

'Where are the stitches?'

'I'm not sure,' Greg lied.

'Are you going to marry her?'

Greg shrugged.

'Do you love her?'

'I guess,' Greg said, motioning for the waitress to bring the bill and allow him to escape Katy's interrogation.

There was a time when he'd have been able to answer Katy's question with an immediate and definite yes. But now he wasn't sure, and he knew from experience that this lack of certainty meant that he no longer did. It was the story of all his relationships. He'd fall in love and then, just as easily, fall out of love, leaving behind him a series of bewildered girlfriends in differing states of emotional disrepair. Although his intention was never to hurt these partners, Greg's farewells were so matter-of-fact and lacking in feeling that it was impossible for them not to be wounded.

The last time it happened had been in a lift. When he'd walked into the elevator on the fifty-third floor of the building, he'd been in love with Vicky Hughes; but by the time they'd descended to the ground floor, he no longer was. Rather than postpone the inevitable, he'd simply told her their relationship was over.

'It's not working,' he'd said. (It was the most any girlfriend got by way of explanation.)

Vicky had stared at him open mouthed. 'You mean *you're* dumping *me*?' she'd asked incredulously.

'I guess.'

'Well *fuck you*, then' Vicky had replied. She'd then punched him hard in the face and ridden the elevator back to her apartment.

It was no surprise that Greg and his exes never kept in touch or remained friends after such break-ups, and when they did meet it was by accident and rarely pleasant. One disgruntled ex had even thrown an empty wine bottle at him during a faculty party – accidentally hitting the Head of the Electrical Engineering Department – while another had tried to stab him with a ballpoint pen when she'd seen him walking on Sixth Street.

The beginning of the end for Greg always happened after the girlfriend of the moment started to talk about *the next step* or taking things to *a different level*. Unfailingly, Greg would decide he was happier remaining in the shallow end of their relationship, where commitment was purely physical and responsibility only notional; the idea of settling down with one person for the rest of his life still filled him with disquiet, and he certainly had no intention of becoming a father.

Yet this was what Cyndi was now signalling, and it dawned on him, while he was waiting for the waitress to return with the bill, that he would be ending their relationship when he returned to America.

When news of his father's death reached him, Cyndi had just had a breast augmentation. Although she'd never actually met Lyle, she'd been thinking of him as a future father-in-law for some time and saw it as her 'wifely' duty to be with Greg during his time of tribulation. After the doctor had told her it would be unwise to travel by plane so soon after the procedure, she'd suggested to Greg that they fly Lyle's body to Austin and have the funeral there.

It had been the charm of her vapidity, as well as her undoubted beauty, that had attracted him to Cyndi in the first place, and dating an ex-cheerleader of the Dallas Cowboys had been a welcome antidote to listening to the intellectual pretensions of his colleagues in the History Department. He didn't, however, want either her support or her concern and viewed both as unwelcome intrusions – indications that she wanted to take things to the fateful next level. Had the tables been turned and it had been Cyndi's father who'd been knocked down by a bus, Greg was in no doubt that he wouldn't have accompanied *her* to North Dakota for the funeral.

Greg gave an involuntary sigh, which coincided with the waitress placing the bill in front of him.

'You've got enough money, haven't you?' Katy asked worriedly. 'I didn't bring mine with me.'

'Sure I have,' Greg said. 'I was sighing about something else.'

'The waitress was nice, wasn't she?' Katy said. 'Shall we give her a big tip?'

'Yes, let's do that,' Greg said. 'Do you want to give it to her?'

Katy nodded.

Greg walked slowly out of the restaurant area while Katy went to the waitress and gave her a five pound note. He increased his speed immediately, however, when he heard Katy's voice.

'Thank you very much, Emily. You're a wanker.'

3

Crack

It was now Sunday morning, and Greg and Billy were standing at the back of their father's house looking up at a long horizontal crack. It started just below the bathroom window and ended three feet into the adjoining property owned by Mrs Turton. The fissure in the rendering was approximately twenty feet long and at its widest point about two inches. The concrete sill of the bedroom window appeared to have exploded.

'How long's that been there?' Greg asked.

'I've no idea,' Billy replied. 'I can't remember the last time I was even in the back garden.'

Greg raised an eyebrow.

'The lock on the back door's been broken for years and I've always entered and left the house through the front,' Billy explained. 'Dad had a gardener, so there was never any need for me to come here. I just fixed things inside the house.'

'What do you think's caused it – subsidence?' Greg asked.

'I hope not or we'll never sell it,' Billy replied, scratching his head. 'I don't understand it. The house has been here for over seventy years. Why would it start sliding down the hill now? There aren't any mines in the area, I know that for a fact, but the soil here is clay so I suppose there could have been some ground movement – especially when you consider the dry summers we've been having. I think we should get a structural engineer to take a look.'

'I can arrange that,' Greg said. 'I'll look through the Yellow Pages and get someone out this week. Should I mention the crack to Mrs Turton? Maybe she could split the cost.'

'I wouldn't bother,' Billy said. 'She signed the house over to Barry in case she has to go into a nursing home, and he'd let the house fall down before putting his hand in his pocket. Have you seen their window frames? They've been rotten for years and he still won't do anything about them. You'd think someone who complained about litter all the time would be a bit more house-proud, wouldn't you?'

Billy looked at his watch. 'I'd best be going, Greg. I have to pick up Jean and Katy from church, and if I don't leave now I'm going to be late.'

The two brothers walked to the front of the property. The flagstones were uneven, some had sunk and others wobbled; and the metal drainpipes they passed were rusting, and the grates full of debris. The middle of the three steps leading to the front door and veranda also rocked, and the paint on the bay window was peeling and some of the wood rotten.

'You're sure you won't change your mind and stay at Spinney Cottage?' Billy asked.

'Thanks, but I think it's easier if I stay here. I can spend more time working on the house if I do that and, if I'm honest, I think I'd find it a bit awkward being there alone with Jean.'

'Okay, but if you need anything just give a shout. I'll be back on Friday night.'

'What are you doing in Denmark? I'd have thought the universities would be deserted in the summer.'

'Oh, just bits and pieces,' Billy said, keeping things vague.

He handed a set of keys to Greg – one key for the front door, one for the cellar and another for the garage – and then shook hands with his brother. Greg watched as Billy drove out of the quiet cul-de-sac and up the Grove, and then turned to the house. He saw Mrs Turton standing in her window and waved. Mrs Turton smiled and waved back.

The last time Greg had been in the house was seven years ago; the last time he'd actually lived there nearer twenty. The redolence of family life had all but disappeared and the house now smelled of an old man: an old man who had lived by himself and never opened windows.

He left his suitcase in the hallway and walked to the kitchen, the room where his father had drunk the white spirit and afterwards walked to his death. The glasses containing the petroleum distillate and liquid antibiotics had been washed and placed in a dish rack, but the paintbrush his father had used was in the sink, its bristles hardened and unusable. Greg picked up the brush and turned it slowly in his hands, as if by touching the last object his father had held he would somehow be reunited with the man.

Absent-mindedly, he placed the brush in his pocket and turned his attention to opening the kitchen window. He released the catch and pushed, but the window wouldn't budge. He climbed on to the draining board, carefully positioned himself and then thumped the frame several times with the palm of his hand. The window moved and then suddenly sprang open. Greg was about to congratulate himself on a job well done when two tiles, jolted by the sudden vibration, fell from the wall. He climbed down, picked up the pieces and placed them on the counter. It appeared in that moment that the whole house was in danger of falling to pieces; certainly, it wasn't the house he remembered.

While his mother had been alive, the house had always been state of the art, a show house for the neighbourhood that had pioneered new technologies and embraced modern comforts. If the neighbours hadn't looked up to his parents – which they had – then they'd certainly looked up to the house. But that was almost thirty years ago, and since then little if anything had changed. After a quick inspection of the downstairs rooms, however, it became clear that the house wasn't in danger of falling to pieces as he'd first imagined, but was simply tired. It was a house that had given up on life. And Greg knew why.

His mother had been the one to furnish the house and, after her death, the appliances and furnishings she'd chosen were all that remained to give her a presence. It was no longer a family of Lyle, Mary, Billy and Greg, but a family comprising Lyle, Billy, Greg and, standing in for his mother, a twin-tub washing machine, a spin dryer, a refrigerator, a three-piece suite, six chairs, two tables, three beds, and an array of carpets and curtains. Rather than buy new when something broke or became worn, his father would simply have them repaired or patched. In this way, the house became frozen in time, a time capsule encapsulating the essence of their dead mother.

Apart from the fact that he dusted and vacuumed every week, in many ways Lyle Bowman became the male equivalent of Miss Havisham – who, in all probability, also had perfect command of the gerund.

Greg carried his suitcase upstairs and placed it on the floor of the back bedroom – Billy's old room, and the room he used to covet.

As the last member of the family to arrive, Greg had been given the box room at the front of the house. It was the smallest of the three bedrooms, and there was a gap of no more than two feet between the single bed adjacent to the exterior wall and the wardrobe-cum-desk-cum-chest of drawers placed against the interior wall adjoining his parents' bedroom. When Billy's height had stalled permanently at 5′ 7″ and his own climbed to a fraction over 6′, Greg had suggested to his brother that they swap rooms. Billy had told him to take a hike and his father, after being brought into the discussion, had agreed with Billy: things were fine as they were; there was no need for change. It was another way of saying they should keep things as they were – the way they'd been when their mother had been alive.

Greg cleared a couple of drawers in the tallboy, rearranged the clothes hanging in the wardrobe and unpacked his suitcase. He took his toilet bag to the bathroom and placed it on the shelf above the pink washbasin. His father's toothbrush was still wedged in the metal holder above the pink toilet, its bristles worn and misshapen, and globs of dried toothpaste clinging to its handle like coral to a reef. Greg could only guess the kinds of bacteria lurking there – the same way he could only guess what had possessed his parents to buy a *pink* bathroom suite.

The bed in Billy's room had an eiderdown thrown over it, but was otherwise unmade. Greg went to his parents' room and searched the drawers for clean sheets and a pillowcase. The room still smelled strongly of his father, an aroma that was musky and, if truth be told, unpleasant. He'd either read or heard somewhere that it was natural for families to find each other's scents disagreeable. Supposedly, it was nature's way of guarding against incest, though the times he'd mentioned this to anyone his comments had always been roundly dismissed.

Eventually, he located the sheets on the top shelf of the wardrobe next to his father's hats. The wardrobe was sectioned into two, and Billy was surprised to find his mother's clothes still hanging in the left side compartment. For some reason, he'd assumed that his father had taken them to a charity shop after her death, but now, on reflection, realised that such an action would have been out of keeping with the man's determined curatorship of the past.

Indeed, such stewardship had led Lyle to continue sleeping on the same mattress he'd shared with Mary. Whether such an old mattress could ever have been physically comfortable after more than thirty years of use was debatable, but there was no doubting the emotional comfort it would have afforded his father. Over the years, the mattress had been turned and re-turned, turned and turned again, and for periods of time Lyle would have slept on the very part of the mattress Mary herself had slept on. His father, however, had remained sleeping on the left side of the bed, the side of the bed he'd slept on when his wife had been alive.

A lump formed in Greg's throat as he remembered his mother. He rarely thought of her, had forced himself over the years not to think of her. The memories were always too painful, her loss still unbearable. She was the one he'd loved the most, more than Billy and more than his father. And there was no doubting that he'd also been his mother's favourite.

Greg had been eight when she died. There'd been no build-up to her death and no time to prepare for her loss. One day she'd been alive and the next day dead. A congenital defect, the doctors said, a freak thrombosis that torpedoed her brain and – if government statistics were to be believed – sent her to the Promised Land forty-three years too soon.

He'd been at school the day she died. He still remembered the headmaster coming into the classroom and asking for him, accompanying him to his office where his Auntie Irene was waiting. He could tell she'd been crying, that something was wrong. He thought something had happened to his father or Billy, but not for a moment to his mother. And then Auntie Irene had spoken...

The rest was a blur. Tea at Auntie Irene's house with Billy and Uncle Frank. The arrival of his father, ashen-faced and trembling. Returning to an empty house and the scent of his mother. Days at home and life on hold. Numbness. Disbelief.

A packed church and a tearful farewell. The dawn of a new reality: no Mother.

His father had done his best to fill the void, but it had been an impossible task and Lyle knew this more than anyone. Routine changed by necessity. Instead of going home for lunch, Greg and Billy would eat cooked meals at school and after school go to Auntie Irene's house and wait there for their father to collect them. Lyle would arrive shortly after six, sooner if at all possible, and drive the boys home. There he would prepare them a cold tea, ask them about their days and then start doing chores: washing and ironing clothes, sewing buttons on shirts and darning socks. Although he proved surprisingly adept at mending their material world, he had greater difficulty repairing the boys' emotional worlds, especially Greg's.

Lyle had never wanted Billy and Greg to forget their mother and he would forever regale them with stories: how they'd met, her love for music, the exquisite way she'd danced, the things she'd said and, above all, how much she'd loved them both. It all became too much for Greg, who could only cope by forgetting his mother.

'Shut up, Dad, just shut up! I don't want to talk about her anymore. She's dead! She's got nothing to do with my life!' he blurted one evening, and then dashed from the room leaving Lyle and Billy staring at each another.

His mother, of course, had everything to do with his life, and therapists would have been more than happy to interpret the impact of her death. While Greg would have argued that the death of his mother had alerted him to the fragility of life and the importance of living life to its full, irrespective of consequence, analysts would have posited that her loss had instilled in him a morbid fear of future loss. Not only did it explain his disassociation from the family, but also his reluctance to form long-term relationships. They would have further submitted that his mother's death had left him angry and resentful – of both her and the world – and in all likelihood accounted for his youthful delinquency.

There was no doubting that Greg had acted up in his youth, but the only person to have ever called him a *delinquent* was the owner of an abandoned hen hut he'd set on fire. To Greg's way of thinking it had been an experiment with matches that had gone wrong rather than anything malicious, and fortunately for him his father had believed him. In return for the hen hut owner not calling the police, Lyle had paid the man over the odds for the damage sustained to his derelict property, and then grounded Greg for three weeks.

Groundings for Greg became as much a routine for the denuded family as eating school dinners and visiting Auntie Irene's. At various times and various ages, Greg was grounded for truancy, underage smoking and drinking, for taking Lyle's car without permission and crashing it into a tree, and for stealing a cheap propelling pencil from the local newsagents – a misdemeanour unnoticed by the owner but witnessed by Mrs Turton, who was more than happy to tell his father.

It was the drugs, however, that concerned Lyle most. He'd grown up in an age when all drugs had been considered dangerous and an expressway to either living on the street, prison or death. He was therefore unconvinced by Greg's argument that the marijuana in his room was a harmless organic put on earth by God for the same reason He'd planted hops and grapes: to give people a fucking break, Dad!

Unsurprisingly, it had been Uncle Frank who'd spoken up for Greg when Lyle confided in him that his youngest son was smoking dope.

'Is he hurting anyone?' Uncle Frank had asked, who at heart was a libertarian and resentful of any interference in his own life.

'Only himself,' Lyle had replied.

'The lad got straight As in his GCSEs, didn't he?'

Lyle acknowledged that he had, though wondered how his son had managed such a feat considering the amount of studying he did.

'Then ask me again when his grades start to slip. I'll reconsider the matter then.'

Greg's grades, however, didn't slip. He sailed through his A-levels, gained a first class honours degree, then a master's degree and, a week after Billy's marriage to Jean, announced to his father that he'd won a scholarship to study at the University of Arizona. As always, Lyle had been proud of his son's achievement, but also puzzled. Why, he wondered, had things never been this easy for Billy?

And Billy probably wondered the same thing.

If not a straight 'A' student, Billy had more than made up for it by being a straight 'A' son. Lyle had no doubts that his first born would grow up to be a model citizen, and neither had the neighbourhood, which considered Billy the politest boy to have ever lived. He bade a cheery hello to all he met, doffing his school cap or, if hatless, touching his brow with two closed fingers. When funeral corteges passed in the street, he would come to a halt and bow his head until they passed.

Although Billy's anachronistic behaviour impressed those of his father's generation and beyond, his own peers and those younger found his manner risible, and Greg was one of these. As far as he was concerned Billy was an embarrassment, a goody two-shoes who, irrespective of intent, always ended up making life more difficult for him: Billy the church-goer, Billy the Boy Scout, Billy the boy who never swore or answered back, Billy the son who helped his father with the chores, Billy the brother who endlessly nagged him about the stupid things he did, and Billy, the example he was always exhorted to follow.

There was a difference of four years between the brothers but, as far as Greg was concerned, it could have been forty.

Ghost

When Greg and Katy returned from The Tearoom the previous day, his suitcase had been standing conspicuously in the kitchen.

'Your suitcase arrived,' Jean announced unnecessarily. 'I suppose you'll be leaving tomorrow?'

Despite protestations from Billy and Katy, Greg acknowledged that he would. The sooner his father's house was made shipshape, the sooner he could return to Texas.

'Greg's got a girlfriend called Cyndi,' Katy said.

'No doubt next year she'll be called something else,' Jean said. 'Now go upstairs and practise your dance steps, darling. You know what Mrs Parkinson says: *practice makes perfect.* And put some effort into it, too: you need to burn off those cake calories. You know there isn't a call for fat dancers in the world.'

'There is in Mauritania,' Greg said. 'Fat women are considered attractive in that country.'

'Well, if you haven't noticed, Greg, this isn't Mauritania, and I'd appreciate it if you'd keep your comments to yourself while you're living in my house.'

'Sorry, Jean,' Greg said, and then after a slight pause: 'Is it okay if I phone my opinions through once I'm living in Dad's house?'

Jean ignored his question and left the room with Katy in tow.

'I think she's warming to you,' Billy said.

'I sense that too,' Greg replied.

They looked at each other and burst out laughing.

After a somewhat awkward dinner when Jean again pushed out the boat and served fish fingers, Greg and Billy retired to the lounge to discuss their father's house. Over a bottle of wine and the last of Greg's whisky, they agreed that Greg would clean the house and make a list of everything requiring attention before it could be put on the market. The kitchen and bathroom, however, were to be exempted, as both rooms now qualified as period pieces and would be gutted by anyone purchasing the property.

'I could be wrong,' Billy said, 'but from memory the only areas needing a complete repaint are the hallway and dining room. Dad was a great toucher-upper but his eyesight was poor and he never appreciated that the new magnolia he was dabbing on to the walls and woodwork was of a completely different hue from the magnolia paint that had been there for twenty years.'

How right Billy was, Greg thought when he saw the rooms. Both looked to be studies in impressionism, more likely to have been painted by an early Claude Monet than the late Lyle Bowman.

It was early evening by the time Greg finished cleaning the house and completing his to-do list. He went to the kitchen and looked through the cupboards, found a tin of stew and opened it. (The can opener was in the same place it had always been; everything was as it was on the day he'd left – and also the day his mother had left.)

He took the warmed stew into the dining room and sat down in his father's rocking chair. Strangely, something about this room *was* different; something *had* changed. There was no television! Greg put down his plate and went into the lounge, a room that had always been reserved for special occasions and entertaining visitors. But there was no television in this room either.

Greg felt slightly panicked. 'How the hell am I supposed to entertain myself?' he wondered out loud.

'I'll talk to you, son,' a voice said.

Greg froze.

'It's me, kid, your old Dad,' Lyle said. 'Turn around and let me take a look at you.'

Greg turned slowly, nervously, wondering if the voice was in his head or an intruder was in the house. It was neither. Standing by the door was his father – or at least an opalescent outline of his father. He was naked, his full frontal rhythm section swinging from side to side like a metronome, and he talked with an American accent.

For a moment Greg couldn't speak and stood transfixed.

'Cat got your tongue, son?' Lyle smiled.

Greg still couldn't speak. He worked his jaw, tried to get some moisture back into his mouth and stared at the apparition. He told himself this wasn't happening – couldn't be happening! It was a trick of the mind – that's all it could be – and occasioned in all probability by the circumstances of the day: being in his parents' house again, stirring the past and resurrecting memories. He'd been thinking of his father and now he was picturing him. He was having a hallucination!

He closed his eyes and kept them closed, fully expecting the manifestation to have disappeared by the time he opened them again. But, when he did open them, the illusion stubbornly remained and once more he heard a voice.

'I know this is weird for you, Greg – it's weird for me too, kid, believe it or not. But you have to get with the programme. You have to accept that I'm here. Isn't there anything you want to say to your old man?'

Still Greg didn't speak. Slowly and reluctantly, however, his mind started to accept the changed reality. There appeared to be no other option. And getting with the programme, he reasoned – if, in fact, he was reasoning – might well be the only way of ever understanding this mystifying turn of events. But what to say to his father after all this time? He stammered the obvious: 'You... you haven't got any clothes on, Dad.'

'Tell me something I don't know, kid,' his father shot back. 'You wouldn't have any clothes on if someone stuck you in an oven and turned up the volume. What did you think I was wearing – an asbestos suit? And whose goddamn idea was it to put me in a *bamboo* coffin?'

'That was Jean's idea,' Greg said, his voice still tentative. 'She's concerned about the environment.'

'And I bet Billy went right along with her, didn't he?' Lyle said. 'That boy needs to get himself a pair of balls. He lets that woman walk right over him.'

While Greg could agree with the sentiments his father expressed, he found it difficult to equate them with anything his father might have said while he'd been alive. His father had never spoken ill of anyone – especially family.

'If you don't mind me saying so, Dad: you're sounding a bit... how shall I put this... a bit hot under the collar.'

'I am hot under the collar! I'm two thousand degrees Fahrenheit hot under the collar, if you must know. I wanted to be buried next to your mother, not put in a goddamn incinerator. That's where they burn rubbish – not people!'

'I was in America when that decision was made,' Greg replied, in an effort to extricate himself from any guilt his father might be imparting.

'You're always in America,' his father shot back. 'That's where you live, for God's sake! You can't use that as an excuse. You've got a goddamn phone like everyone else, haven't you? Huh! Any chance of avoiding responsibility and you'll take it, lad. You were always that way!'

Greg was unsettled by the anger, by the accusation – even if he did know it to be true – and he sought to take command of this strange conversation. 'Is there anything in particular you want, Dad?' he asked.

'There are a lot of things I want, Greg, but most of them I can't have now. That's the problem with being dead. How long have I been dead, anyway?'

'Just over three weeks. The funeral service was on Friday.'

'Three weeks? It feels more like three years! Three years of being bandied from pillar to post and now back to bloody square one. Jesus Christ!'

Lyle paused when he saw his son's expression and his tone became more conciliatory. 'I'm sorry, Greg. I shouldn't be talking to you like this. Taking things out on you. It's you I came to see, lad – you I wanted to see. I think I'll go up to the loft for a bit. Get some rest and calm down. I'll be different when I return, I promise you. More like my old self. Bear with me, son. It's important you bear with me.'

Greg nodded. 'When you come back, Dad, can you wear some clothes? I'm not trying to be rude or anything, but those dangly bits of yours are a bit of a distraction.'

Lyle looked down at his pecker and was surprised to see it swaying around like a divining rod.

'I see what you mean,' he said. 'What time is it?'

Greg looked at his watch. 'Going on for eight-thirty.'

'I'll be back at ten, then. Don't go anywhere!'

Lyle's outline disappeared and Greg was once more alone in the room. He stood there immobile, his arms hanging limply. Slightly dazed and totally confused, he walked to the dining room and picked up the bowl of stew he'd been eating. It was now stone cold and he scraped the contents into the sink and turned on the tap. When the last of the hash had disappeared down the plughole he went to the pantry in search of something more substantial – alcohol – and found his father's Christmas sherry.

He poured a generous amount into a beaker he found in the kitchen cupboard and moved to the dining room. There, he took a piece of scrap paper and the pen his father kept by the telephone, sat down in one of the easy chairs and, resting the paper on an old dictionary, started to write a narrative of his strange experience – and also a list of questions to ask his father if, in the event, his father did return.

But how could his father return? His father was dead. The prismatic outline had been a daydream, a trick of the mind; there had to be a rational explanation for its appearance. But what was it? Delayed jetlag came to mind, but he quickly discounted the idea; he was more than familiar with its discomforts and just as aware now that he wasn't suffering from any of them. It had to be something else.

He retraced the events of the day. He'd climbed out of bed, showered and then gone downstairs and joined Billy at the breakfast table. Jean had handed him an orange juice and… that was odd. When had Jean ever poured him an orange juice before? She'd always banged the carton down on the table and told him to help himself. What if she'd slipped something into the juice, a slow-releasing Mickey or something? The more he thought about this the more convinced he became that his grudge-bearing sister-in-law had drugged him. 'What a bitch,' he muttered, though more out of relief than anger. That would explain everything. But how would squeaky-clean Jean know where to get hold of such a drug? She'd never moved in the right circles.

It was then that a more uncomfortable thought crossed his mind: he'd moved in those circles! Maybe Jean hadn't drugged him after all; perhaps he'd experienced a delayed reaction to one or another of the drugs he'd *voluntarily* taken as a youth. But what drug, and why after all this time would he suffer its after-effects when he'd never suffered from flashbacks before? It made no sense. No sense at all. The sherry, however, continued to make sense, and he poured himself another generous measure.

The more of the fortified wine he drank, the less he believed his father would return, that his appearance – if indeed he had appeared – had been a one-off mental aberration that would forever be unaccountable. Oddly though, the more he believed this, the more he found himself *wanting* his father to return. He'd always preferred the unusual to the humdrum.

Greg wasn't to be disappointed. At precisely ten o'clock, the door to the dining room opened and Lyle walked in wearing a red ruche taffeta ball gown and a flat corduroy cap.

'How's this?' he asked. 'Is this better?'

Greg, who was by now on his sixth sherry, answered his father directly: 'Yes, much better, Dad. But why did you choose to wear one of Mum's dresses when you have your own clothes hanging in the wardrobe?'

'For one thing it's more comfortable,' Lyle said. 'My todger's still going like the clappers down there and the dress gives it room for manoeuvre. For another, I don't seem to be able to wear trousers anymore. I can wear things that hang from the shoulders, but nothing that requires tightening around the waist. There's no point asking me why because I don't know why. All this is new to me.'

He then sat down in the chair next to his son and let out a quiet sigh of satisfaction.

'I loved this chair, Greg. Me and your mother bought it. It cost a fair bit but it was quality – and quality lasts. That's a fact worth remembering. And about earlier: I think I owe you an apology for some of the things I said. I probably meant them, but I shouldn't have said them. I never used to talk like that and I certainly didn't use to cuss when I was alive. But I think I'm more myself now, so let's enjoy the time we have together. I'm not due back for another twenty days.'

This was more like the mild-mannered man Greg remembered, but whether he wanted to spend the next twenty days in the company of this strange apparition was another matter entirely. He glanced at the notes he'd made on the scrap of paper and cleared his throat.

'This is all a bit weird for me, Dad. I mean – don't get me wrong – I'm glad to see you and everything, but I can't help thinking that I'm not seeing you, that I'm having a dream or a sort of breakdown and that I'm talking to myself.'

'Completely understandable, Greg. Completely understandable. But I'm here. You're not having a dream or a breakdown.'

'And you're dead?'

'Dead as a herring, son.'

'So why are you here then? Why am I seeing you?'

'There's something I need you to do for me, Greg – for the family. I'm counting on you.'

'You're counting on me?' Greg exclaimed. 'I'm the last person people count on. You know that better than anyone, Dad. You said earlier that if there was a chance of me avoiding responsibility then I'd take it. And you're right. I'm not proud of the fact, but that's the way I am – the way I've always been. Wouldn't you do better talking to Billy?'

'I can't. Billy's a part of the problem you have to fix. Now hear me out, will you?

'There's probably no convenient time for a person to die, but my death came at the worst time possible. There were matters needing my attention that I'd been putting off for too long. Family matters. And Billy's one of them.

'It's always been a great sorrow to me that you and your brother never really got along, and that for the last few years you haven't even been talking to each other.'

'We're talking now,' Greg said.

'And what did it take for that to happen? My death is what! Don't you think it would have been better if you'd started talking to each other while I was still alive? I don't know the ins and outs of what went on between you two, but I do know one thing: you were always hard on your brother and, in my opinion, unfairly so. That's something you need to understand.'

Greg poured more sherry into his beaker and braced himself for a lecture. It was familiar ground.

'You had it all, Greg – the looks and the brains. You never had to try. Everything came easily to you. You won a scholarship to the grammar school, sailed through exams with the minimum of effort and got accepted by good universities. And no sooner had you graduated from the University of Arizona than you walked into a well-paying job in Texas and became some hot-shot academic.

'Billy, meanwhile, fails to get into the grammar school – and how you rubbed that into his face. You never let up on him, did you? Always told him he was stupid. He wasn't stupid: he just wasn't as bright as you were. But something he was that you never were was a tryer. It used to break my heart when he only scraped through his exams when he put so much effort into them. Do you know how disappointed he was when he didn't get into university and had to settle for a polytechnic? Probably not, or you wouldn't have kept ribbing him about that either, telling him he was as thick as two short planks.'

'I didn't mean those things, Dad – and I certainly never meant to hurt him. I was just teasing him. That's all it ever was. But you have to admit, Billy was a bit of a geek when he was growing up: all that lifting his cap and touching his forelock. Everyone thought he was odd.'

'If a geek's a person who's polite, a person who doesn't swear and a person who doesn't break the law and get into trouble, then I guess you're right: he was a geek. But if that's what a geek is, then you can give me a geek as a son any day of the week.'

His father fell silent for a moment and so too did Greg.

Home truths had never been his favourite subject.

'He worked hard at polytechnic, Greg,' Lyle continued, 'got a degree in textile engineering and found a job in a mill. And no sooner had he started to do well there than the mill closed and the textile industry upped sticks and headed to the Far East. He tried accountancy after that, but no matter how hard he studied he could never get the hang of it and had to find something else.

'When he went into sales, I admired him. It went against his nature, took him outside his comfort zone. He was never particularly confident or outgoing – and a part of that's your doing. But he's made a good fist of it, and he's even got a couple of people reporting to him now.

'But when it comes to real promotions, he's always been passed over. I could be wrong, but to my way of thinking there's only so high a person of 5' 7" can climb in the corporate world. When it comes to choosing between tall people and short people, charisma and substance, the tall person with charisma wins out every time. It's why this country's in the mess it's in. I'll admit that Billy's a bit light on the charisma front, but the lad's always had substance.'

'So, what's the matter with Billy?' Greg asked. 'You said he was part of the problem I have to fix?'

'I don't rightly know,' Lyle answered. 'That's what you have to find out. I know for a fact though that there is something wrong. I could always read Billy like an open book and I know when something's troubling him. I thought for a while he was having problems with Jean, but he assured me he wasn't – or at least no more than usual.'

'But if I ask him what the problem is, he's not going to tell me, is he, Dad?' Greg said. 'We've only just started talking again. Wouldn't it be better if Uncle Frank asked him?'

'No, this is a matter for you to sort out, Greg. It's up to you to find a way. Besides, Uncle Frank is the other family matter you have to sort out. I don't know the full story here, either, but at least I know the start of it: he keeps handing himself in to the police.'

Uncle Frank's unexplained behaviour had started about a year ago, after a large jeweller's store in the city centre had been robbed. The robbery, Lyle said, had been front-page news in the local paper and, the day after the story appeared, his uncle had gone to the police station and claimed responsibility.

Although the police had immediately discounted Frank's claim – both robbers had been in their twenties and a good foot taller than the old man now standing in front of them – procedures required that they question him before eliminating him from their enquiries. Frank was therefore taken to a small room and interviewed by a junior officer.

'So, Frank, tell me what happened,' the officer had said.

'It's Mr Bowman to you, young man,' Uncle Frank had replied. 'And, if you don't mind, I'd like a cup of tea.'

Over a cup of tea and two Rich Tea biscuits the officer had generously thrown in, Uncle Frank told him he'd met his accomplice at a bus stop and that they'd only decided to rob the jeweller's store after the bus they were waiting for had failed to arrive. Since privatisation, he added, the bus service had gone to pot.

It was a spur of the moment thing, Uncle Frank explained, and no, he didn't know his accomplice's name – it wasn't as if they were friends or anything. What did they take? Jewels, of course! What kinds of jewels? Shiny ones. Any watches? Maybe – he couldn't vouch for what his accomplice took. Where are the jewels now? He'd lost them. Why are you here, Mr Bowman? It was his duty as a citizen. Do you have a wife, children – any relatives?

It was then that Lyle had been called to the station. No longer having a car of his own and in the middle of a delicate paint job, it had taken him an hour to get there. He was asked by a detective if his brother had ever been sectioned or was currently being treated for a psychological disorder. Lyle had answered a simple no to both questions, but when asked if his brother led a full life, had replied dismissively that no person their age led a full life.

Lyle and Uncle Frank left the station together, Uncle Frank waving a cheery goodbye to Pete, the junior officer who was now allowed to call him Frank. 'See you later, Pete,' Uncle Frank called out to him.

And see him later he did.

On three subsequent occasions, his uncle returned to the station and admitted responsibility for other robberies: a branch bank, a building society and a travel agent's, all of which had been reported in the local newspaper. Each time Lyle had been called to the station to escort his brother home, and each time Uncle Frank had bade a fond farewell to his growing number of friends there: 'Bye Pete. See you later, Dave. Mind how you go, Carol – and thanks for the digestives.'

'It beats me why they never charged him with wasting police time,' Lyle said. 'I think they just saw him as a lonely old man with too much time on his hands and, when you think about it, that's exactly what he is. They liked him, though, that was apparent. Always treated him with respect. It wouldn't surprise me if they even looked forward to his visits.'

'Did he ever say why he did this?' Greg asked, intrigued by the story his father told him.

'No. He refused to talk about it. I tried reasoning with him – even shouted at him – but he never would tell me. All he'd say was that he had a plan and I could rest assured that he wasn't losing his marbles. He said his silence on the matter was for my own good, but God knows what he meant by that.'

'Can you remember if anything happened just before he started doing this?' Greg asked.

Lyle thought for a moment. 'There was one thing,' he said thoughtfully, 'but it made no sense. He said the government had turned off his television.'

'Why would he think that?'

'I haven't a clue, Greg. I haven't had a television for six years. It got to the point where I wasn't prepared to pay a licence fee for the drivel they were broadcasting. Syd was of the same opinion, but kept his television for when his grandchildren visited.'

'So you want me to find out what he's up to?'

'Him and Billy, both,' Lyle said. 'Billy will be the toughest nut to crack, but your uncle's always had a soft spot for you. If he's going to open up to anyone, it will be you. Your emails were always the highlight of his week.'

(The emails Greg sent his uncle weren't exactly emails. Uncle Frank had heard of emails, wanted to tell the few people he knew that he received emails, but had no computer. Greg had therefore written emails, printed them off and then put them in an envelope and posted them. In all but name, the emails were simply old-fashioned letters.)

'I'm tired, Greg,' his father announced. 'I'm going back to the loft. What are your plans for tomorrow?'

'Buy some paint and get hold of a structural engineer. Did you know there's a crack in the back wall?'

'No, but the house is old – like me. It's not dying though, so I wouldn't worry about it too much. By the way, I found an old war helmet and gas mask in the loft. I'll put them on the landing and save you a climb. You never know, they might be worth something. Sleep well, son. I'll see you tomorrow at eight pm.'

Without ceremony, Lyle disappeared.

Greg looked down at the list of questions he'd prepared and crossed out those his father had answered. Two remained: why was his father speaking with an American accent and what was the Afterlife like?

Frontier

It was in the early hours before Greg fell asleep. For a long time he lay thinking about what his father had said, not only about him but about the way he'd treated Billy. Had he really been that insensitive and dismissive of his brother's feelings? The answer troubled him, for the answer was probably yes. Although he'd told his father it had never been his intention to hurt Billy, that his remarks were no more than brotherly teasing, he knew this wasn't true.

Billy's straightforward life had always irritated him, especially after their mother's death when it appeared that his brother's life had continued as before, as if untroubled by her loss. Billy hadn't cried at his mother's funeral and neither had his father; he'd been the only one to shed tears. Thereafter, he realised he'd been happy to stick a spoke in his brother's wheel at every opportunity. Even his supposed concern for Billy when he announced his engagement to Jean was a sham: he wasn't worried for his brother – he'd simply disliked Jean.

Greg had never known that Billy had tried as hard as he had at school, and neither was he aware of the acute disappointment he'd felt when his efforts went unrewarded. He'd been happy when Billy failed, when the family's perfect son came to grief. Greg had never been there to pick up the pieces of his brother's life, only to scatter them further. What kind of a person did those things – and was that person still him?

For the first time he understood what Billy had meant by *you always have to know best, don't you*? He was, he realised, the know-it-all younger brother who'd dismissed his older brother's opinions out of hand, short-changed him at every opportunity and, as his father had asserted, probably contributed to his lack of confidence. The clarity of the image disturbed him. It was as if he'd been staring at a Magic Eye picture his whole life and seen only a meaningless pattern of dots; now that he concentrated and allowed his eyes to bifurcate, he saw the truth of the three-dimensional picture hidden there.

Unexpectedly, he thought of Cyndi, and was reminded of his father's assertion that everything in life came easily to him. Certainly this was true when it came to relationships, and also a possible explanation of why he never valued them. Cyndi was only the most recent of a long line of girlfriends and there was little to differentiate her attributes from those of her predecessors. Greg's tastes were superficial and based solely on physical appearance. He didn't date for conversation or an intellectual exchange of ideas.

Greg's male friendships were similarly of the moment, friends who didn't bother or need him. He drank with them, went to ball games with them, but there was always an unwritten agreement that neither associate would place demands on the other or burden them with personal troubles. Such demands were the preserve of lifetime friends and Greg made a point of not having any. The only long-term relationship he had was with impermanence.

There were two people, however, that Greg had kept in contact with: his father and Uncle Frank. Communication with his father had always been more out of duty than anything else, for although he loved the man, he could never think of much to talk to him about during their weekly phone conversations and had been more than happy for his father to simply recount the minutiae of his last seven days – which, in the event, always tended to be the same as the minutiae of the previous seven days.

Uncle Frank, however, was a different kettle of fish and had always been his favourite relative. Cantankerous and obdurate though the man was, his heart was good and his spirit free, and in him Greg found not only an occasional ally but also a mentor. Indeed, if it hadn't been for his uncle, it was doubtful that he would now be living in Texas and teaching American history.

The bond between them had formed after the death of his mother, when he and Billy had spent more and more of their time at Auntie Irene's house, where Uncle Frank also lived. (In truth, the house belonged equally to both Irene and Frank, but it was always described as Auntie Irene's house, as if somehow Uncle Frank lacked both the responsibility and the means to own a dwelling.)

Uncle Frank's passion was for the Wild West. It started on his sixth birthday, after his mother had taken him to see *Stagecoach* at the local picture house, and never ended. That Christmas his parents bought him the first of many cowboy outfits, and thereafter he roamed the neighbourhood with a marshal's star pinned to his small leather waistcoat, drawing his gun from its holster and firing paper caps into the air. The obsession was nurtured by other films and, after the family bought their first television set, the adventures of *The Lone Ranger*, *The Cisco Kid* and *Hopalong Cassidy*. He saved his spending money and bought stories set in the West, books written by Jack Schaefer, Elmer Kelton and Louis L'Amour.

The West that Uncle Frank observed on the screen and read about in books was a wild frontier. It was a time of the loner, the nomad, of cowboys and gunfighters who drifted from one small frontier town to the next, living by their own codes of honour and dispensing their own forms of justice to the wrongdoers who crossed them. Their loyalty was to themselves and their immediate circle only, never to the wider community or its abstract laws. It was a world that Uncle Frank could understand, a world that made more sense to him than the one he'd been born into.

Frank's pride and joy was his collection of model cowboys,

Indians and American soldiers. After his parents died, he remained in the small box room rather than move into a larger bedroom, and with his sister Irene's permission – though never her approval – set about converting their parents' room into the American West.

He bought three trestle tables and arranged them in the form of an H, a shape that allowed him access to all areas of the frontier he was building. Using sand from the beach and modelling mountains out of papier-mâché, he created the arid and desolate landscape of his imagination. He made small towns from cardboard and old matches, built saloons, livery stables and jailhouses. He constructed ranches with fencing and herds of cattle, Indian encampments with wigwams and totem poles, and turreted stockades for the soldiers. He would spend his evenings and weekends in this room, inventing scenarios of his own or restaging events he'd witnessed on film or read about in books.

This was the world he introduced Greg to when his nephew visited the house, and in doing so allowed the boy into his own world. Greg's interest in history was born in this room and then nurtured at grammar school by an eccentric teacher who spent entire lessons standing on a desk. Although Greg briefly equivocated between studying history or geography at university, it was his uncle's salutary words that swayed him. 'Hell's teeth, Greg! Geography's just about maps. History's about *chaps*!'

The rest, so to speak, *was* history. Greg graduated from the University of Arizona and without too much effort landed a position teaching history at the Austin branch of the University of Texas. To be awarded tenure, however, he needed publications to his name.

His doctoral dissertation had been a biography of a little known socialist presidential candidate who had garnered fewer than 20,000 votes. (He'd chosen the subject not for any interest in socialism, but for the more mundane reason that the library held the candidate's papers in their Special Collections Department and was within easy walking distance of his apartment.)

The contents of the dissertation provided him with two articles that were accepted for publication by reputable journals, and then, as usual, happenstance took Greg by the hand and led him through doorways and down alleyways to a cornucopia of publishable topics that his associates spent lifetimes trying to discover. In quick succession, he had two books published: one on the West Virginia mining war of 1921 – which Syd had alluded to at the funeral – and the other on a 1919 massacre of trade unionists in a small town in Washington State. (The description of Greg as a Labour Historian on the flyleaves of these books came as a surprise to his father: to his knowledge, his son had never done a day's work in his life.)

Greg fell into a troubled sleep and awoke the next morning with a pounding headache. The bedclothes had fallen to the floor during the night and he was perspiring. He lay there for a long time and went to the bathroom only after his saliva glands had started to work overtime. He spat the seemingly never-ending supply of juice into the washbasin and wondered if he was going to be sick. He lifted the lid of the toilet as a precaution and recoiled. Floating there was a large disintegrating stool, the remnant of his father's last earthly bowel movement.

The wondering stopped and Greg threw up.

He clung helplessly to the toilet bowl as the contents of his stomach splashed into the water. He retched twice and remained kneeling until the feeling of nausea passed. He stood up slowly and washed his hands in the basin and rinsed his mouth with water. He looked at his ashen-faced reflection in the magnified shaving mirror and resolved never to drink sherry again.

He sat down on the side of the bath and held his head, gathered his thoughts and tried to make sense of them. Had he been talking to his father last night or had it been a drunken dream? And, if it hadn't been a drunken dream, had he in some inexplicable way been haunted by his father's turd? And, if it had been the turd haunting him and the turd was now flushed, would the haunting stop?

He sighed, the same way he remembered his father sighing, and made his way back to the bedroom. His attention was drawn to something lying on the landing, something that hadn't been there when he'd gone to bed. He went to pick up the objects and the penny dropped: he was looking at a World War I helmet and gas mask.

He knew then that he had been talking to his father and, moreover, that his father would be returning.

4

Myanmar

Greg drank only coffee for breakfast, and afterwards took the Yellow Pages from the sideboard drawer and looked for names of structural engineers. He located several in the section headed Surveyors and Valuers and, in the hope that the man was as down to earth and no-nonsense as his name suggested, decided upon Fred Stubbington. He dialled the number and arranged for Mr Stubbington to visit the house at ten the following morning. He then phoned the offices of the three estate agents Billy had suggested and arranged for them to call at staggered times on the afternoon of the same day.

The rest of the morning was taken up with errands. He bought groceries from a supermarket; paint, filler, and brushes from a DIY store; and sandwiches for lunch from a local bakery. No sooner had he returned to the house than the phone rang.

'Hello, Gregory, it's Mrs Turton. I was wondering if you'd like to come round for coffee this afternoon.'

'Sure, Mrs Turton. What time do you have in mind? Three? That's fine. Okay, I'll see you then.'

Greg still held a grudge against Mrs Turton for telling his father about the propelling pencil he'd stolen from the newsagent, and the idea of spending an afternoon in her company didn't appeal. He reminded himself, however, that she'd been a good neighbour to his father over the years and that it had been her who'd first raised the alarm for his mother's well-being after seeing her prostrate on the lounge floor – though why she'd been looking through the bay window that day had never been fully explained.

Three o'clock arrived and Greg knocked on Mrs Turton's door.

She opened it slightly, sufficient only to see who was standing there. Even after recognising Greg as the caller she still kept the door in the same position.

'Hello, Gregory,' she said, eyeing him suspiciously. 'What do you want?'

'You invited me for coffee, Mrs Turton. I could come back if it's not convenient.'

She thought for a moment. 'Oh, of course I did! I forgot all about it, Gregory. Barry says I'd forget my head if it wasn't screwed on. Come on in, will you.'

Greg stepped through the door and was told to wipe his feet on the mat.

While his parents had always lived in the back room, Mrs Turton preferred to live in the front room and use her dining room for storage. Even so, the lounge was still overflowing with bric-a-brac, and a selection of stuffed bears had to be moved from the settee before Greg could sit down.

'Make yourself comfortable, Gregory, and I'll go and make the coffee,' she said.

She returned a few minutes later with two coffees and a plate of custard cream biscuits.

'Custard creams are my favourite, Mrs Turton,' Greg said. 'They're one of the few things I miss about England. I think my Dad's funeral was the first time I'd seen any in years.'

Mrs Turton looked uncomfortable for a moment, wondering if Greg had seen her taking the biscuits from the funeral buffet. 'Mine too,' she said guardedly.

They chatted about this and that, old times and new, and the sadness of Mr Bowman's passing. (His father and Mrs Turton – like most people of their generation – had clung to the etiquette of addressing each other formally. Lyle had always been Mr Bowman and Doris had always been Mrs Turton.)

Mrs Turton then raised the subject of the Collards.

'We're still not speaking,' she said. 'And they're still refusing to lower that wall of theirs, even though they don't have a dog now.'

The building of the wall that separated her property from theirs was the source of the conflict that now divided the two neighbours.

The rift had started when the Collards bought a collie. Constantly worrying that the dog they called Sam might escape from the garden and follow its instincts to herd sheep, they determined to secure its borders. Fence panels already divided their property from that of their attached neighbours, but nothing separated their drive from Mrs Turton's. Consequently, they hired a builder and asked him to build a wall measuring six feet from base to capstones. Although the builder doubted the necessity for a wall so high, he kept the reservation to himself and duly obliged.

Despite these precautions – and the fact that there were no sheep in the area to herd – the dog escaped the property on the day Margaret Collard forgot to close the gate behind her. Two miles from the house, and on a road close to the motorway, Sam was knocked down and killed by a lorry transporting pet food.

'It's such an eyesore,' Mrs Turton said. 'And it's not even made from real stone, either. Barry calls it the Berlin Wall. Anyway, I've told them flat that as long as the wall's there I'm not speaking to them. Maybe it's not the most Christian of things to say, but I've talked it over with the minister and he says he can fully understand my feelings.'

She paused for a moment and then confided in Greg: 'The minister says I haven't got an unchristian bone in my body.'

Greg nodded his head and murmured sympathetically, wondering how much longer he'd have to sit there before politely excusing himself.

'There are all kinds I suppose, and goodness knows we've got enough of them living in this city,' Mrs Turton said. 'Newcomers,' she added, when she saw Greg looking puzzled.

Greg – or Gregory, as Mrs Turton insisted on calling him – was still mystified by her comment. 'What newcomers are you talking about, Mrs Turton?'

Mrs Turton shuffled uneasily in her seat and almost whispered the answer. 'The ones from Myanmar, Gregory.'

'I didn't know we had any Burmese people living here. When did they arrive?'

'They've been coming here since the sixties,' Mrs Turton said, herself now baffled by Greg's remark. 'But they're not from Burma. Maybe I've got the name wrong. I'll phone Barry – he'll know.'

Mrs Turton looked for her phone but couldn't locate it. 'I wonder where that's got to. I was only using it this morning. You're not sitting on it are you, Gregory?'

Greg stood up. There was no phone in his chair, but he did notice one half-hidden by some knitting on the table next to Mrs Turton. 'Is that your phone?' he asked, pointing to it.

'Well, what the deary me,' Mrs Turton laughed. 'Right next to me all the time.'

'What are you knitting?' Greg asked.

'It's a scarf for one of the orphans in India, Gregory.'

'It looks to be about ten feet long, Mrs Turton. How big are their necks?'

'It's fifteen feet actually,' Mrs Turton replied with a smile.

'And I still haven't finished knitting it. This is going to be a special scarf, Gregory – the longest scarf in the world! It's Barry's idea really. He says that once I've knitted it I should call the local newspaper and get them to write an article about the work I do for other people. He says I should stop hiding my light under a bushel and take some credit for a change. That boy: he's always thinking of me... that reminds me, I was going to phone him, wasn't I?'

She pressed a number on the speed dial.

'Hello, Barry, it's your Mum, love. No, nothing's wrong. I've got Gregory here with me. No, of course he won't take anything.' She looked across and smiled at Greg. 'Barry says you haven't got to steal anything.'

Greg was astonished by her remark, but smiled back.

'I was telling him about the newcomers, Barry. Where are they from again? No, not the ones from Poland – the ones that have been here longer. Mirpur, that's it! What did I tell you it was called, Gregory?'

'Myanmar.'

'I told him it was Myanmar, but he said that was Burma. Did you know that? No, me neither. Is Diane doing all right? Three pounds? Well, that's not the direction we were hoping for, is it? Have you been keeping her away from the bread? I know you can't watch her all the time, love. I'm not going on, Barry: I just want what's best for her. Okay then. Call me when you get home then. Bye.'

Mrs Turton put the telephone back on the table and shook her head. 'That girl is a fool to herself. She's already the size of an elephant. How big does she want to get? Now where were we? That's it, Mirpur.'

'I presume that's a part of Pakistan then,' Greg said.

'Yes, that's right, Gregory. When the newcomers first came here, it was like having a year-round Nativity in the city – you know, the way they dressed and everything – but then, more and more of them started to come and they're half the population now. It doesn't bother me, but I think it bothered your father. He never said anything, but I could tell from his eyes and the way he sighed when I talked to him about them.'

'I don't remember my father ever saying anything derogatory about them, Mrs Turton. Are you sure you've got that right?'

Mrs Turton nodded. 'You can't blame people for feeling the way they do, Gregory, and I certainly didn't blame your father. If they'd tried to fit in more and become more westernised, I don't think there'd have been a problem. But very few of them have done. That's why Barry says we should celebrate those that have – people like Lenny Henry.'

'Lenny Henry's British,' Greg said. 'And his parents were from Jamaica, not Pakistan.'

'Yes, but you know what I mean, Gregory. He's fitted in, hasn't he? And he's always got that nice smile on his face. If I'm honest, though, I can't say that I find him particularly funny. I watched him on television the other week and I didn't laugh once. I wouldn't have bothered, but the *Radio Times* gave him a good write-up and described him as a comic genius. I think that was stretching it a bit. They probably only said that because his show was on BBC1.

'I mean he looks like he should be funny, doesn't he, but he's not – or at least I don't think he is. Barry likes him though, and he's forever shouting out *Katanga*! That's one of his catchphrases. Now what the Dickens are the names of those other two characters of his that Barry goes on about?' Mrs Turton studied for a moment and then announced their names triumphantly. 'Delbert Wilkins and Theophilus P. Wildebeeste! Barry says they're funnier than Mr Pastry.'

Greg glanced at his watch.

'I'm not sure I agree with him there, though,' Mrs Turton continued. 'In my opinion, Mr Pastry was a lot funnier. But

Barry's a lot more forgiving than I am, believe it or not, and he always looks for the positives in people. He'll find something good to say about anyone – even Robert Kilroy-Silk. He doesn't like the man's politics – they're a bit too left-wing for Barry – but he does give him credit for having tidy hair. And Barry says that even if I don't find Lenny Henry funny, I should still give him his due for the work he does in Africa for Comic Relief and his Premier Inn adverts.'

'And the fact that he was a trailblazer for other black comedians, I suppose,' Greg said.

'I'm sorry, Gregory, but I don't allow words like that in this house.'

'What words?'

'You know very well what I'm talking about. Words like B-L-A-C-K,' she said, spelling out the letters. 'It's racist.'

'But he is black, Mrs Turton, and what's more he's probably proud of being black. Black's a positive word – just like white. It's not being racist to say a person's black.'

'I think we'll have to disagree on that, Gregory, but while you're in my house I'd appreciate it if you didn't use that word.'

First Jean telling him how to behave under her roof and now Mrs Turton! What the hell had happened to free speech in his absence? He looked to see how much of the foul-tasting brew was left to drink and was disappointed to find his cup still half full. He was about to drain it when Mrs Turton continued the conversation, as if the intervening unpleasantness had never happened.

'Anyway, going back to what I was saying, Gregory. Barry says that we should celebrate newcomers who make an effort to fit in, and he wrote to the company that makes Robertson's Golden Shred to try and get them to back one of his ideas. He said that now they'd stopped putting paper golliwogs behind their labels, maybe they should consider putting photographs of people like Lenny Henry and Moira Stuart there – Barry was as upset as anybody when Moira lost her job for being too old. She wasn't even pension age, you know.'

'And what did Robertson's have to say about this?' Greg asked, incredulous that Barry could be so blind to the mores of the time.

'To tell you the truth, I don't think they took him seriously,' Mrs Turton said. 'They just wrote back thanking him for his interest in Golden Shred and asked him if he'd tried any Hartley's jam recently.'

Greg dissolved into laughter and started to guffaw uncontrollably. Mrs Turton stared at him po-faced.

'I don't think it's anything to laugh about, Gregory,' she said. 'What's the matter with you – are you on drugs?'

'No… no, Mrs Turton,' he gasped. 'I think I'm just tired. I didn't sleep very well last night.'

Still smiling, Greg drained his cup, winced involuntarily and then gathered himself. He stood, thanked Mrs Turton for her hospitality and then moved towards the door. 'You don't want to frisk me before I leave, do you?' he asked light-heartedly.

Mrs Turton declined his offer with a straight face and said that she'd know soon enough if anything was missing.

As Mrs Turton closed the door behind him, only one thought passed through her mind. Whatever Gregory might have said to the contrary, there was no doubt in her mind that Mr Bowman's youngest son was still taking drugs. 'Poor Mr Bowman,' she said quietly to herself. 'He'll be turning in his grave.'

She picked up the phone and called Barry.

Rather than return to his father's house, Greg chose to put as much distance between him and Mrs Turton as possible and headed for the pub. The rubbish that woman talked. Why, he wondered, had he sat there so placidly while she'd intimated his father was a racist and that, by dint of his vocabulary, so too was he? And that son of hers suggesting he was a thief, and her that he was under the influence of drugs. Jesus Christ!

The Brown Cow was as it had always been. It had withstood the calls for modernisation and remained an establishment where people could drink in peace without being distracted by loud music and the noise of fruit machines. He ordered a pint and moved to a corner table. There were only two other people in the pub and they too were sitting alone, one reading a newspaper and the other puzzling over a crossword.

He'd been there only a few minutes when Ian Collard walked through the door wearing a neck brace. He saw Greg and brought his pint over to the table.

'Is it all right if I join you, Greg, or would you prefer to be alone? You look to be deep in thought, young man.'

'Please do, Ian,' Greg said, pulling out a chair for him. 'What happened to your neck?'

'Car crash,' Ian replied matter-of-factly. 'Hit from behind when I was driving Margaret home from the Beech Hotel. Hedgehog runs into the road, I brake hard and the car behind goes slap-bang into the back of me. Car got off light, but the old neck took a bit of a hammering. Brace probably makes it look worse than it is though.'

'How's Margaret? Is she okay?'

'Margaret's fine but the marriage is on the rocks! Not really,' he laughed. 'I was just joking when I said that. We are having a bit of a disagreement though. She wants me to call a personal injury lawyer and make a claim for compensation. I'm refusing point-blank – just like your dad would have done. I'm a traditionalist, Greg, and I don't go in for that kind of thing.

'Margaret does though. She watches daytime television – too much for my liking – and sees adverts telling people to contact them on a No Win No Fee basis. I don't believe in it. It's not the culture I grew up with and it's not a culture I like.

And your father didn't like it either. He said it encouraged untruths and personal irresponsibility, and stoked the belief that you could always get something for nothing if you blamed other people for your stupidity. It drives up the costs of car insurance too. My own premium went up over twenty per cent last year. Can you believe that?

'Anyway, I'm not claiming and that's that! Besides, I think the accident was my fault. I know it's human nature to brake for a living animal – unless you're driving a lorry load of pet food, that is – but even so, I should have looked in my rear-view mirror before I braked. I didn't give the car behind me a snowball's chance in hell. To cap it all, it turned out that it wasn't even a hedgehog I braked for: it was a brown paper bag that someone had screwed into a ball and thrown out of their car window.

'And I'll tell you another thing, Greg: I read in the newspaper the other week that there are more claims for whiplash in this country than any other country in Europe. No one's going to tell me that British necks are weaker than continental ones – we'd have never won any wars if that was the case. It doesn't make any sense. It's a con is what it is and the only people benefitting from it are those ambulance-chasing lawyers. I've no time for them, and neither had your dad.'

He took off his hat, placed it on the chair next to him and ran his fingers through his thinning hair.

'Apart from my dad, I think you and my Uncle Frank are the only people I know who still wear hats,' Greg commented.

'I'm afraid hat wearers are a dying breed, Greg. Your dad had a nice trilby, though. Always wore it when he went out. And, if he painted outside the house, he wore a flat cap. If I'm not mistaken it was made of moleskin.'

'Corduroy,' Greg corrected. It was the cap his father had been wearing the previous evening.

'Two things I wouldn't want to be making today are hats

and ties. No one wears them anymore. Your dad did though. Even after he retired from work he still wore a tie, irrespective of whether he was inside or outside the house. He said he was trying to set an example. Are you staying at the house, by the way? Margaret says she's seen a car parked in the drive.'

'Yes, I'm helping Billy get it ready for sale.'

'Good luck to you with that then. The market's tough these days. There was a time when any house in the Grove sold in a couple of weeks and for its asking price. Those days are long gone, Greg. People still ask for those prices, but they don't get them. That's why you see so many For Sale notices in the same gardens for months on end – sometimes years.'

'You haven't by any chance got a crack in the back wall of your house, have you?' Greg asked.

'I'm glad to report that I haven't, young man. I presume you have. Is it horizontal or vertical?'

'Horizontal.'

'Shouldn't be too much of a problem, then. Vertical cracks are the ones you have to worry about. How big is it?'

'It runs the full length of the back wall and into Mrs Turton's. I gather Barry owns her house now.'

'He owns it all right but he doesn't maintain it. Mrs Turton's got a right cheek complaining about our wall when her own windows are practically falling out of their frames. Have you seen her since you've been back?'

'I went round for coffee this afternoon.' Greg replied.

'And how was she?'

'Put it this way, Ian: if you ever decide to add another three feet to that wall of yours, I'll give you a hand.'

'Hah! That's a good one, that is,' Ian laughed. 'Wait till I tell Margaret that.'

They chatted for a while longer, mainly about Mrs Turton and her Christian bones, and then Ian drained his glass. 'I'd best be getting home, Greg. Margaret's going to be wondering where I've got to. Can I give you a lift anywhere?'

Greg thanked him but declined. He waited while Ian left the pub and then went to the bar and ordered another pint of beer and a plate of sausage and mash. He glanced at the clock behind the bar.

'How long will the food take?' he asked the woman who'd taken his order.

'No more than fifteen minutes, love. Are you in a rush?'

'Not particularly,' Greg replied. 'But I have to be somewhere at eight.'

'A hot date?' she smiled.

'More like an appointment with death,' he said, returning her smile.

China

When his father appeared that evening, Greg was staring out of the back window. The views from the house were panoramic and Greg could see the sprawl of the city below him and the moors rising in the distance. Like Rome, the city had been built on a series of hills, but there the comparison ended.

'It looks like an old carpet that's been left out in the rain, doesn't it?' Lyle said.

Greg turned quickly. Even though he was expecting his father, the voice still made him jump. Lyle had changed clothes and was now wearing a black paloma long dress and a trilby.

'So, what do you think?' Lyle asked, giving him a twirl.

'It becomes you, Dad – as long as you're not expecting me to dance with you.'

'I'll spare you that pleasure, Greg. The only person I could ever dance with was your mother. If I danced with another woman I'd always lose my rhythm and forget the steps – tread on a good few toes, too.'

Greg turned to look through the window again. 'What happened to the city, Dad? It never used to be like this. When I first went to America and people asked me where I was from, I was always proud to tell them. I used to say that if you had to live in a northern industrial city then there was no better place than this. I'm not sure I'd say that now.'

'I guess it lost its way,' Lyle replied. 'When your Mum and me first came to live in the house, we could look out of this window and count up to three hundred mill chimneys – one supposedly big enough for a man to drive a horse and cart around the top. In the days before the city went smokeless, you could see smoke belching out of all of them. The air quality wasn't up to much and we used to get some real pea-souper fogs in the autumn, but somehow the pollution was reassuring. You knew that the city was working and that people had jobs.

'There are no jobs now – not to speak of anyway. The city had all its eggs in one basket and once the woollen industry was gone there was nothing to take its place. Most people today seem to drive taxis for a living. You see long lines of them in the city centre – sitting there for most of the time – and people climbing into them who don't look as if they've got two ha'pennies to rub together. Beats me how they afford them.'

Greg turned the conversation to one of his two outstanding questions. 'Tell me, Dad. Why are you talking with an American accent?'

'I didn't know I was,' Lyle said. 'But I guess things change when you die. I still can't believe I got knocked down by a bus. I used to cross that road practically every day.'

'You were drunk, Dad, and you crossed at a blind spot.'

'Drunk! How could I have been drunk? I don't drink.'

'You accidentally drank some white spirit. You put your paintbrush in the antibiotics and drank from the wrong glass

– or that's what people think happened. What's the betting you weren't wearing your glasses?'

'Well, I'll be,' Lyle said. 'I thought it tasted a bit sharp… And no, I wasn't wearing my glasses. Who in the name of King Arthur wears glasses when they're painting?'

'Usually people with bad eyesight.'

'I didn't come here to debate my eyes, Greg. I want to know what you've been doing to fix the family.'

'Jesus, Dad! You only told me last night that there was something to fix, and I've been busy all day. Besides, Billy's in Denmark and won't be back until Friday. I phoned Uncle Frank though and I'm seeing him on Thursday.'

'What day is it today?'

'Monday.'

'What's wrong with seeing him tomorrow or Wednesday?'

'I've got a structural engineer coming to have a look at the crack in the wall tomorrow morning and three estate agents in the afternoon. I suggested Wednesday to Uncle Frank, but he said that was his day for fish and chips and that Thursday would be more convenient. It's not as if I've been sitting on my backside all day.'

'Sorry to nag you, son, but I've only got twenty days.'

'And nineteen of them are still left. We've got plenty of time.'

'If you say so,' Lyle shrugged. 'So tell me: what *did* you do today?'

'I made appointments, ran errands and had coffee with Mrs Turton.'

Lyle smiled. 'And how's Mrs Turton keeping?'

'As usual, not to herself. I don't even know why she bothered inviting me round. She thinks I'm a thief and accused me of being on drugs.'

'And were you?'

'Of course I wasn't! You know I stopped taking drugs after

Billy's wedding.' (If not the absolute truth, Greg's answer was nearer the truth than a lie.)

Lyle smiled his approval and then laughed. 'That reminds me,' he said. 'Mrs Turton once accused the couple opposite her of dealing drugs. She called the police and told them that strange people were calling at the house all hours and that there was a pungent smell every time the garage door opened. They sent a van with lights flashing and six policemen climbed out. All they found were hundreds and hundreds of scented candles. It turned out the couple had a Yankee Candle franchise. Ha!'

'I wonder why that doesn't surprise me,' Greg said. 'By the way, you didn't get off scot-free. She practically called you a racist.'

'That's balderdash! The only thing I ever said that might have given her that impression was that there were too many Scottish people on television – and there are, especially in the weather and sports departments. Frank thinks so too.'

Greg doubted the wisdom of citing Uncle Frank's views as proof of anything, but let the matter pass. 'She never mentioned that to me. She was talking about newcomers, which I gather is her codeword for immigrants. She even accused me of being racist because I used the word black when I was describing Lenny Henry.'

'That woman!' Lyle said shaking his head. 'She's not the sharpest knife in the drawer, that's for sure, and she'd do better not listening to that son of hers. The older Barry gets the weirder he becomes. It wouldn't surprise me if he had a Nazi uniform hanging in his wardrobe.

'What you have to realise about Mrs Turton,' Lyle explained, 'is that she channels her own views through the mouths of other people, and if these people happen to be dead then all the better, because dead people can't contradict her. She'll claim to her dying day that immigration hasn't affected her, because if it had she wouldn't be the Christian woman she believes herself to be… I presume she told you about that church minister telling her she didn't have an unchristian bone in her body? She tells everyone that. The guy must be addled.

'No, son, I'm afraid Mrs Turton used me for her own purposes. She has her good points, I'll grant her that, and she was always a good neighbour to me – especially after your mother passed – but she thinks the same way most people of her generation do. I don't approve of it, but I can understand it. Maybe I should have said something to her while I was still here, but people at that time of their lives aren't going to go changing their minds. I'd have been wasting my breath.'

Lyle paused for a moment, pulled a face and adjusted the dress around his groin area.

'I remember the first time I saw someone of a different colour,' he went on. 'I must have been five at the time, and a Chinese family moved into the neighbourhood. A whole bunch of us kids would go and stand outside their house and wait for them to appear. We'd never seen anyone like them before. They'd smile at us and we'd smile back at them, and we'd follow them to the bus stop and wait with them while the bus came. To us, they were like celebrities.

'And I don't mean these two-bit celebrities you get nowadays, people famous for their stupidity and wrongdoing, or for taking their clothes off in public. These Chinese people were real celebrities. Think about it: they'd travelled half-way across the world to a country they knew nothing about and didn't even speak its language. That took guts.

'People never do something like that without good reason. Things have got to be bad in their own country for them to leave family and friends behind, and they have to believe that things are going to be a whole lot better in the country they're going to. I take my hat off to these people, I really do. But I can understand why it's easier for people to welcome a single family into their community rather than thousands.'

The immigrants who came to the city from the late 1950s onward, Lyle said, were for the most part from a rural area of Pakistan called Azad Kashmir. They were subsistence farmers in their own country, poor and largely illiterate, and needed little persuasion from the British government to move to a city thousands of miles away whose mills were in desperate need of cheap and unskilled labour. In the blink of an eye, these incomers from Mirpur moved from mediaeval to modern times.

They congregated in ghettoes within the inner ring road, but instead of making the city their new home, made it their home away from home and continued to live in the style and times of the country they'd left behind. They retained their identity, their customs and continued to speak their own language. In doing so they became marginalised from the wider society. The city fathers turned a blind eye to the fragmentation that was going on in their own backyard and pretended that all was well, preached multiculturalism and urged other cities to follow its example.

But then the manufacturing base of the city collapsed.

'That's when the real problem started,' Lyle said. 'When there's full employment people just get on with their lives, but when jobs are scarce or non-existent they start looking for scapegoats. It's always easier to blame others for your own misfortune. You'll know this from studying history.'

And the others in this case were the immigrants. Over the years their number had grown exponentially and their visibility marked. They moved into neighbourhoods beyond the ring road, opened businesses and built mosques, and the old-time dwellers of the city started to fear for their identity. There were murmurings, rumblings and then riots – as often as not provoked by outsiders. No longer was the city an example that others aspired to follow.

'I blame both sides,' Lyle said. 'The people of the city should have brought the immigrants into the fold earlier, given them a real welcome and encouraged them to assimilate instead of letting them go their own way. How else are you going to get a culture that's common to all, a culture that everyone can feel a part of? The obligation was on both sides though, and the immigrants should have been more ready to enter that fold. You can't go to a new country and expect your life not to change, to go on living as if nothing's happened. The worst thing you can do is cut yourself off from the culture you enter.'

Greg remembered his father being a man of few words, a man who communicated as much through sighs as he did language, and certainly not a man who shared viewpoints.

'How come we never talked like this when you were alive, Dad? I can't recall a single conversation we had. I can remember you telling me not to do this and not to do that, but other than that, not a thing. I left home thinking you didn't have an opinion on anything.'

'I don't rightly know, son,' Lyle said, giving the matter careful thought. 'I always figured other people's opinions were a waste of time and that mine would be no different. I know this isn't always the case, but in my experience most opinions are borne of ignorance and the people with the strongest opinions are usually the most ignorant. Besides, I wanted you and Billy to make up your own minds about things and not parrot some dumb thing I might have said.

'Anyway, it takes two to talk, and I can't remember you ever volunteering your services on that front. You either stayed in your room or went out. It was like having a lodger in the house rather than a son. You never used to be like that when your mother was alive.'

Greg averted his eyes and Lyle abruptly changed the subject, the way he'd always sidestepped emotion. 'Have you and Billy given much thought to selling the house? I want £150,000 for it. It's bigger than the other houses on the Grove and it's got more land.' (The dining room had been extended by three feet and the back garden by ten yards.)

'I don't know whether we'll get that, Dad. I bumped into Ian Collard in the Brown Cow and he said that the market was in a slump and that house prices were falling. He gave me the impression that £130,000 would be a more realistic figure.'

'You'd be crazy to sell the house for that, Greg! I know Ian talks a lot of common sense, but Syd reckons the house is worth a good £15,000 more than the other houses on the Grove, and he's got no reason to be biased.'

'He might be unbiased, Dad, but he isn't an estate agent, is he? What did he do when he was working?'

'He owned a small garage. Did repairs and sold second-hand cars. I presume he was at the funeral?'

Greg nodded.

'Who else was there?'

'Me, Billy, Jean, Katy, Uncle Frank, Jean's mother, Mrs Turton, Barry, Syd, and Ian and Margaret Collard. The minister told Billy he'd seen a young woman there, but she left before we had a chance to meet her. You don't know who she was, do you?'

Lyle looked out of the window. 'I've no idea, Greg.'

Greg sensed that his father wasn't telling him the truth. Lyle Bowman, he surmised, knew exactly who the young woman was.

Heathrow

Lyle continued to stare out of the window. 'There are still some fine Victorian buildings down there,' he said, pointing to the city's centre, 'but most of them were demolished in the sixties and replaced with ugly modern things. Most of those have been torn down now, and some of their sites are sill derelict. Anything they build nowadays is functional and cheap, without architectural value. Syd says they look as if they've been constructed from materials bought at Wickes!

'Oddly enough,' he smiled, 'this was probably the safest place to live when the IRA was targeting the mainland. Everyone knew they wouldn't waste their bombs on a city that already looked as if it had been blown up.'

They moved away from the window and sat in the two easy chairs facing each other.

'What's it like in the Afterlife, Dad?' (This was the second of Greg's outstanding questions.)

'I don't rightly know, son. I haven't made it that far yet.'

Greg looked at his father quizzically.

'You know the stories you hear about people dying on the operating table and coming back to life?' Greg nodded. 'Well, my experience was nothing like theirs. I was never drawn to an intense white light or overcome with feelings of inner peace. The nearest thing I can liken it to is that Big Dipper ride we took when we went to Blackpool one year. You remember the time: I was sitting behind you and your Mum with Billy, and Billy threw up?'

Again, Greg nodded. It was him Billy had thrown up on.

Lyle described how he'd *woken up* in a small rollercoaster car with no seat, no sides and no bar to hold on to. He presumed it had been attached to other cars, but couldn't say for sure as it had been pitch-black and he'd been lying on the floor. For a long time the car hadn't moved, but then it started to climb steeply and make strange clickety-clack noises as if it was running on a track. At first, it was doing no more than 5mph, and the higher it got the slower it went. For a moment he'd thought it was going to stall and roll backwards, but then, all of a sudden, there'd been an almighty jolt and the car had hurtled forwards, then downwards, corkscrewed upwards and then plunged again.

'I tell you, Greg, there were times when I thought I was going to be thrown out of the car. It was an experience I wouldn't wish on my worst enemy.'

When the car finally came to a standstill, Lyle lay there thinking he was going to throw up; he couldn't move and he couldn't breathe. 'I think that's the whole idea of the ride,' he said. 'To soften people up for whatever comes next.'

Lyle's journey had been completed in darkness, but the landing place was bright enough to have been illuminated by a thousand floodlights, and for a time he was blinded. There was no one there to greet him, but intuitively he'd known what to do. Once able, he climbed out of the car and joined a line of people, who he presumed had arrived in similar fashion. No one spoke; they just stood there, inching forward when space permitted. Some of them wore their Sunday best (the Burieds), and the rest of them were naked (the Cremates).

It reminded Lyle of the time he'd visited Greg in Texas and had to stand in line at the check-in at Heathrow Airport for three hours. 'And just like then,' he said, 'no one came round to explain what the delay was or offer you a sandwich.'

'Jesus, I'm sorry, Dad!' Greg apologised, reminded that he was the host. 'Can I get you something to eat or drink?'

'Thanks, lad, but there's no need. I don't eat or drink anymore. It's funny, when I stopped smoking my pipe I missed it for years, but I haven't missed food or liquids for a second – not even chocolate. How strange is that?

'Anyway, when the last person in front of me disappeared – and that's what they did: they just disappeared into thin air – and I was standing at the front of the line, I was suddenly sucked upwards, whizzed around a couple of times and then deposited on a chair in a small windowless room. It was a process that reminded me of those old aerial delivery systems they used to operate in big department stores.'

Greg looked at his father inquiringly.

'When you bought something in a shop in those days,' Lyle explained, 'you'd hand your money to the salesgirl who'd served you, and she'd put the notes and a bill of sale into a small metal pneumatic tube. She'd attach it to a rail and pull a cord. The tube would go flying overhead to a cashier sitting on a dais somewhere in the middle of the floor, and the tube would then be returned with your change and receipt inside it. Now do you understand?'

Greg nodded.

'So I whizz from nowhere into a small white room and find myself sitting opposite a man who looks like a person in reverse, a bit like a photographic negative. I learned later that they call these men and women X-ray people.

'He was sitting behind a desk flicking through a file and for a long time he didn't look up. He said he'd be with me in a minute and told me to watch a short film he was about to play. He wasn't kidding when he said it was short: from beginning to end it was no more than fifteen seconds, and all it showed was me being knocked down by a bus, put in a bamboo coffin and then set on fire. When the film ended, he looked up at me and gave me one of those smiles that puts you on your guard. "Hello, Lyle," he said. "How are you today?"'

'I told him I wasn't sure how I was, but that if I wasn't dead I was having one hell of a bad day. He asked me what I'd prefer the outcome to be, and I said a bad day. He shook his head – the way a person does when you give them a wrong answer – and made a note in my file. He then put down his pen, clasped his hands together and told me I was dead.

'He asked me how I felt about this, and I answered that I wasn't particularly thrilled by the idea as I'd been in the middle of a paint job and still had a few family matters to attend to. He picked up his pen again and made some more notes, and then asked me what my favourite animal was, what my least favourite animal was and what I thought of glass.'

'How did you answer those questions?' Greg asked, his curiosity roused.

'Hippopotamus to the first, cat to the second and okay to the third. The glass question was the hardest one to answer. I've seen some beautiful glass ornaments in my time – and it's always good to have windows to look through, isn't it – but I once cut my finger on a shard when I was weeding the back garden and had to go to hospital for some stitches and a tetanus shot.

'Anyway, he noted all this down and then took three cards from a drawer and asked me what I saw on them. For a time they just looked like black splodges, but after a while I started to see shapes: on the first card was a hippopotamus, on the second a cat and on the third a glass window. I asked him if this was some kind of conjuring trick, but he just smiled and said nothing.

'He asked me then if I had any questions, and when I asked him if I was going to see Mary again his brow wrinkled. He asked me who Mary was, and I told him she was my wife who'd probably passed this way some twenty-nine years earlier. He checked his file again and told me there was no mention of any Mary in it, and that according to his records I was a bachelor. When I told him I was a widower with two sons called Billy and Greg he looked at me and said: "You're not Lyle Bowman from Buffalo, New York, then?" I told him I wasn't and that I was from England, and asked him if this meant I could go back home again.'

'"I'm afraid not, Lyle," he said. "I might have the wrong paperwork in front of me, but you're still dead. However, if you're not Lyle Bowman of Buffalo, New York, then it might mean that your answers make more sense than I first thought. We can sort out the bureaucracy later, but in the meantime I'd advise you to ask questions. This is the only opportunity you'll have."'

'So I asked him if I was going to meet God and he said he didn't know, but that stranger things had happened. When I asked him if I was going to see Jesus he just looked at me strangely and asked who Jesus was. I told him He was the Son of God – surely he'd heard of him – but all he did was shrug his shoulders and tell me there were a lot of people called Jesus there – just as there were a lot of people called Mohammed.

'To tell you the truth, Greg, I gave up on the man after that. I was going to ask him if he was an angel, but figured he wasn't or he'd have known who Jesus was. He didn't seem to know much about anything and he took offence when I asked him if he was a trainee. He got all hoity-toity and started lecturing me. He said that 155,000 people passed through there every day of the week, every week of the year, and that some mistakes were inevitable.'

'So does God exist then?' Greg asked, still trying to come to terms with his father's story.

'I have absolutely no idea, Greg. There's obviously something, but I don't know what that something is. I'm hoping that once I pass through the transit camp I'll get a better idea. I'm hoping there is, because I've believed in God my whole life, and I was sure it was Him who'd got me through your mother's death. But if the guy I was talking to hadn't even heard of Jesus, then it makes you wonder, doesn't it?'

'So you've no idea what comes next?'

'No. You hear rumours of course, but none of them make any sense. One old guy said we were on our way to a giant warehouse with millions of pigeon holes inside it. He told us that the compartments were the size of a small apple and each one could house four people. He was in the same boat we were in though, so there's no reason why he should have known this. I think he was just one of those clever Dicks who likes to show off.'

'What happened to you after you left the room then, Dad – after you'd finished talking to this X-ray man?'

'I was sent to a lounge reserved for Americans,' Lyle replied. 'They had me down as a Yank so I had to stay with them until my paperwork got sorted. I kept to myself in the early days, turned myself into a golf ball and hibernated – that's something the X-rays encourage you to do. No doubt it's another form of crowd control that makes life easier for them, but it's pleasant enough, and at least you don't think about things when you're in that state.'

'You can actually turn yourself into a golf ball?' Greg asked.

'Not as such,' Lyle replied. 'That's just X-ray-speak. It's more like a standby light. Anyway, I was in this mode when a truckload of GIs arrived in the lounge and woke me up. They were a good bunch of guys to hang out with though, and they told great stories, so I decided to stay awake after that. They'd all been blown up by an IED in Afghanistan and every man jack of them swore like a trooper. Maybe that's why I was cussing like I was yesterday: their language must have rubbed off on me.'

'And that's probably the reason you have an American accent,' Greg concluded. 'But how did you manage to get back here again? Why did they let you return?'

'I got lucky, I guess. You know how I mentioned earlier that when I first got there I was reminded of Heathrow Airport? Well, the whole place *is* like an airport. It's not just the queuing and the lounges: there are announcements detailing departure numbers, and when people hear their number they simply get up and leave. I think there are actual flights out!

'The number I'd been given was Z87, but when they announced that number they said that the departure was overbooked and they were looking for five people to give up their places and take a later departure. They said that anyone prepared to do this would be given a free upgrade when they left.

'So I went up to the X-ray woman standing behind the reception desk and told her that even though I'd been assigned the number Z87 I wasn't the Lyle Bowman they had me down as – the one from Buffalo – and I was more than happy to wait for another number until the right paperwork came through. She made a few tut-tutting noises when she heard this and told me to stand completely still. She then pressed a button and, like before, I was sucked into the air and plonked down on a chair in another white room.'

It was a larger room than the one Lyle had previously been in, and this time there were three X-ray people sitting there, all with a copy of his file open before them. The X-ray who sat in the middle was a woman and she apologised to Lyle for the mistake made in wrongly identifying him as Lyle Bowman of Buffalo, New York. She assured him that the X-ray who'd made the error and not rectified it would be disciplined. There was no excuse for poor customer service.

She told Lyle that he would remain there until his documentation had been corrected and would then be given a departure upgrade as promised. It would, however, take time for this to happen. In view of his poor experience of death to date, and the fact that the first X-ray had classified him as a *Reluctant Dead* because of some unresolved family matters, they were prepared to give him the opportunity of returning to the world for a short time.

Lyle then described the restrictions of his furlough. He was limited to one physical location and could reveal himself to only one person – both of which had to be decided then and there. He would be able to touch and move objects, but unable to touch or be touched by a living person.

'The house was an obvious choice,' Lyle said, 'but I was never sure you'd be there. I figured that sooner or later you would show up, but it was still a gamble. Fortunately it's paid off.'

The maximum time he could spend in the world was twenty days – it was the most they allowed anyone in his category. Once that time had elapsed, he would be recalled automatically. If, however, he chose to return earlier, all he had to do was move beyond the physical location he'd chosen. Unfortunately, the sensation of travel he'd experienced on first dying would have to be endured for a second time: there was, they told him, no easy way around this.

'That's the bit I'm not looking forward to,' Lyle said.

'Is there any point in me bringing Billy and Uncle Frank to see you?' Greg asked.

'Not really. I'd be able to see them, but they wouldn't be able to see or hear me. The only thing they'd see is you talking to yourself and that wouldn't look good. For your own sake, you have to keep our meetings private. If you tell them you're talking to me they'll think you've lost your mind – and who's going to accept the help of a crazy person?'

Greg wasn't sure about Billy, but had no doubts that his Uncle Frank would jump at the chance.

'Don't you think they'll get a bit suspicious when I know all this stuff about them? How am I supposed to explain it to them?'

'You'll think of something, Greg. Tell them we discussed things on the phone, or think of something else. You were always good at lying.'

It was a compliment of sorts, Greg supposed, but doubted that this credential alone made him the right person for the job. In all likelihood, his father would return to Heathrow Airport a disappointed man.

5

Callers

Fred Stubbington knocked on the door at precisely ten o'clock.

'Mr Bowman? Fred Stubbington. I'm here to look at the crack.'

He had a firm handshake and was, as Greg had hoped, no-nonsense and to the point. Greg was confident that at least Mr Stubbington was the right man for the job.

They walked to the rear of the house and Greg pointed to the crack. On seeing it, Fred Stubbington sprang to life.

'Classic wall-tie failure!' he exclaimed. 'No doubt about it.'

'Is that bad?' Greg asked, having no idea what wall-tie failure was.

'It's something that happens, Mr Bowman – especially in houses as old as this – but you can rest assured that it's not the end of the world – or the house.'

Most houses, Mr Stubbington explained, were built with inner and outer walls. There was a space between the walls called a cavity, and hence the term cavity walling. For a cavity wall to have structural integrity, the inner and outer leaves of masonry had to be 'tied' together with fasteners. These fasteners were called wall-ties and were made of metal. Over time, however, the metal corroded – especially if it was iron – and eventually the rusting would cause a tie to snap. If a sufficient number of ties snapped, the integrity of the wall would be compromised and, in some instances, crack.

'Considering the age of the house, Mr Bowman, I'd say the builders used iron fish-tails, and this type of tie is particularly susceptible to rusting. You wouldn't think moisture would find its way through a thick layer of pebble dashing like this, would you? But it does, and this rear wall of yours is also the weather wall – the one that gets the brunt of the wind and rain. This explains why the crack is here and not in the side or front walls.'

Mr Stubbington walked down the steps to the side of the cellar door where a large piece of rendering had fallen from the wall. 'Hmm, just as I suspected,' he said. 'They've used black ash mortar.'

'Shouldn't they have done that?' Greg asked.

'There's no law forbidding it, Mr Bowman, but it wouldn't have been my choice. This particular type of mortar is acidic, and acid corrodes wall-ties just as much as moisture. Not to worry though: it's all fixable.'

'So what do we do next?'

'We call in a firm of specialists and get them to replace the wall-ties.'

Mr Stubbington told him the name of a company he trusted. 'They charge reasonably,' he said, 'and, what's more, they guarantee their work for twenty years.'

Greg accepted his suggestion, and it was agreed that Mr Stubbington would send a copy of his report to them. 'I'll suggest they use the vertical twist rather than the double triangle ties. All types are made from stainless steel these days, but the vertical twist has a plastic coating.'

'Do we just replace the ties in this wall?'

'No. You have them all done. Even though there aren't any cracks showing in the other walls, the ties there will have weakened and eventually they'll start to crack too. Any surveyor acting for a potential purchaser would insist on this work being carried out.'

'How long will it take to do this?' Greg asked.

'No more than a day. They'll drill holes in the walls and insert the ties through them, and then they'll fill in the crack. There won't be any need for scaffolding. Do you want them to replace the sill while they're at it?'

Greg agreed to his suggestion. 'How much do you think this is going to cost, Mr Stubbington?'

'No more than £1,500, Mr Bowman. If the house was in London you'd be paying twice that amount. People down there don't know the value of money.'

Mr Stubbington went inside the house with Greg and phoned the firm he'd recommended. 'Is Thursday of next week alright for you, Mr Bowman?' he asked. 'Okay, Bill,' he said to the person at the other end of the phone. 'He'll expect you then.'

Greg walked with Mr Stubbington to his car and turned to see Mrs Turton standing in her bay window. He didn't wave and neither did she. It appeared they had arrived at an understanding.

Greg saw little point in starting any work inside the house until after the estate agents had visited. The first of them, he noted, would be arriving in just over two hours and he decided to use the time clearing out the garage. He unlocked the door with the small key Billy had given him and started to poke around. Apart from his father's tools and gardening implements, there appeared to be little of value. There was a pile of wood and a stack of old bricks at the far end of the garage, a jumble of empty paint cans closer to the door and some cardboard boxes containing only detritus – plastic plant pots, dirty rags, jam jars and empty margarine tubs. The only thing of any substance was an old four-bar electric fire, and he doubted that Billy would have any use for this.

He was filling a dustbin bag with rubbish when the first of the estate agents arrived. A man slightly younger than himself walked down the drive and introduced himself as Darren Coates. He was from the largest of the three estate agencies and his manner was suitably perfunctory. He wished to inspect the house alone, he said, and declined Greg's offer of a tour.

Having already decided not to put the house in Darren's hands, Greg returned to the garage. Darren joined him there thirty minutes later.

'I suggest we put the house on the market for £129,950, Mr Bowman – but don't expect to get that price. The house needs too much doing to it, and the fact that it's been extended is immaterial in the current market. If I were you, I'd seriously consider any offer over £110,000.'

He handed Greg a shiny coloured brochure and his business card. 'Call me if you'd like to take advantage of our services. We're the biggest in the city and you won't find any better.'

Greg watched while Darren drove away, and then put the brochure and business card with the rest of the rubbish.

The second agent to arrive was a woman in her early forties who believed herself to be more attractive than she actually was. As Greg led her from room to room, she flirted with him unabashedly and, on reaching the back bedroom, sat down on his bed and applied a new coat of lipstick. Her valuation of the house, however, was the same as Darren's: £129,950. 'And remember, Greg, if you sign with our agency, you'll be getting my very own special attention – and I mean special!' She then winked at him.

Kevin Dangerfield, the third of the estate agents, had a nervous affliction that caused him to flinch every few minutes. 'Sorry about the flinching, Mr Bowman. It happens sometimes. Is it all right if I call you Greg?'

'Sure, Kevin. Let me show you round the house.'

'I'm not very good at this, yet,' Kevin confessed. 'I'm more used to selling novelties for a living than houses, but the company I worked for went belly-up and I had to look for something else. I've only been an estate agent for a month and this is the first time I've been out of the office on my own. In fact, the only reason you're seeing me today, instead of someone who knows what they're doing, is because we're a bit short staffed at the moment. I promise you I'll do my best though, and I'm happy to take on board anything you have to say.'

Greg took an instant liking to Kevin. There was no side to him, no airs and graces, and he was unreservedly honest – probably too honest for his own good. He impressed Greg as a tryer; someone who would put his full weight – which was considerable – behind the sale of the house. The fact that he hadn't yet mastered his electronic tape measure and had the dining room measuring thirty-six yards by four feet mattered little to Greg, who was more than happy to show him how it worked – even though he'd never seen one before.

Kevin was the only agent to tell Greg that he actually liked the house – he'd grown up in one just like it. He nodded appreciatively when Greg showed him how the dining room had been built out and the garden extended, and whistled in amazement when he took in the views from the rear windows.

Greg made coffee and they sat down to determine a selling price. With little discussion they decided on £135,000 which, they both agreed, could be reduced if the right buyer came along. Kevin handed Greg some sheets of paper held together with a clip and wrote his name on the front.

'I haven't got a business card yet,' he explained. 'What do you think I should put on it when I do: KP Dangerfield or Kevin?'

'I'd go with Kevin. KP makes you sound like a nut.'

Kevin laughed and shook Greg's hand. 'It's a bit damp, I'm afraid, but I like to think it's firm. It's been very nice meeting you, Greg, and I'm sorry to hear about your father. Thanks again for giving me your time and showing me how to use the tape measure.'

He then made to leave the house.

'Well, do you want the business or don't you?' Greg asked him.

'You want *me* to sell your house?' Kevin asked in amazement.

'I wouldn't have it any other way,' Greg said. 'And tell your boss it was you who swung the decision, and not the name of the agency.'

'Well I'll be!' he said.

Kevin left the house whistling, and Greg returned to the garage smiling. He continued to sort the rubbish into piles and then took a brush and swept the floor. It was while he was carrying the electric fire to the car that the truth dawned on him:

He'd just hired Billy.

Some things in life never change and, fortunately for Greg, neither had the location of the refuse tip. The internal arrangement of the dump, however, had changed considerably since he'd last visited and there were now numerous and separate skips for different kinds of rubbish: paper, cardboard, plastic, metal, garden waste and so on. He was wondering where to make a start when Syd Butterfield approached him.

'It's Greg, isn't it?' Syd enquired.

'Hello, Syd!' Greg said, surprised to meet anyone he knew at the dump. 'What brings you here?'

'I've been off-loading some leylandii clippings, Greg. Those trees make fine hedges, but if you don't keep on top of them and cut them back every year, they'll grow tall enough to interfere with air traffic. What are you up to? Clearing out your dad's house?'

'I'm making a start – all this is from the garage,' he said, pointing to the car. 'I was just wondering which skip to put what in.'

'Dump it all in the skip marked General Waste,' Syd told him. 'That's what me and your dad did. We weren't prepared to waste what precious time we had left on earth accommodating the lazy buggers who work here. And what's more, it's only since we joined the EU that we've had to do this – and neither me nor your dad voted for that! What in the name of God are we supposed to have in common with the French?

'Anyway, you'd best get cracking. The dump closes at five and there's no one here works a minute longer than they have to. I'll get my gloves and give you a hand.'

They took the bags and boxes out of the car and, as Syd had suggested, threw them all into the same skip. All that remained was the electric fire.

'I could take that off your hands, if you like,' Syd said. 'I could use it for heating my garage, and the warmth would remind me of your father.'

Greg was happy to oblige him. He carried the fire to Syd's car and placed it carefully on the back seat. The two of them then leaned against the side of the car.

'It was at this dump that I met your father,' Syd reminisced. 'He was throwing out an old television.'

At the time of their meeting Lyle had already been a widower, and five years later Syd was also bereaved. While Lyle's wife, Mary, had died of a thrombosis, Syd's wife died of a brain tumour.

After that, the two of them had started to do their weekly shops at Tesco together, taking it in turns to drive there until Lyle accidentally killed a motorcyclist and then sold his car. Although Lyle hadn't been at fault in the collision, his confidence behind the wheel was as shattered as the car windscreen the motorcyclist had sailed through, and thereafter it had been Syd who'd driven, picking up Lyle at his house every Thursday morning at ten and returning there for coffee afterwards.

'I'm going to miss our Thursdays together,' Syd said. 'Your father was a good man, Greg; the best friend I ever had. In all the time I knew him I don't think we ever had a cross word. It's too late for me to find another friend now, but at least I have my family – three daughters, two sons-in-law and five grandchildren...'

Greg knew Syd's family tree backwards, but pretended he was hearing it for the first time. Every week, for as long as he could remember, his father had recited the names, heights and occupations of Syd's daughters as though a litany.

The eldest was Lorna. At 6' 2" she was the tallest of the three sisters and lived in The Netherlands close to Haarlem. She was married to a Dutchman five inches taller than herself and had two young sons, no doubt destined for gianthood. She was a stay-at-home mum these days, but had worked in the marketing department of Heineken.

The middle daughter, Alice, was an inch shorter than Lorna and lived in London. She was married to an architect and also had two small children – a boy and a girl. Despite the demands of motherhood, she worked part-time as a primary school teacher.

The third daughter, Catherine, was the shortest of the three sisters, but still 5' 11". She worked in the city as a probation officer, lived over the brush with a career student called Derek and had one son born on the wrong side of the blanket. (Despite these apparently disapproving judgements, Catherine had been Lyle's favourite, and he'd often accompanied her to the Gilbert & Sullivan performances of her father.)

Hearing their names again, Greg was reminded of the

mysterious young woman who'd been at the funeral and asked Syd if any of his daughters had been there.

'They were there in spirit, Greg, but I'm afraid none of them could make it in person.'

'You knew my father as well as anyone, Syd,' Greg continued. 'Did he ever date younger women?'

Syd laughed out loud. 'Your dad was a one-woman man, Greg – and that woman was your mother. She might have been dead, but he was still in love with her. He had no interest in meeting or marrying anyone else. Why are you asking me this?'

'There was a woman at the funeral and no one seems to know who she was. It's been puzzling me.'

'I can't help you there, I'm afraid. I never even saw her. It's a pity your dad's not here to tell you.'

His father *was* here, Greg thought, and his father knew exactly who the young woman was. It was just that his father wasn't telling.

Lyle appeared again that night, but stayed for only a short time. He'd changed out of the paloma long dress into a turquoise bustle back ball gown, but looked tired, and his opalescent form had lost some of its shimmer.

'You okay, Dad?' Greg asked him. 'You're looking a bit drawn.'

'I'm weary, son, but I'm fine. I made the mistake of not changing myself into a golf ball last night and I think the old batteries have got a bit worn down. I'll be okay tomorrow. So tell me, what have you done today?'

Greg told him about Fred Stubbington and that the crack would be fixed next week. He described the three estate agents, the one he'd decided upon and the price they were going to ask for the house.

'I was hoping for more,' his father sighed. 'But if that's what the estate agent says.'

Greg then told him about bumping into Syd at the dump and Syd describing him as his best friend.

'He was mine too,' Lyle smiled. 'It's funny: if someone had told me that my best friend would be a second-hand car dealer I probably wouldn't have believed them. People in that line of work never enjoyed much of a reputation. Strange old world, isn't it?

'I don't know if I ever told you this, but Syd's got three daughters and they're all as tall as skyscrapers? Lorna, she's the eldest...'

Grandparents

The following morning Greg made three further trips to the dump and then washed and changed. Today was the day he'd arranged to take Uncle Frank for lunch, and the day he would have to broach the man's strange behaviour. It wasn't something he looked forward to.

Uncle Frank lived in the first of a row of four terraced houses with garden on three sides. Greg opened the gate and made his way to the side door – the used door – knocked, and turned the handle. Unusually, it was locked. He knocked again and waited, but there was still no answer. Strains of loud rock music seeped from the house and Greg could only surmise that his uncle was deaf to his knocking – as he was deaf to all things when he wasn't wearing his hearing aid.

He walked to the back of the house and peered through the window. Uncle Frank was standing in the middle of the room twitching his body and flailing his arms and, if not in the middle of an Apache war dance, appeared to be having a fit. Greg knocked hard on the window and was relieved when his uncle turned. Uncle Frank looked sheepish for a moment and then broke into a broad grin.

'What's going on in here? You having a party?' Greg asked, once inside the house.

'What, lad? I can't hear you.'

'Turn down the music and put your hearing aid in, will you? The radio's loud enough for your neighbours to hear it.'

Uncle Frank did both, and then asked Greg to repeat what he'd said.

'I said your neighbours are going to be deafened. I could hear the music outside.'

'I don't give a damn about my neighbours!' Uncle Frank said. 'I'm sick to death of them.'

'Why, what have they done now?'

'It's their son! He's out of control and they just make excuses for him.'

Greg had noticed a small boy of about seven bouncing on a trampoline. 'He looked harmless enough to me, Uncle Frank. He didn't strike me as being a tearaway.'

'You don't know him!' Uncle Frank retorted. 'He keeps kicking my fence down. When I went round to complain, his father just shrugged and said his son had special knees. What kind of a damn-fool answer is that? I told him his boy wasn't using his knees to kick my fence down, he was using his *feet*, and if it happened again I'd call the police. I told him I had friends in the police force.' (Greg knew this to be true: Uncle Frank did indeed have friends in the constabulary.)

'I think your neighbour was telling you his son had special *needs*,' Greg said.

'Why would he have a special need for wood?' Uncle Frank said. 'He's a kid, not some damn cabinetmaker.'

'I'll explain in the car, Uncle Frank. Now go and get yourself ready.'

His uncle left the room and then, just as quickly, returned. 'I like this song,' he said, turning up the volume and disappearing again.

Greg sat down on the pouffe his aunt had used for resting her legs on and smiled: there was no way his uncle would be playing music like this in the house if Auntie Irene had still been alive.

Although her golf and tennis trophies continued to adorn the sideboard, Auntie Irene had died thirteen years ago, shortly after Billy married. She herself had never married, and had instead spent much of her life looking after ageing parents. She had at one time, however, been engaged to a man called René and, after his unexpected death from scarlet fever, had looked upon herself as a widow rather than a spinster. Irene had been thirty-six at the time, and the news of his death hit her with the force of a sledgehammer. It was a blow she never recovered from, and René forever remained her one and only.

For her parents, however, Irene's tragedy and decision to eschew further ideas of marriage had been a blessing in disguise. Old, and in their own minds increasingly infirm, they now encouraged their daughter to leave her job in one of the city's two department stores and tend to their needs. Her father, her mother said, was now suffering the effects of a gas attack he'd endured during World War I; and her mother, her father said, was so worn out she was in danger of hopping the twig. They led Irene to believe that without her help they, like René, would suffer untimely deaths – though probably not from scarlet fever as they'd both already had the disease.

Eventually, Irene submitted to their pleas and agreed to become their carer. The day she resigned from her job, her parents climbed the stairs and took to their beds, staying there for the next fifteen years and only venturing down for special occasions. One such occasion had been the time Lyle had brought Mary home to meet them.

Mary described the meeting to Greg in one of their frequent tête-à-têtes, when just the two of them were in the house. She was nervous, she said, as anyone would be on meeting their future in-laws for the first time, but it had struck her that Lyle was even more apprehensive.

Grandpa and Grandma Bowman had been sitting in the lounge in their pyjamas, dressing gowns and slippers; Grandpa smoking his chewed pipe and Grandma knitting a pair of bed socks. Neither had stood when Lyle introduced her, and it was apparent that they were surprised by her young age. 'They were probably wondering if Lyle was intending to adopt rather than marry me,' Mary laughed. They asked about her parents rather than herself and appeared disappointed when she told them her mother was dead and that her father worked in a lumber yard.

'Do you have any brothers or sisters?' Grandma Bowman had enquired with a weak smile.

'I have a sister called Rita, Mrs Bowman, but she emigrated to New Zealand. She's two years older than I am.'

Grandpa Bowman muttered that Rita may as well be dead too then, as the chances were good that Mary would never see her again. When Mary had replied that she was hoping to visit her one day, he'd retorted that it was unlikely she'd be affording the trip on Lyle's wages. Lyle was about to enter the discussion when Frank walked into the room and Grandpa Bowman turned his attention to him.

'Go and put that damned eye patch on!' he shouted. 'And make sure you wash your hands well: we don't want any rat droppings on the table!'

(Frank had woken up two weeks earlier with one side of his face paralysed, and despite his protestations to the doctor that he'd never even met anyone by that name, was diagnosed as having Bell's palsy. It was a condition that caused the left side of his face to droop alarmingly and his left eye to remain stubbornly open.)

Frank rolled his eyes – or at least one of them. 'How many

times do I have to tell you, Father? I work in the office, not in the field.'

'It's the same thing,' his father countered. 'And don't use that tone with me, boy. While you're living under my roof, you'll show me respect.'

Grandpa Bowman turned to Mary. 'Never in a million years did I think a son of mine would end up as a rat catcher.'

He then turned his attention back to Frank. 'Do you know how embarrassing it is when people ask me what you do for a living and I have to tell them you catch rats? It's probably how you got that damn palsy in the first place – caught it from a rat! The sooner you get yourself a proper job the better. Now get that ugly face of yours upstairs and sort yourself out.'

'I'll admit he looked a sight, Gregory, but there was no need for his father to talk to him like that, especially in front of me.'

After Frank had left the room – with literally only half a smile on his face – Mary had tried to lighten the atmosphere by saying she liked the wallpaper.

Grandpa Bowman glanced at the raised swirly-patterned paper and told her it was Anaglypta, the most sanitary wallpaper on the market. (The antiseptic nature of the house, Mary later found out, came to a crescendo in the bathroom, where she found a block of orange Coal Tar soap and a box of medicated Izal toilet paper – little better than greaseproof, she commented.)

Irene had been busying herself preparing a salad for their tea, and it was only after they'd sat down at the table that Mary had a chance to talk to her. Irene, she told Greg, had a no-nonsense, almost gruff manner and smiled rarely. In her own way, however, she was warm and welcoming towards her, and though Frank eventually became her favourite in-law, Irene was always the one she'd confide in – something she'd have never done with Lyle's parents.

Grandma Bowman had said little during the meal, deferring

the whole time to her husband who, with the exception of Irene, appeared to believe that his fatherly duty was to belittle rather than praise his offspring – Frank, in particular.

Mary recalled for Greg the moment when the tomatoes in the bowl had dwindled to one and Grandpa Bowman had asked if she'd like it. Sensibly, she'd declined. It was then that Frank had said he'd have it. 'No you won't, you greedy little bugger!' Grandpa Bowman had snapped. 'This is my house and I'm having it! You're fat enough, boy. You go on eating the way you do and you'll end up looking like a beach ball. Now, pass me the bowl!'

'It's difficult to believe your Daddy was cut from the same cloth as that man, Gregory. I only wish you could have known my father. He was a good man. There was no kinder.'

Greg remembered visiting his grandparents only once, recalling his grandmother propped up on pillows eating a bag of Pontefract cakes and his grandfather lying next to her staring at the ceiling and sucking on a Fox's Glacier Mint. After insisting that he and Billy kiss them on the cheek, they effectively ignored the boys and talked only to their parents.

Greg and Billy were spared further visits to their grandparents when, shortly after that visit, both Grandpa and Grandma Bowman died on the same day – a washday.

Grandpa Bowman had been suffering from a chest infection and had coughed and spluttered for two weeks. When his wife noticed that he hadn't coughed for a good twenty minutes, she turned to him and said it sounded like he was getting better. He didn't respond, which wasn't unusual for Grandpa Bowman as he rarely saw any need to respond to anything his wife said, and Grandma Bowman went back to reading her magazine unconcerned. After a while, however, his continued silence began to trouble her and she examined him more closely. It was then she realised he was no longer breathing.

Frantically, she rang the bell for Irene, called her by name and urged her to hurry: something had happened to her father, something awful! Irene, however, was oblivious to the alarms of her mother. The day was Monday, a washday, and while her father was pegging out inside the house, Irene was busy pegging out outside the house.

In growing desperation, Grandma Bowman climbed out of bed on jellied legs weakened by years of inactivity. She walked unsteadily to the landing, lurching from the bedside table to a chest of drawers and from the door jamb to the banister. When her calls for help still went unanswered, she walked to the top of the stairs and took hold of the balustrade with both hands. She took a deep breath, tilted her head backward and gave an almighty yell: 'Ireeeeeene!'

The sudden exhalation of so much air left her dizzy and disoriented, and what strength remained in her decrepit body quickly drained. Her legs gave way beneath her and her hands slipped from the balustrade. She lost balance and, in a silence punctuated only by thuds, toppled headlong down the stairs.

Needless to say, things weren't quite the same when Irene went back into the house.

The deaths of his grandparents had meant nothing to Greg and neither, it seemed, did they mean much to his mother, who had long believed that Lyle's parents were taking Auntie Irene for a ride. She doubted Grandpa Bowman's claims that he was suffering from the effects of a gas attack, doubted even that he'd ever found his way to a trench in World War I, and was of the firm opinion that both he and his wife were simply lazy. 'At least now Irene's got her life back,' she'd said to Lyle. 'I just hope she does something with her hair!'

Just as René's death had been a blessing in disguise for her parents, so too were her parents' deaths a blessing in disguise for Irene. Although she never went in search of romance, as Mary had hoped she would, at the age of fifty-two she returned to the store where she'd previously worked and took a part-time job in the glove and scarf department. She also rejoined the tennis club where she'd met René, and started playing golf. She won trophies and made friends, went on holidays and started to smile.

Irene and Frank continued to live together and chores were divided as before: Irene taking charge of the house and Frank the garden. Theoretically they were now joint owners of the property, but it was Irene's voice that held sway. Frank had no quarrel with this and was more than satisfied to come home to cooked meals and laundered clothes. Although he never once mentioned this to his sister, he was also much happier returning to a house where his father no longer lived.

The amicable arrangement came to an end a year after Frank retired from pest control when, at the age of seventy-two, Irene died. For the first time in his life Frank now had to take care of himself. Guided by Lyle, he learned how to cook, use the washing machine and iron clothes. He dusted, cleaned and kept the house in good repair, preferring to maintain rather than change its character. In one way, however, the house did change.

Although Frank missed his sister, he never once missed her choice in music and, while happy to keep her sporting trophies on display, was unprepared to keep any of her records in the house. A week after the funeral, therefore, he took the entirety of her collection and dumped it in the dustbin, which to his way of thinking was the only suitable place for the likes of musicals and crooners.

That same day he unpacked the radio Billy had bought him for Christmas and, after a lot of twiddling and false starts, found the station of his dreams: Planet Rock. He pushed the store button, turned up the volume and, in the privacy of his own house, started to dance!

Greg looked at his watch. According to the DJ, *Nantucket Sleighride*, the song that had been playing when his uncle left the room, had been 'five minutes and forty-nine seconds of pure heaven' (recorded, Greg noted, four years before he was even born), and since then there'd been an advertisement for Autoglass and at least two minutes of a song recorded when Greg had been two. He went into the hallway and shouted up the stairs.

'How much longer are you going to be, Uncle Frank?'

'You'll have to give me a few minutes, Greg. I've just pissed on my pants!'

Greg sighed – worryingly, he realised, like his father – and returned to the dining room. His eyes fell on the television and he noticed that it wasn't plugged into the socket. He rolled his eyes: no wonder the television wasn't working if it wasn't even plugged in! He knelt down and pushed the plug into the socket, switched on the current and then turned on the television. The screen was immediately filled with thousands of hissing and dancing dots, and whichever station he chose or button on the control he pressed, the static remained.

'I told you it didn't work,' Uncle Frank said, having just re-entered the room. 'I don't know why people don't believe me.'

'You're sure there's nothing wrong with your TV?' Greg asked, still puzzling the situation.

'Of course I'm sure. I've already told you: it's the government. Those people are buggers!'

Village

Greg started the car engine and waited for his uncle to fasten his safety belt.

'What are you waiting for?' Uncle Frank asked him.

'I'm waiting for you to fasten your seat belt.'

'Why do I have to do that? I don't like seat belts.'

'Well, first of all, the law requires it,' Greg replied, 'and secondly, I don't want to listen to that pinging noise for the next forty minutes.'

Uncle Frank made an exasperated grunting noise and reluctantly fastened his belt. 'I still don't see why I have to do this. What's it got to do with the government if I wear a seat belt or not? It's my business if I go through the windscreen, not theirs. And I'll tell you another thing: I'd prefer to go through a windscreen than go to The Dales again! You're not taking me there, are you?'

'No, but what have you got against The Dales? People travel from all over the world to see them.'

'I've seen them too many times already,' Uncle Frank replied. 'I'm bored with them. Now, where are you taking me?'

'Across the big divide,' Greg smiled. 'We're going to a small village in Lancashire.' Uncle Frank looked at him for an explanation. 'I went there on a school trip once,' Greg said. 'It's pretty. Dates back to the tenth-century. People used to make their livings from farming sheep and weaving wool, but when the power loom was invented most of them moved away and settled closer to the new mills and the village was abandoned. The teacher who took us there said it was an early example of deindustrialisation.'

'Nowadays he could just hire a bus and drive you round the city,' Uncle Frank said. 'All the industry's gone from there, too.'

'That's what my father says – or rather said,' Greg replied, hurriedly correcting himself.

'Pull over by the post box, will you,' Uncle Frank interrupted. 'I've got a letter for the BBC.'

Greg waited while his uncle popped the letter into the box. 'Why are you writing to the BBC?' he asked, once his uncle was back in the car.

'I'm complaining about *Bells on Sunday*,' he replied. 'I want it taken off the air.'

Bells on Sunday, Uncle Frank explained to his unknowing nephew, was a two minute segment that aired every Sunday morning on Radio 4 at 05:43 precisely when, unfortunately, he was already awake. Each week, he said, the programme came from a different church. An announcer described the church and its history, and then detailed the age and weight of the bells and the changes the bell ringers would be ringing.

'This morning we're visiting the church of St Edith's in the picturesque Ribble Valley,' he mimicked, in a slow and solemn voice. 'It's been there for some time and has a congregation of six. There are five bells in the tower. One of them weighs 8cwt and was cast in the sixteenth-century, while the other four were made by students at the local technical college during a lunch break. The peal they'll ring today is in the key of "A" and a programme favourite: the Winchendon Place Doubles. Take it away, St Edith's: pull those ropes and get those bells clanging. Let's piss Frank Bowman off!'

'Every damn peal sounds the same, Greg. It's just a lot of depressing noise. I don't want to turn on my radio and hear the sound of some bloody bells ringing first thing in the morning – and I doubt anyone else does either. The programme's run its course and it's time it went.'

'Why don't you just tune your radio to Planet Rock?' Greg asked. 'Wake up to *Stairway to Heaven* or something.'

'I can't get Planet Rock on my upstairs radio.'

'Why not?'

'I don't know,' Uncle Frank shrugged. 'Why do you think?'

'There's no point asking me, Uncle Frank: I haven't lived in this country for fifteen years. Billy's your best bet. I'll ask him to take a look at it.'

'How are things with you and Billy? The two of you getting on?'

'We're doing okay, thanks. We do better when Horse-Face isn't around.'

Uncle Frank snorted with laughter. Horse-Face was his and Greg's private name for Jean who, although pretty, had an unusually long face. In the past, and in Jean's presence, they'd competed with each other to coin phrases of an equine nature and insert them into the conversation; phrases such as: it's good to see that you and Billy have a *stable* relationship, Jean. I think you need to start *reining* her in, Billy. Don't *saddle* me with your problems, Jean. I wonder what *triggered* that response, Greg? Do you think Jean's *jockeying* for position, Uncle Frank? And so on.

Their mutual dislike of Jean and Jean's mutual dislike for them was another bond that tied uncle to nephew. While Uncle Frank dismissed Jean for her airs and graces, Jean ridiculed him for his lack of hair and choice of cowboy-patterned braces. At first, Jean had followed her mother's lead in disapproving of Frank, but soon had reasons enough of her own, and prime amongst these was her belief that Uncle Frank didn't love Katy – or, at least, not enough.

It was a misunderstanding that happened when the battery in Uncle Frank's hearing aid was running low. She and Billy had made a rare, and therefore special, visit to see Uncle Frank when Katy had gone away for the weekend with Betty. Jean had taken one of Katy's paintings with them, supposedly a portrait of her great-uncle, and had handed it to Uncle Frank. Under the impression that Jean herself had painted the picture of him, he asked her if it was some kind of joke and made to hand it back. Jean assured him that it wasn't a joke and said that the picture was his to keep. 'Mine to do with as I please?' Uncle Frank had asked.

Jean had nodded, not quite sure what Uncle Frank was talking about, but thought no more about it until she and Billy were leaving the house and she saw the painting lying on a kitchen work surface torn into four pieces. 'The ungrateful bastard!' she'd said to Billy when they were back in the car. 'I'm just glad we didn't bring Katy with us. It could have scarred her for life.'

'Can we make a detour to Sainsbury's on the way back?' Uncle Frank asked.

'What's wrong with the Co-op? It's closer to you.'

'I don't shop there anymore.'

'Why's that – too socialist for you?'

Uncle Frank shifted uncomfortably in his seat. 'No, there was an altercation,' he mumbled.

'An altercation!' Greg laughed. 'You mean you got into a fight?'

'Not as such, but I got accused of queue jumping. I'd rather not talk about it, if it's all the same with you?'

'Man alive, Uncle Frank. You're not doing too well these days, are you – falling out with your neighbours and being persona non grata at the local shop. Next thing you know, you'll be an outlaw with a price on your head. Ha!'

Poor old Uncle Frank, the world was always against him. He'd been the runt of a litter, bullied by his father and in all probability at school. While most people completely recovered from Bell's palsy, his uncle had been marked for life by the disease, his left eye and the corner of his mouth forever misshapen. The effects of the palsy, his diminutive stature and his choice of career in pest control had left him a reluctant bachelor, a spectator of life rather than a participant. He'd never once received a Valentine's card, and the nearest he'd ever got to romance was the day he'd been walking to a bus stop and an approaching girl had smiled at him. He hadn't believed his luck and had smiled back falteringly. He was about to say hello when she brushed past him and threw her arms around the man walking immediately behind him. 'I suppose I should have known better,' he'd confessed to Greg, 'but you live in hope, don't you?'

If women in his life were non-existent, so too were friends of any kind. And, if this wasn't misfortune enough, the local Co-op had now banned him from shopping there. It was true that life hadn't dealt his uncle the kindest of hands, but by choosing to kick the world he perceived to have kicked him, Greg couldn't help but think that Uncle Frank only made matters worse for himself. The man's cantankerousness had been legendary even before he'd left for America, but in his absence appeared to have reached new heights. If proof were needed it came at that very moment when an overtaking car pulled sharply in front of them and Greg had to brake hard.

'What the hell!' Uncle Frank exclaimed. 'That bugger could have killed us!' Without warning, he reached across Greg and punched the horn.

'Whoa, take it easy, will you? We don't want an incident. This is supposed to be a fun day out, remember?' He held up his hand to let the driver know there was no problem.

'People shouldn't be allowed to get away with things like that. They should be taught a lesson!' Uncle Frank said, getting up a steam. 'Hell, if I had a gun I'd shoot the man's tyres out!'

'Well, thank goodness you don't have a gun,' Greg replied, and then, remembering the conversation with his father, a worrying thought struck him. He turned serious and looked at his uncle: 'You *don't* have a gun, do you?'

'I have two revolvers and a rifle,' Uncle Frank replied matter-of-factly. 'And I've got a Bowie knife and a tomahawk too.'

Greg shuddered. 'Real ones?'

'Nah, plastic. I've had them since I was a kid.'

Greg breathed a sigh of relief.

They left the city behind them and drove west on narrow roads that twisted and climbed into the South Pennines, a remote area of wild barren moorland and dark sandstone walls – scenery as far removed from The Dales as the moon was from the sun. Eventually, Greg turned off the road and parked on an unmade area of land intended for cars. The two of them climbed out and looked around.

'By heck, lad, this is a bit bleak, isn't it?' Uncle Frank said. 'I'm glad I brought my coat with me.'

Greg helped his uncle over the stile and continued to hold his arm as they followed the steep footpath down to the village. They entered a dry gully that ran alongside an old vaccary wall made from slabs of millstone and interspersed with hawthorns and holly trees. The incline levelled off here and Uncle Frank shook free of his nephew to take a closer look at a series of molehills.

'How many moles do you suppose made these hills?' he asked Greg.

Greg shrugged. 'I don't know. Three, maybe four?'

'Just one,' Uncle Frank said, drawing on his years in pest control.

'Because of the way they look, most people think moles are loveable, especially if they've read *Wind in the Willows*. But they're not. They're unsociable varmints, and if they catch another mole in one of their tunnels they kill it.

'I'll give them their due, though: they're hard workers – and considering they eat half their own weight in worms every day, I suppose they have to be. It's hard to believe, but a mole can dig a twenty yard tunnel in a single day. One of the lads at work told me that the amount of soil a mole shifts at any one time is the equivalent of a miner moving four tons of coal in a twenty minute period.'

Greg waited while his uncle prodded one of the molehills with a stick and then continued walking. 'Come on, Uncle Frank. I'm getting hungry.'

They reached the village twenty minutes later, a hamlet of old ruins and reclaimed old ruins. Two ancient pedestrian bridges straddled the slow-moving beck and picnic tables had been placed next to a small pond where mallard ducks swam. They kept their sightseeing to a minimum and walked to the licensed tearoom, a converted old barn that sold gifts and served pies and sandwiches. Uncle Frank took a seat at one of the tables and studied the menu while Greg went to the bar and ordered drinks.

When Greg sat down, Uncle Frank tugged at his sleeve and pulled him closer. 'Is that Dickie Bird?' he whispered. 'Him over there in the corner.'

Greg looked at the man. There was a resemblance to the cricket umpire, but this man was too old to be Dickie Bird. 'I don't think so,' he said.

'But look at him, he's crying. Dickie Bird's the only man I know who cries in public.'

This was true: Dickie Bird did do a lot of crying in public – usually while being interviewed on television about his career or a recent honour. But this man was simply wiping sweat from his brow. 'No, it's not him,' Greg said. 'Now, what do you want to eat?'

'Cheese and onion pie with mushy peas, please,' Uncle Frank replied, still staring at the man. 'Did I tell you I was thinking of adding Dickie Bird to the list?'

'The Tombstone List?'

Uncle Frank nodded.

The list had been in existence for as long as Greg could remember. At first, it comprised the names of people who, in some way or another, Uncle Frank believed to have slighted him: the cleaner who'd left the windows smudged, a bus conductor who'd wrong-changed him or a sales assistant who'd sold him a shirt with faulty buttons. It was called the Tombstone List after the town in Arizona where the *Gunfight at the OK Corral* had taken place, and where scores had been settled unilaterally.

In time, however, his uncle had started to add pet hates to the list – golf, brass bands and Morris dancers – and include those people in the national arena who, in his eyes, were either smug little bastards or had got too big for their boots. Anyone proclaimed a 'national treasure' was sure to be included, as was anyone dubbed the nation's favourite. The Queen Mother, when she'd been alive, had been included for being the nation's favourite grandmother, as had Eric Morecambe for being the nation's favourite comedian; and Vera Lynn was still on the list for being the nation's favourite sweetheart. Uncle Frank resented being told who his favourite people were.

If he was to add Dickie Bird to the list, however, Uncle Frank knew he was in danger of overloading it with 'professional' Yorkshiremen, who in his mind gave the county a bad name. He was puzzling over whether to take Michael Parkinson or Geoffrey Boycott off the list when his nose started to run and he reached in his pocket for a handkerchief.

'Well, bugger me sideways,' he exclaimed, 'I forgot to put a handkerchief in my pocket when I changed my trousers. You haven't got a spare one on you, have you, Greg?'

'I don't own any handkerchiefs: I use tissues. And I've only got the one with me. Why don't you use the paper napkin?'

'Tissues? Men don't blow their noses on tissues: they use handkerchiefs. Cowboys never set foot outside the bunkroom without a handkerchief tied round their neck, and there's no way an outlaw would have robbed a bank holding a piece of tissue paper over his face. What the deary me, lad. What's become of you?'

A thought struck him. 'If Billy doesn't want your Dad's handkerchiefs, can I have them? He had some nice ones, he did, and they'd make a nice keepsake.'

'Sure you can. I doubt very much that Billy will want them.'

Greg looked through the menu and decided that his uncle's choice of cheese and onion pie was as good anything. He walked around the corner to the food counter and waited for someone to take his order.

As Uncle Frank was finishing up wiping his nose on the napkin, Billy walked into the tearoom. He took one look at his uncle and turned on his heel – though not before Uncle Frank had seen him.

'Hey, Billy,' Uncle Frank called out. 'It's me! Uncle Frank!'

Uncle Frank left his seat and followed his fleeing nephew. He caught sight of him running down the main street and watched as he crossed one of the bridges. 'Billy! Billy!' he shouted after him. 'Can I have your Dad's handkerchiefs?'

'Where have you been?' Greg asked, when his uncle returned to the table.

'Billy was here!' Uncle Frank said. 'He came in and then left. It was as if he didn't want me to see him.'

Greg looked puzzled. 'Billy's in Denmark. He's not due back till tomorrow.'

'I'm telling you, it was Billy! My hearing might not be worth a damn, but my eyesight's as good as it ever was. I know my own nephew when I see him.'

'Well, that's strange,' Greg admitted. 'I'll give him a call when I get back and find out what he's up to.'

'Don't forget to ask him about your Dad's handkerchiefs, will you?'

A waitress brought their food to the table and, as his uncle always preferred, they ate in silence. Once the plates had been cleared and they were left drinking their beers, Greg plucked up courage and prepared to confront his uncle about his recent behaviour.

'Uncle Frank, there's…'

'What's wrong with your teeth?' Uncle Frank interrupted. 'They're a bit strange looking, aren't they?'

'My teeth?' Greg said, off-balanced by the question. 'Nothing's wrong with my teeth. I've just had them whitened.'

Uncle Frank looked at him and shook his head. 'Billy the Kid never had *his* teeth whitened.'

'He never had time to go to the dentist. He was too busy killing people, remember. Anyway, it's you I want to talk about, not Billy the Kid.'

'Gunned down at the age of twenty-one,' Uncle Frank lamented. 'Pat Garrett...'

'Uncle Frank!' Greg interrupted. 'There's something we have to talk about...'

6

Feet

Of all the tea joints, in all the villages, in all the world, Uncle Frank walks into mine, Billy brooded. What kind of sheer bad luck was that?

He had a feeling that someone had voiced the same thought before him, but couldn't for the life of him remember who. He doubted, however, that the words related to a predicament in any way similar to his own, and in supposing this he was correct: Humphrey Bogart had never been afraid of feet.

Billy had pitched his tent in this part of the world for the simple reason that Jean and Betty refused to travel here. Both hated the area's desolation, and Betty had questioned why anyone not suffering from depression would want to go there in the first place. That his Uncle Frank might turn up in the village had never once crossed his mind, and if his uncle was here, then so too was his brother.

Billy flopped down on his sleeping bag and tried to catch his breath. He hadn't exercised in years and the run through the village had exhausted him. He stared at the canvas walls of the tent and listened to the bleats of the sheep outside. He envied them. They didn't worry about things or lead complicated lives. They ate grass and had their coats sheared once a year, and that was about it. If only he'd been born a sheep instead of Billy Bowman, he lamented: a man suspended from his job and ordered to see a therapist; a husband deceiving his wife; and now a nephew running from his uncle. How in God's name had he got himself into such a mess?

The answer, or at least the source of his troubles, stared at him from a distance of no more than 5' 7": his feet – or, more precisely, his fear of other people's feet.

As far as Billy could remember, his fear of feet had started when he was about seven or eight – certainly he could never recall being discomfited by them before that age. Seemingly overnight, in much the same way as the palsy had descended on Uncle Frank, Billy had woken up one morning with a nagging urge to cover his feet. He couldn't explain why, but their appearance suddenly troubled him. From that day onwards he dressed his feet first, pulling on his socks and shoes even before his underpants, and at night bared them only for the briefest of moments before hiding them under the bedcovers.

He was soon unwilling to even touch his feet or allow others to touch them. He started to wear gloves when he cut his toenails and use a flannel when he washed his feet. Visits to shoe shops, once enjoyable, turned into nightmares. He sat in chairs and squeezed his mother's hand, closed his eyes and tried to ignore the sickly feeling that welled in his stomach when assistants placed his foot in a measuring block or eased shoes on to his feet. Often, he would accept the first shoe brought to him, irrespective of whether he liked the style or if the shoe fitted comfortably. (When old enough to buy shoes for himself, Billy would simply point to a shoe, tell the salesperson his size and then buy the pair without first trying them on.)

While his own feet disquieted him, he never grew to hate them. Once covered, the anxiety they caused soon faded, and he was also cognisant of the fact that without them he wouldn't be able to walk very far. Other people's feet, however, terrified him.

Feet walking around in everyday life and minding their own business didn't unduly bother him, but feet that came close or touched his scared the living daylights out of him. Unfortunately, such situations were hard to avoid at school, where feet were plentiful, constantly within range and, in changing rooms and swimming baths, invariably bare. The fear, if not the actuality of a foot touching him during periods of physical activity, filled Billy with feelings of indescribable dread. His heart would start to race and his breathing grow laboured; he'd break into a cold sweat and feel light-headed and, on occasion, suffer panic attacks.

When some of his classmates realised that Billy's discomfort was caused by their touch, they touched him all the more and made a sport of grabbing his feet. It was good old-fashioned schoolboy fun at the expense of a weaker party, the kind that had propelled the Nazis to power in a bygone age and made *Britain's Got Talent* a ratings success. Had they known that the happiest day of Billy's young life was the day he left school and escaped their good humour, they would have been surprised but unrepentant. How the hell could anyone in their right mind be scared of feet?

And Billy wondered the same thing. He was embarrassed by his phobia and admitted it to no one. Rather than confide in his parents and teachers or talk it through with a doctor, he suffered in silence. They'd have told him he was being ridiculous and that his fear was irrational – and they'd have been right. He knew this as well as anyone.

There was a difference as deep as the Mariana Trench, however, between him knowing something and being able to do anything about it. In the thrall of the phobia he was powerless. Rather than confront the condition head-on, he resigned himself to a life of managing the disorder and avoiding potentially stressful situations, and for a time this strategy worked. What the stratagem hadn't provided for, however, was that Billy would fall in love with the daughter of a podiatrist.

Jean had never mentioned that her father was a chiropodist, only that he was a successful businessman and magistrate, and consequently the bomb fell from a clear blue sky on the evening Billy first went to Spinney Cottage for dinner.

Although he'd shared a table with Jean's parents at a charity event, Billy had never been formally introduced to them and, effectively, this was their first meeting. All had gone well until they'd sat down for dinner and Henry Halliwell had started to describe how he'd removed a nail from a client's toe the previous day. Billy had been smoothing pâté on a small finger of toast at the time and the unnecessarily gruesome account disquieted him. It also left him wondering if such torture practices were common in big business.

Betty noticed the look of consternation on Billy's face. 'Henry's a chiropodist,' she explained. 'If you ever want him to take a look at your feet, just say the word.'

At this point the blood drained from Billy's face and a cold shiver ran through his body. The familiar feeling of dread returned and, despite his best efforts to ignore the portent, he started to hyperventilate.

'Quick, Jean. Get a brown paper bag!' Henry commanded.

Billy came round lying on the couch with his head propped on a cushion. He mumbled embarrassed apologies, and sought to explain the event by wondering out loud if a small piece of toast had gone down his throat the wrong way.

'I doubt it, lad,' Henry said. 'My guess is that you're squeamish.'

'I think I might be, Mr Halliwell,' Billy admitted.

'Maybe you shouldn't talk about your work at the table, Henry,' Betty suggested.

'It's my work that *puts* food on the damned table, Betty! There's no more suitable place to talk about it,' Henry replied.

And until his death – and even though it had been decided that Billy was squeamish – Henry Halliwell continued to regale his family with tales of podiatry: stories of corns and in-growing toenails, verrucae and bunions, chilblains and athlete's foot. Billy tried to block these stories by placing small wads of cotton wool in both ears and droning quietly to himself while Henry spoke, and if these tactics failed – which they often did – he would excuse himself from the room and make unnecessary visits to the downstairs toilet, passing the time there by combing his hair or brushing dandruff from his shoulders.

'That boy's got one hell of a weak bladder,' Henry once commented.

There was one story, however, that intrigued Billy as much as it disgusted Jean and Betty. It concerned a patient whose toes were so twisted and jammed from wearing winkle pickers that Henry had been forced to refer him to the hospital for two toe amputations, one from each foot. This, to Billy, was an affirming story of feet disappearing – albeit bit by bit – and he started to envisage a world without feet, a utopia he'd never before dared to imagine. And then, out of the blue, an image of a woman with no feet popped into his head and his body stiffened.

'What's wrong, Billy?' Jean asked.

'Nothing's the matter, love. I was just day dreaming.'

The unfaithful thought troubled him and he took Jean's hand and squeezed it. 'I love you,' he whispered.

The image of the woman with no feet, however, lingered and refused to go away.

Billy had no intentions of betraying his wife at this stage of their relationship. He loved Jean and she loved him, and her feet never overly troubled him. He viewed them almost, though not quite, as he viewed his own feet, and though he made a point of minimising contact with them, he appreciated that some contact was unavoidable, especially if they were to have sex.

The exhilaration of the act was, at first, distraction enough for Billy not to notice when Jean's feet touched his, but as time wore on the touch of her feet started to niggle him. He sought to remedy matters by researching sex manuals for positions where feet never came into contact, and with this end in mind, made a visit to a distant branch of Waterstones. He read the books he found there furtively, carefully memorised the postures that didn't require professional gymnasts to perform them, and then returned to his car and sketched diagrams. (His suggestion to Jean that she wear boots when they have sex – other than the ones she wore for hiking – came to him after an even more secretive visit to an adult bookstore.)

Jean took his suggestions in her stride, pleased that the man she'd married was so experimental in the bedroom. When she suggested he try sucking her toes, however, Billy turned her down flat and became quite agitated.

'I don't know why not,' Jean had said sulkily. 'The Duchess of York has her toes sucked.'

'And look what's happened to her,' Billy snapped. 'The only time you see her these days is when she's on *The Oprah Winfrey Show* confessing another of her problems. I don't want you ending up on that woman's couch, Jean!'

Issues in the bedroom were further resolved after Billy started wearing thick socks to bed. He explained to Jean that his circulation had worsened and he was now suffering from cold feet. It wasn't his idea, he added, just something the doctor had suggested. (Billy was aware that in his attempts to hide his phobia from Jean, he hadn't painted the most flattering portrait of himself over the years: squeamish, weak-bladdered and now cold-footed.)

Jean accepted the socks, but drew a line in the sand when Billy attempted to climb into bed wearing his slippers one night.

Things in the bedroom ran smoothly after that, and eventually Jean became pregnant with Katy. During the last three months of her pregnancy, however, Jean started to have problems in her lower legs, especially when she lay in bed. She experienced a kind of itching sensation, as if ants were crawling inside her legs, and without warning her lower limbs would spasm and jerk in Billy's direction. The condition was diagnosed as Restless Leg Syndrome, a harmless disorder the doctors said, but with no known causes and no known cure.

While the doctors described the syndrome as innocuous, Billy had very different ideas. When he went to bed at night now, he felt threatened and in constant danger of being attacked by feet no longer in his wife's control. He wanted to barricade himself, build a wall of blankets between himself and Jean or tie her fidgety legs to the bed rail. The dread that had always lurked once again returned and for long periods he would lie awake at night, his heart palpitating and his stomach churning. When he did fall asleep, he would dream of the callused and deformed feet Henry Halliwell had described in such detail, and would wake in the morning exhausted and drenched in sweat.

Once more, the image of the woman with no feet crept silently into his head, and this time Billy felt no guilt.

The crisis in sleeping arrangements was resolved after Jean suggested they move into the twin-bedded room. Conscious of the fact that she was now sleeping as well as eating for two, Jean was ever more aware that she was having difficulty enough sleeping for one. His anxiety, she complained to Billy, was not only palpable but contagious. How was she supposed to sleep at night when he tossed and turned the whole time and made strange noises in his sleep? The doctor, she continued, had told her that stressful situations only exacerbated her rhythmic leg movements, and there was nothing more stressful in her life at this time than sleeping next to Billy. She'd concluded, therefore – reluctantly, and with sorrow in her heart – that she and Billy needed to avoid each other at night.

The arrangement, which was only intended to be a temporary measure, suited Billy down to the ground. If circumstances demanded, he was now free to wear even his shoes to bed!

The arrangement, however, became permanent. Although the Restless Leg Syndrome went on extended vacations, it always returned unexpectedly and made a long-term commitment to a double bed impossible. The two foot gap separating their beds became symbolic of the growing gap in their relationship, which had morphed from romance to domesticity. They continued to have sex, but only occasionally and always hurriedly, and set aside their true passions for discussions of utility bills, Katy's schooling and the whereabouts of Betty.

And then, shortly after Katy's sixth birthday, the domesticity of Billy's life was blown apart when he met the woman who'd been stalking him for the past seventeen years – the woman with no feet.

Polly

The offices of the company Billy worked for were located in a small sleepy town on the south coast of England, sited there for the simple reason that the man charged with establishing a European base for the American conglomerate was a keen sailor and a smooth talker, who legitimised his choice by pointing to the savings the company would make by not having to pay London salaries.

In the past, Billy had travelled there only for biannual sales meetings but, after being unexpectedly promoted to the no-man's land of sub-middle management, had been encouraged, seemingly for political rather than practical reasons, to spend more of his time in the office and attend meetings on subject matters he barely understood.

He didn't enjoy these trips which, depending on the traffic conditions of the day, could take anything from seven to twelve hours. They also took him away from Jean and Katy for three-day periods and necessitated him staying in soulless hotels and eating evening meals alone. But more than this, it was the language spoken in the office that troubled him: it was simply indecipherable!

Several years previously he'd attended a conference of textbook publishers and academic booksellers where speaker after speaker had climbed to the platform and incorporated the phrase 24/7 into their addresses. He'd had absolutely no idea what the expression meant but, for fear of appearing stupid, had been too reticent to ask the person sitting next to him for an explanation. By the time he'd learned its significance the idiom was already passé and had, in the meetings he now attended, been replaced by even more inscrutable expressions. People talked of blue ocean opportunities and green field thinking, boiling frogs and putting socks on octopuses, reverse infallibility and zombie projects; and variously described people as either negatrons, goldbrickers or duck shufflers.

Billy said little in these meetings and instead chose to nod his head knowingly. (He'd mastered this disingenuous knack of feigning comprehension while visiting lecturers of quantum physics and pure maths, subject matters he found equally impenetrable.)

Between meetings, he would sit at a hot desk in the open-planned area of the office and do work he could have done at home. The only person he knew there was his immediate boss, but most of the time he was either missing or in meetings too important for Billy to attend. He knew the faces of some of the marketing people in the department, but none seemed interested in conversation and he was never invited to join them for after-work drinks.

Billy wondered sometimes if people thought he was dull, something that had already crossed his mind at sales meetings. He'd noticed then that while his colleagues in the department walked to the designated restaurant in twos and threes, he usually walked there alone. It seemed that people rarely sought out his company. It also struck him as odd that he still had only four friends after so many years.

He was pondering this curious state of affairs when his boss came over to his desk waving an expenses sheet. Unbeknownst to Billy, the form he'd used had been superseded by a newer document and his claims had been placed in now out-of-date boxes. He was advised to go down to the accounts department 'tout de suite' and get an explanation of the new form from someone called Polly.

Billy put his laptop in sleep mode and headed down the stairs to the accounts department, wondering if he was going to be told off. He'd always worried about small things, and still remembered the time in primary school when a class teacher had thrown a fit after consecutive pupils had brought work to him not ruled off at the bottom of the page. The teacher, whose name was Mr Hodgson, warned the class that the next pupil to bring him work not ruled off would be in trouble – serious trouble!

Billy's essay had come to a natural end on the very last line of the page and he was unsure what to do. Flustered, and not wanting to get into trouble, he'd taken another piece of paper and ruled a line across its top and then taken both sheets to the teacher. He could still recall Mr Hodgson's words: 'Well, if this doesn't take the biscuit, Billy!' The teacher had then held up both pieces of paper to the class and made Billy stand in the corner and face the wall for thirty minutes.

On asking for Polly, Billy was directed to one of three offices lining the far wall. He knocked softly and walked in, and found Polly sitting behind a large desk with two large computer screens open and an in-tray piled high with different coloured files.

'Hi, Polly. I'm Billy Bowman from Academic Sales. I've been told I've been filling in the wrong expenses form.'

'Don't worry about it, you're not the only one,' Polly said. 'It would have helped if someone had actually sent out an email telling people we'd changed the form. Most people here don't bother themselves with details, but for me they're what life's all about. It's probably why I became an accountant.'

'I tried accountancy once,' Billy said, sitting down in the chair opposite her. 'I couldn't understand it. That's probably why I became a sales rep.'

Polly had an easy manner and a ready smile. She was slightly on the plump side of life – as jolly people, in Billy's experience, tended to be – and had the prettiest of faces.

'You're in the field most of the time, aren't you?' she asked. 'It must be strange spending time in the office.'

Billy admitted that it was. He felt unusually at ease in her company and confessed that he didn't have a clue what people were talking about most of the time.

'Join the club, Billy,' she laughed. 'People here talk bollocks, and the more bollocks they talk the higher up the ladder they climb. Someone should coin a phrase for it. Bollocksurfing or something like that. You know my favourite? *Deferred success.* That's failure to you and me. Ha!'

Billy laughed. 'That's a good one, Polly. I might have that engraved on my headstone,' he said, wondering when he'd last been so amusing.

She handed a copy of the new form to him and went

through the columns and boxes one at a time, indicating the expected location of each future expense claim. Surprisingly, Billy understood every word and returned to his desk feeling strangely good about life. He was certain in his own mind that he'd just made a new friend!

He manufactured reasons to return to Polly's office after that, either feigning a misunderstanding or checking that the two reps who reported to him were also filling in their expenses forms correctly. Often, if Polly wasn't too busy, he'd get a couple of fair-trade coffees from the machine closest to her office and chat for a while. He found himself sitting in meetings on core competencies and knowledge growth, nodding his head sagely while replaying every word of their conversations.

About two months after their first meeting – when Billy was in her office on yet another pretext – Polly looked at her watch. 'It's lunchtime,' she announced. 'How about we finish this conversation in the Slug and Lettuce?'

Billy was happy to. He stood up and waited for Polly to stand, but instead she wheeled herself from behind the desk. 'You don't mind pushing, do you?'

Billy had had no idea that Polly was disabled, but then remembered he'd never actually seen her when she hadn't been sitting behind her desk. 'Happy to,' he said, hoping that his voice had remained neutral and not betrayed an element of surprise.

The Slug and Lettuce was about three hundred yards from the office in the direction of the promenade. Billy manoeuvred Polly's chair down the ramp at the front of the office and then pushed her along uneven pavements to the pub, careful not to jolt her when they went up or down kerbs. Once inside the Slug, he cleared two chairs from a table to make room for her wheelchair and then went to the bar to order a baked potato with cheese for her and a ham sandwich for him. He returned with a glass of white wine and a coca-cola.

'You're not drinking?' she asked.

'If I drink at lunchtime I fall asleep in the afternoon,' Billy replied. 'Besides, I'm driving.'

They laughed at his joke, and once again Billy wondered when he'd last been so amusing. The answer was obvious: it was the last time he'd been with Polly!

He took a sip of his coke and then asked Polly how long she'd been in the wheelchair. Strangely, he didn't feel the least bit uncomfortable asking her this question. Conversation was always so easy with Polly.

Polly looked at her watch. 'Let's see, I climbed into the wheelchair at eight o'clock this morning and it's now one o'clock in the afternoon, so I'd say about five hours.'

'Oh, now I see,' Billy said. 'Something happened to you last night! I was thinking that you were *confined* to the wheelchair. Did you have a fall or something?'

Polly laughed. 'You're a bit credulous, aren't you, Billy? But it's a nice quality to have.'

Billy looked confused. 'You haven't just been in the wheelchair for five hours then?'

'I've been in it since I got up this morning – that's the five hours I was referring to,' Polly smiled. 'I suppose I shouldn't make light of the situation but it's my situation, so why not? I don't see any point in getting depressed about it.'

'Is it spinal?' Billy ventured. 'Are your legs paralysed?'

'My spine and legs are fine, thanks. It's my feet – I don't have any.'

Billy had just taken a drink of coke and some of the fizzy drink now found its way down his nose.

'Oh Polly,' he gasped. 'That's fantastic! – I mean, fantastic*ally* bad luck!' he quickly added, hoping that his joy wasn't detectable.

'So those aren't your feet then,' he said, pointing to her shoes.

'No, they're prosthetics. I can walk with sticks, but it's more comfortable using a wheelchair. I've always liked sitting.'

'Me too,' Billy said. 'I've always preferred sitting to walking as well. Jean and her mother go walking together but I never join them. I've always thought feet were overrated.'

'I wouldn't go that far!' Polly said, annoyed by his remark. 'If I had to choose between having feet and not having feet, then I'd have feet any day of the week. They allow you more freedom.'

'What… what happened?' Billy asked, slightly disappointed by her reaction.

'I was in a car accident – a bad one,' Polly said. 'The only way they could get me out was by amputating my feet.'

'How awful,' Billy sympathised. 'Were you driving?'

'No, my boyfriend was. We'd been arguing, and he decided that the best way to resolve the argument was by getting me home and out of his car as quickly as possible. He took a bend too quickly and lost control, smashed into a tree. That was seven years ago.'

'What an idiot!' Billy blurted out. 'What a stupid idiot! And I bet he climbed out without a scratch on him, didn't he?'

'Not quite,' Polly said. 'He was killed on impact.'

Billy was about to say something to the effect of how it had served him right, when he saw the look in Polly's eyes (green ones, he noticed). 'I'm sorry to hear that, Polly. Very sorry. I shouldn't have said that.'

A barman brought their food to the table and conversation drifted to more mundane matters, namely Polly's baked potato and his ham sandwich. Billy wondered why she'd chosen cheese as her topping rather than tuna and sweetcorn, and she asked him why he'd opted for white bread instead of brown. 'I never eat white bread,' she said. 'Wholemeal's a lot healthier.'

After they'd finished their meals Billy picked up the tab and Polly, determined that this should be a corporate rather than a personal expense, told him which column to put the claim in. 'It was a work related conversation, remember,' she said.

That evening, Billy sat in the hotel bar drinking pints of lager. He had a lot of thinking to do. Could Polly really be the woman who'd haunted his thoughts for so many years, the soul mate his phobic mind had longed for?

Although the image of a woman with no feet had first popped into his head when Henry Halliwell had been describing the plight of a patient, it had taken up permanent residence there after Jean's legs had started to travel independently from her body and the two of them had moved into separate beds. He remembered that Jean had been pregnant with Katy at the time and that Katy was now almost seven. He did the sums and realised that it was the same time Polly had been in the car crash. Surely, there was more to this than just coincidence!

He recalled his first meeting with Polly, his immediate ease in her company. Not for one moment had he ever felt anxious or threatened when he was with her. Although the fact of her handicap had only been revealed to him that day, he believed now that he'd always intuitively known she had no feet.

He thought of Jean and wondered if he still loved her. He thought he did, but couldn't decide if it was love or just the fact that he'd got used to living with her. If Polly was the woman he was meant to be with though, how would he break the news to Jean, and how hurt would she be? Probably not too hurt, he eventually decided – more likely inconvenienced.

But if he left Jean and moved south, how would he ever maintain a close relationship with his daughter? Katy he *did* love. Maybe she could move south with him, he thought, but then wondered how on earth he'd ever afford a house in the south of England.

The stupidity of the thought suddenly struck him. He didn't need to buy a house. He and Katy could move in with Polly!

But then Billy caught himself. He knew that he loved Polly – there was no other way to describe his feelings for her – but how did Polly feel about him? Did she feel the same way or see him only as a friend? Would she even want him and Katy to move in with her and, more to the point, would she allow them to eat white bread? There was no point planning anything until he knew the answers to these questions, and at this stage in their relationship he didn't feel comfortable asking Polly outright.

He needed to be more subtle, he decided, make her realise she loved him without actually suggesting it to her. But how? It was then he remembered something Polly had said over lunch – something about feet giving a person more freedom than a wheelchair – and a plan of action fell into place as if purposely presented to him on a plate. That's exactly how he'd do it! He'd make the town wheelchair friendly for her and make her realise that feet weren't the be-all and end-all of life and that she was no worse off without them. And he could do this in the evenings and on his own time instead of kicking his heels in the hotel.

On subsequent and unnecessarily frequent visits to the office, Billy put his plan into action. For two months he visited pubs and restaurants in the town and checked access and toilet facilities for people confined to wheelchairs, and where he found shortcomings he asked for the manager and reported his findings, mentioning in an off-hand way that he worked for the biggest consumer of services in town.

All appeared to be going well until the day he was asked to step into his boss's office for a chat. ('Chat' was such an innocent word, but its connotations were always ominous.)

'Billy, I've been asked to have a quiet word with you,' his boss said.

'What have I done?' Billy asked nervously. 'Am I in trouble?'

'You will be if you don't stop going around town telling people how to run their businesses. It's not within your managerial remit to speak on behalf of the company and threaten them with a boycott unless they improve their facilities for the handicapped.'

'I don't think I've ever threatened that,' Billy said cautiously. 'I certainly never intended to.'

'Whether it was your intention or not, they thought there was an implication to your words. It's not your business to make places wheelchair-friendly, Billy, and it's not mine. That's what governments and local councils are for.'

'I was only trying to help things along,' Billy replied. 'It's not always easy for people like Polly to get around.'

'And that's another thing,' his boss continued. 'Have you been dipping your pen in company ink?'

'No,' Billy replied carefully. 'I don't even have a fountain pen.'

His boss smiled and shook his head. 'Let me put it another way, Billy: Have you been *fucking* Polly?'

'Me? Good grief, no! We're just friends. Why on earth would you ask such a thing?'

'Because Polly's had an *off the record* word with HR, and believe me you don't want to get to the stage where it's *on* the record. You'll really find yourself behind the eight ball then!'

His boss told him that Polly was starting to feel pestered by Billy's constant visits to her office, his numerous texts and emails, and certainly didn't appreciate being called at home in the middle of the night.

'She says she's told you this time and again but that you don't listen. And another thing, she thinks you've got a weird fascination with her prosthetics and it's making her feel uncomfortable.'

Billy left the office gobsmacked. How could Polly have said

those things, told those lies? She made him sound like some kind of pervert. He didn't remember her ever telling *him* those things. He wanted to confront her there and then, but remembered his boss telling him that her office was now out of bounds to him. This was so wrong, so very, very wrong.

Even though it was only 3:45pm, Billy packed away his laptop and returned to the hotel. The bar was shut and so he headed to the Hole in the Wall, an all-day pub by the pier with an indiscriminate clientele. He looked out of place in his suit and wished he'd changed into a pair of jeans before leaving the hotel. Ignoring the stares, he ordered a pint of lager and took it to a corner table in the back room. There was so much to think about, so much he had to put right.

In hindsight, lunch with Polly at the Slug and Lettuce had been the apogee of their short non-relationship, but they had lunched at the George about three weeks later when Billy had updated her on his crusade to make the town more wheelchair-friendly.

'I hope you're not doing this for my sake,' Polly had said.

Of course he was doing it for her sake! How could she not realise this?

'No, I'm doing it for *all* the town's handicapped,' he'd lied.

Looking back on things now, maybe the George hadn't been the right occasion to tell Polly that he'd been dreaming of her for seventeen years. Certainly she hadn't taken it as the compliment he'd intended, and it was disconcerting to have her stare at him for so long with her mouth open.

After that, the conversation had dipped and become stilted. Billy blamed himself for this: he always became nervous and tongue-tied when relationships transitioned and there was no guarantee of a happy ending. Too much now hinged on his relationship with Polly for him to simply relax and enjoy her company and, as always happened in such situations, he said the wrong things and became as dull as dishwater. He'd worried at the time that Polly might have noticed this, but after a nightcap in the bar that evening decided she hadn't and that their relationship was still on track.

Billy asked Polly out several times after that but she'd always declined, saying she was too busy and planning to eat at her desk – *al desco* dining, as the bollocksurfers called it. He'd still found excuses to drop by her office, but wondered now why he'd needed an excuse. Why couldn't he have just dropped by? That's what friends did, wasn't it, and he and Polly were definitely friends. In fact, he remembered her emphasising that point to him on a number of occasions, certainly the time he'd invited her out for dinner. Come to think of it though, hadn't she used the phrase *just* friends and unnecessarily reminded him that he had a wife and daughter.

He'd asked her at the time – hypothetically of course – if her answer would have been different if he'd been single, and she'd told him no. She looked upon him as a friend (she'd used that word again!), and was anyhow romantically involved with another – a doctor.

The news that she was seeing someone jolted Billy, and he'd returned to his desk despondent. Having misheard her, however, and thinking that she'd said *her* doctor instead of *a* doctor, he'd done some research on the net and returned to her office the next day with the sad news that their relationship was unethical, and that if the practice ever got wind of it her doctor friend might well be struck off – not that he himself had any intention of telling the practice.

He remembered her getting annoyed, raising her voice and telling him that her personal business was hers and hers alone, but that if he really wanted to know, the doctor she was seeing was an academic doctor and not a medical practitioner, and that he'd lost a leg in a skiing accident and wasn't too happy about having a missing limb either, unless of course Billy wanted to phone him and tell him that legs were overrated too!

This news made Billy more despondent still. How could he compete with someone who was a doctor *and* an amputee? 'I'm only looking out for you, Polly,' he'd stammered. 'It's your best interests I have at heart. You must realise this.'

But it appeared that Polly didn't realise this. Why else would she complain to HR about his late night phone call? All he'd said to her was that she'd left the bathroom light on. Surely, it wasn't a crime for one friend to be concerned about another friend's electricity bill and, come to think of it, what was so wrong about sitting outside someone's house listening to the car radio at night? It was a free country, wasn't it?

And that time he'd followed her and another girl from the office to the train station and been caught by Polly observing her from behind a pillar. There was nothing peculiar about that. He'd explained to her at the time that he was just concerned about the amount of metal in her wheelchair and wanted to make sure she didn't fall on the track and get electrocuted. This was normal behaviour by any standard. Why did she have to make it sound so sinister?

After finishing his third pint, Billy left the Hole in the Wall and walked to the nearest restaurant and ordered a pizza. He drank a large glass of Chianti while waiting for the food, and another while he ate his meal. He looked around the room and saw couples talking, laughing, touching. He was the only person sitting alone. Why wasn't he there with Polly? He should have asked Polly to join him for dinner. They could have talked things through and committed to a fresh start. They were made for each other – surely she realised this? It wasn't by chance they'd met. It was… fate. Yes that was the word – fate! They were *fated* to be together. Polly needed to know this and he was the only person who could make her understand. He drained the last of his wine and resolved to make this clear to her in the morning. This time tomorrow, he told himself, everything would be fine, everything hunky-dory.

Billy left the restaurant and, on the spur of the moment, bought a packet of cigarettes from a late-night shop. Tobacco, he'd heard, focused the mind, and it was imperative that his thoughts were marshalled to military precision by the time he spoke to Polly the next day.

The first cigarette made him cough and feel lightheaded, and the second, which he'd lit from the glowing embers of the first, made him feel sick. He threw up in a skip at the back of the hotel, but took the unpleasantness in his stride: there was no gain without pain, he reasoned.

He reached his hotel room and splashed water on his face and rinsed out his mouth. He opened the mini-bar and the room's windows: he needed to drink alcohol, smoke cigarettes and get himself in shape for the morning's encounter with Polly. There was no time for sleep.

Despite his best efforts to remain awake, however, Billy fell asleep on the floor shortly after 4am and woke up four hours later. He looked at the blurry image on his watch face and cursed: 'Jiminy Cricket!' Polly would already be on her way to the office. He had to get there before she made it through the door and went off-limits!

His head hurt like a tractor had run over it during the night, but there was no time to shower or change into fresh clothes, shave, comb his hair or brush his teeth. He left the hotel and half-walked and half-ran to the company offices, struggling to maintain a straight course and occasionally losing balance and bumping into other pedestrians on the street. He arrived out of breath, just in time to see Polly wheeling herself across the still largely deserted car park.

'Polly! Polly!' he gasped. 'I need to talk to you,' he said – or at least these were the words he was intending to pronounce.

Polly just heard strange noises, and was alarmed by Billy's dishevelled appearance. 'Christ, Billy! Just leave me alone, will you? What the hell's the matter with you?'

Polly was almost at the door and Billy had no choice but to take the handles of her wheelchair and push her back in the direction she'd come. She started to scream and Billy tried to calm her. He told her – or at least he was under the impression he was telling her this – that everything was going to be alright, that he was going to save her and make her understand their intended destiny, which, at this moment, appeared to be the far corner of the company car park.

Fortunately for Polly, six members of the Journals Department were returning from an early morning jog and heard her cries for help. (All were in training for the Zola Budd half marathon, an upcoming charity event to raise money for a local children's hospice. The organisers of the run had thought the gimmick of runners competing barefooted would encourage sponsors to dig deeper into their pockets.)

Immediately, they changed direction and surrounded Billy and Polly, demanding to know what was happening. Polly told them she'd been kidnapped by a crazy man from Academic Sales and needed their help. Billy was unable to say anything. Not only was he still drunk and unable to form cogent sentences, but besieged by an army of bare feet he was now in the throes of a panic attack. He fell to the ground gasping for breath, and while one of the runners went to the office to summon help, the others stayed to watch over him – or, at least, watch him.

Slowly, Billy came round, but appeared oblivious to both his surroundings and the seriousness of his situation. His mouth felt incredibly dry and he licked his lips.

'I could do with something to drink,' he said. 'Polly – put the kettle on, will you? We could all have tea before I drive home.'

That morning, Polly made a formal complaint to HR and Billy was suspended.

Therapy

Dr Haffenden diagnosed Billy as a non-psychotic stalker within thirty minutes of first meeting him, but it took a further three sessions for Billy to accept this uncomfortable truth and concede Dr Haffenden's point that only governments and licensed private detectives had the right to monitor and follow people. Although Billy maintained his intention had never been to harm Polly, he now allowed that his unwanted attention and unwarranted behaviour might indeed have caused her distress, and for this he was both ashamed and truly sorry.

Dr Haffenden, however, was still unclear as to why Polly had become the object of Billy's obsession, and on this subject the patient remained stubbornly reticent. If the cause of Billy's neurosis remained undiscovered, it was likely he would relapse and repeat such behaviour. The key to a successful outcome was to unearth the cause, and rather than waste time digging deep into his patient's psyche, Dr Haffenden decided instead to take the shovel and hit Billy over the head with it.

'Why do people call you Billy?' he asked.

'It's my name,' Billy replied after a moment's hesitation. 'Was that a trick question, Dr Haffenden?'

'I don't use artifice, Billy,' the behavioural therapist replied. 'Professional relationships are built on trust, not trickery.'

Billy smiled at him uncertainly.

'You're forty-one years old, Billy, and yet you still go by a child's name. Over time, most Billys become Bills. I'm just wondering why you didn't.'

'Our window cleaner's called Bill,' Billy replied.

Dr Haffenden pondered the reply and stared despairingly at the ceiling.

'Do you ever feel emasculated by the name Billy, Billy?'

Why did Dr Haffenden have to use such big words, Billy wondered, and what did emasculate mean? Surely, he wasn't talking about masking tape. They hadn't even discussed his enthusiasm for DIY yet.

As if sensing Billy's confusion, Dr Haffenden asked the question a different way: did he feel that his name deprived him of masculine vigour?

'Do you mean in the bedroom?' Billy asked guardedly.

'In life generally, Billy,' Dr Haffenden sighed.

'Hmm, I don't rightly know, Dr Haffenden. It's something I've never really considered. I don't think people think I'm gay or anything like that, if that's what you mean.'

Dr Haffenden had yet to make up his mind whether Billy was a naïf or just slow on the uptake, and rather than pussyfoot around the issue any longer decided to take the bull by its horns.

'Were you attracted to Polly because *she* was emasculated? And please don't tell me that she isn't a man because I already know that! I'm using the term loosely to cover her incapacitation. Were you attracted to Polly because she was in a wheelchair?'

Billy remained silent, debating whether to tell Dr Haffenden or not. He was tired of carrying the burden alone, confiding in no one. Their conversations, Dr Haffenden had assured him, were confidential and no different from him whispering his private fears into a hole in the back garden. What did he have to lose? He decided to tell his therapist the truth.

'No,' he said eventually. 'It was because she didn't have any feet. I'm scared of feet, Dr Haffenden.'

He waited nervously, wondering if the therapist would burst out laughing. Instead, Dr Haffenden stood up and shook him by the hand. 'Billy,' he said. 'This is our breakthrough moment.

'See you next week!'

Although Billy's behaviour had been aberrant and reprehensible, it was also out of character, and the HR Department worried that his breakdown might have been caused by overwork. (It was generally recognised within the company that sub-middle management positions were not for the faint-hearted, and differed little from the situations of junior doctors.)

Rather than terminate Billy's employment and run the risk of a possible lawsuit, the HR Department decided to suspend him on full pay for six months and arrange, through their private health insurers, for him to visit a therapist. If, after this time, his mental state had recovered and he still wished to work for the company, the situation would be revisited. (Their hope, however, was that once Billy did come to his senses, he would realise the impossibility of returning to the company and simply hand in his notice.)

Billy had been in no fit state to drive home on the day of the incident and had been forced to phone Jean and tell her he'd be returning the following day. He told her an unexpected meeting had cropped up that was too important for him not to attend.

'You work too hard,' Jean told him.

'I know, love, I know,' he replied. 'But I think people are starting to take notice of me.'

How true that was.

Billy didn't reveal to Jean that he'd been suspended from work, and neither did he tell his father. Instead, he followed his normal pattern of behaviour. On the days he would have worked from home, he went into the small room he used for an office and pretended to manipulate the sales screens he could no longer access; and, if Jean was in hearing range, he would have phantom conversations with lecturers and company personnel while listening to the sound of a dialling tone.

The days he would have travelled to the office he now visited Dr Haffenden in London; and on days he would have visited universities in the north of England, he drove into The Dales and went for long walks. Similarly, extended overnight trips to Scotland and Denmark now became either camping trips to the South Pennines or another cover for his increasing visits to Dr Haffenden, whose rooms were on the ground floor of a large house overlooking Battersea Park. The once hourly sessions with his therapist became two-hourly and, depending on their time of day, Billy would stay in a cheap B&B close to the British Museum the night before or the night after.

It had been a relief to admit his fear to the therapist, and an even greater relief to learn that he wasn't the only person in the world suffering from it. Podophobia, Dr Haffenden had told him, was an unusual condition but, like all phobias, could be cured by a process of systematic desensitisation. 'It's a slow business, Billy, but it works. The idea is to overcome your phobia by confronting each stage of it gradually. Once you realise that nothing bad happens to you, your fear of feet will subside and eventually disappear. Before we start though, I'm going to teach you some relaxation skills. The more relaxed you are, the more receptive you'll be to the treatment.'

Dr Haffenden had then showed Billy how to focus on his breathing, and encouraged him to think happy thoughts while doing this. Once mastered, he said, the skill would see him through most of their sessions and could always be supplemented with anti-anxiety medicine on the few occasions it proved ineffective.

Before Billy left the office that particular day, Dr Haffenden had suggested they make a list of the various types of foot exposure that elicited Billy's phobia and rank them by degrees of unpleasantness: from dressed feet to presumably deformed bare feet.

'We'll start with photographs, Billy, and then move on to the real thing,' Dr Haffenden said. 'One good thing about podophobia is that we can treat it here in the office. Most of the phobias I've treated have always involved visits to the zoo, and I'm about sick of that place.'

In the sessions that followed, Dr Haffenden showed Billy pictures of shoed feet, pictures of socked feet and pictures of bare feet. Billy responded well, and Dr Haffenden then asked Billy to touch his feet. 'Breathe as I taught you, Billy. Deep breaths and happy thoughts, remember.'

Billy gingerly placed his hands on Dr Haffenden's shoes and carefully traced the outline of his feet. He breathed deeply and thought of childhood trips to the seaside. The following week he repeated the exercise on his therapist's socked feet.

It appeared that progress was being made, but when Billy returned to Dr Haffenden's rooms the week after his father's funeral – the week he was supposedly in Denmark – Billy told the therapist of a setback.

'Katy came cartwheeling into the room with no socks and shoes on her feet and I lost it, Dr Haffenden. By now, that shouldn't be happening, should it?'

'Those were unusual circumstances, Billy,' Dr Haffenden reassured him. 'You'd just been to your father's funeral and you were in the company of your brother for the first time in seven years. From what you've said of your relationship with him – and your wife's hostility towards him – I'm not surprised your anxiety levels were high. Katy's feet would have tipped the balance. I wouldn't worry too much about it, if I were you. However, in the circumstances, I think it's best if you take an anti-anxiety pill before touching my feet today. I'll keep my socks on at first, but then I'm going to take them off. Remember, my feet are clean and they hold you no grudge.'

The exercise went better than either Billy or Dr Haffenden had expected: Billy didn't freak out and the massage left the therapist feeling strangely relaxed. It was decided they would repeat the same exercise the following session and then Dr Haffenden would start the process of touching Billy's feet: first shoed, then socked, then bare. Ultimately, the therapist wanted Billy to go for a pedicure.

'That will be the final challenge, Billy. I can't see any point in exposing you to truly deformed feet as even a person without podophobia would shy away from those.'

Driving home to pitch his tent in the remote South Pennines that day, Billy wracked his brains. Dr Haffenden had told him on several occasions that if he could remember the negative past experience that had caused his persistent fear of feet, then the healing process would quicken by leaps and bounds. Billy had suggested hypnotherapy as a means of discovering the cause, but the therapist had brushed the idea aside.

'I doubt the efficacy of hypnotism, Billy. There's too much false memory rattling around in a person's brain to have faith in it. I'm not saying regression is totally futile, but it's difficult to believe a person's going to tell you anything insightful about his present life when he's just been telling you how he was a big shot in some sixteenth-century fiefdom.'

Try as he may Billy couldn't remember a thing. Instead of focusing on the problem any further, he determined to follow Dr Haffenden's advice and touch as many feet as possible before the next session – without drawing undue attention to himself.

It was almost dark by the time he pitched his tent that night. Off and on, he'd been camping there for two months, in a field he'd first bivouacked in as a boy scout. He'd asked the farmer for permission and the farmer had willingly granted it, brushing aside Billy's offer of money.

He unpacked his wash bag and went to the coldwater tap at the far end of the field, washed his face and cleaned his teeth. He returned to the tent and undressed, stared at his white feet and then gently massaged them. Things were looking up. He smiled contentedly and crawled into his sleeping bag. All in all, it had been a good day. He wondered what tomorrow would bring.

It brought Uncle Frank.

7

Robbery

Uncle Frank might have been deaf, but his vision had always been 20/20, and though his ideas were often demented, he himself wasn't. There was, therefore, no reason to doubt that his uncle had seen Billy in the village that afternoon. But why, Greg wondered, was his brother pretending to be in Denmark?

He called Billy's mobile and was instantly connected to the voicemail service. He decided against leaving a message and reluctantly dialled the number for Spinney Cottage, hoping that someone other than Jean would answer the phone.

It rang seven times and then Katy picked up.

'Hello, who is this?'

'It's me, Katy: Uncle Greg.'

'Hello, Uncle Greg. What're you doing?'

'I'm talking to you.'

'I know that!' Katy said. 'I mean what were you doing *before* you phoned?'

'I was with Uncle Frank. We drove out to a small village in the country and had pies and mushy peas for lunch.'

'Was he grumpy?'

'Of course he was grumpy. Uncle Frank's always grumpy. That's his charm.'

'He's deaf as well, isn't he?' Katy said.

'Yes, he is, but he's got good eyesight. Which reminds me, is your Daddy there?'

'He's in our house.'

'I thought he might be. Can I have a quick word with him please?'

'I've already told you, Uncle Greg. He's in *our house!*'

The conversation was going in circles. Greg took a deep breath and asked Katy to put her mother on the phone.

Jean, who had obviously been hovering in the background, took the phone from Katy and spoke brusquely. 'Hello, Greg. What do you want? We're just about to eat dinner.'

'I was wondering if I could have a quick word with Billy. I gather from Katy he's in the house.'

'Billy's in Denmark,' she replied. 'He's in Our House. He won't be back until late tomorrow. Can I give him a message?'

It took a moment for Greg to equate Our House with Aarhus, Denmark's second-largest city – if his A-level geography still served him well.

'Just tell him to give me a call when he gets back, will you? For some reason, I thought he was back today.'

'I'll *ask* him to give you a call, Greg. Bye!'

The phone went dead.

'Bitch!' Greg muttered, and went upstairs to change his shirt.

The garment was soaked in perspiration and drool – most of it Uncle Frank's – and was sticking to his back like an old-fashioned bathing suit. He pulled the shirt over his head and added it to the growing pile of laundry on the bedroom floor, and then went to the bathroom to wash his face and armpits in the basin.

He missed showering, and realised that he admired his adoptive country more for its mastery of water pressure and shower heads than its ability to put a man on the moon. What he wouldn't give for a shower in his own apartment!

He dried himself on a towel and then rummaged through

his suitcase for a T-shirt. He was fast running out of clean clothes, but was unable to do any laundry until Billy showed him how to use the washing machine. And where the hell was Billy? He wasn't in Denmark and he wasn't at home.

Although he now understood Uncle Frank's strange behaviour, his brother's was still a mystery.

There was a radiancy to Lyle that evening, and Greg was pleased to see his father once more looking a picture of ghostly good health. He was wearing the same turquoise bustle back ball gown he'd worn the previous evening, but now had a mink stole draped over his shoulders.

'You're looking chipper, Dad,' Greg said, rising from his chair. 'I take it you managed to recharge your batteries.'

'I did, son, and I'm feeling as good as new again. But sit down, will you. There's no need to stand on my behalf – and you look as if you could do with a seat. What's wrong?'

'Oh… nothing much. I was just on the phone with Cyndi and she hung up on me. She thinks I should be home with her instead of fixing the house. She thinks I don't care about her.'

'And do you?' Lyle asked.

'Not really,' Greg admitted. 'I can't see the two of us being together for much longer.'

Lyle sighed. 'I wish you could find a nice girl and settle down, Greg. You don't want to grow old and end up by yourself. I'd hate to think what my life would have been like if I hadn't met your mother.'

'Do you think Billy should have married Jean?' Greg asked.

'He seems happy enough with her,' Lyle replied without much enthusiasm.

'I'm not so sure he is, Dad. He's lying to her. He told her – and me, for that matter – that he's in Denmark this week, but Uncle Frank saw him in the village we went to for lunch this afternoon. I think you're right about something being wrong.'

'I figured as much,' Lyle said. 'When are you seeing him again?'

'Hopefully this weekend, but I doubt he'll come straight out and tell me what's wrong. I'll have to win his confidence first – and that might take time.'

'Well, don't take too long about it. I'm a dead person on a deadline, remember.'

Greg smiled at his father's joke – if indeed it had been a joke.

'Anyway, how did it go with Frank today? Did you find out why *he's* been acting strange?'

'I did,' Greg crowed. 'He's planning to rob a bank.'

'Oh my giddy aunt!' Lyle exclaimed. 'I think I'd better sit down to hear this.'

While his father made himself comfortable in the armchair, Greg went into the kitchen for the bottle of wine he'd bought at Sainsbury's.

'You don't mind if I pour myself a glass of wine, do you, Dad?' he shouted from the kitchen.

'No, but hurry up, will you. I'm sitting here on tenterhooks.'

Greg unscrewed the cap and returned to the dining room with a large glass of red wine. He took a small sip of the Shiraz and then sat down carefully.

'We'd just finished eating lunch and I told him there was something we needed to talk about…'

'Hang on a minute, lad. I need a Jimmy Riddle.'

'Can't it wait, Uncle Frank?'

'Not when you get to my age, it can't. I'll be back in a jiffy. That's about as long as it takes these days.'

Once his uncle had returned from the lavatory and again taken his seat, Greg got to the point.

'Why do you keep handing yourself into the police and confessing to crimes you haven't committed?'

Uncle Frank eyed him suspiciously. 'What makes you think I do?'

'Dad told me.'

'*Lyle* told you?'

'He's the only Dad I've got.'

'Well I'll be damned!' Uncle Frank said. 'He promised me he wouldn't breathe a word of it to anyone. When did he tell you this?'

'About three weeks ago.'

'Three weeks ago? He was knocked down by a bus three weeks ago. How could he have told you then?'

Greg kicked himself for getting the time frame wrong. 'I mean three weeks *before* he was knocked down. Now are you going to tell me or what?'

Uncle Frank shook his head. 'I can't believe he broke his promise. I trusted your Dad, Greg, and it hurts that he betrayed me.'

'He didn't tell me to hurt you, Uncle Frank. He told me because he cares – I mean cared about you. Some promises have to be broken.'

'And did he tell you I was losing the plot, because if he did he's wrong – I'm not! I'm as sane as the next man.'

'No, he didn't say that. He thought there was a method to your madness, but he didn't know what the madness was. But that's what he called it – madness.'

'It's not madness, it's a plan!'

Uncle Frank paused and drained his glass. 'Get me another half and I'll tell you about it. On second thoughts, make it a pint.'

Greg went to the bar and returned with a pint of bitter for his uncle and a pint of lager for himself. He waited while Dickie Bird and his friends walked past the table and again pressed his uncle.

'Okay, you say it's a plan and not madness. What's the plan?'

'I'm going to become a cowboy,' Uncle Frank replied, 'and the only way I can afford to do that is by robbing a bank.'

Handing himself into the police on a regular basis had been the corner-stone of Uncle Frank's stratagem. He'd wanted them to believe he was a harmless old crank so that when he did actually commit a robbery and confess to it, they'd simply dismiss his claims and automatically rule him out of their enquiries. He'd be the last person they'd be looking for then, and he'd be free to make a leisurely escape to America and buy a ranch in Montana.

Greg stared at his uncle open-mouthed, trying to digest what he'd just heard. Rob a bank. Become a cowboy. Live in Montana. What the fucking hell!

'Don't you think there are a few loose ends to this plan of yours?' Greg asked eventually. 'It's a bit light on details, isn't it?'

Uncle Frank admitted that there were a few gaps to be filled, but was confident that the plan would come together.

'How are you going to rob a bank by yourself?' Greg asked. 'You don't even drive. What are you going to do, just walk out of the bank and wait for a bus?'

'I'm not going to rob it alone. I'm going to form a posse,' his uncle replied.

'I think you mean *gang*, don't you? It's the posse that will be chasing you.'

'Okay, gang then, if you want to be pedantic.'

'And who's going to be in this gang? I hate to say it, Uncle Frank, but you don't have any friends.'

'I'm thinking of asking Syd Butterfield to be the wheelsman,' Uncle Frank said. 'He's got a big car and, from what your Dad says, he drives like the Furies are after him. I'm also toying with the idea of asking Bill to join us.'

'Bill? You mean The Reverend Tinkler?' Greg asked incredulously.

'Yes,' Uncle Frank replied, as if The Reverend Tinkler was

the most obvious of choices. 'He's not a happy man, Greg, and my bet is that he'd break any law in the land if it got him his wife back. Money always helps love – you've only got to look at Bernie Ecclestone's wife to know that. And I'm planning to whittle away his beliefs too, make him realise that he won't have any God to answer to for his actions. I started at your Dad's funeral, cast doubt on the story of Noah's Ark, and I've got lots more ammunition like that up my sleeve. You wouldn't believe some of the stuff there is in the Bible.'

'Jesus, Uncle Frank! That's the longest shot in history! But just supposing Syd and The Reverend Tinkler do lose their minds and decide to throw in their lot with you, how are three old men with no criminal expertise going to pull off a bank job without having heart attacks or being picked up by CCTV cameras?'

'I can't see a children's television station being there to film us,' Uncle Frank replied, puzzled by the idea.

'You've completely lost me there, Uncle Frank,' Greg said. 'I don't know what *you're* talking about, but I'm talking about *surveillance cameras*. You can't walk ten yards in this country without being picked up by one. They're all over the place! And how are you going to evade the bank's own security systems? It's not the Wild West anymore. You can't just walk into a bank and then ride off into the sunset.'

Uncle Frank started to look crestfallen. He'd had no idea that the world had got so complicated – so nosey.

'I'll... I'll think of something,' he said without much certitude.

'Look Uncle, even if you did think of something, how are you going to get a visa to live in the United States? I grant you they've allowed people with money to enter the country in the past, but they're as paranoid as hell these days. Everyone they admit has to prove they've come by their wealth legally, and you wouldn't be able to do that.

'And if, say, you did manage to slip into the country illegally – which you wouldn't be able to do – and you deposited thousands of dollars in a bank, by law the bank would have to report you to the authorities. Large sums of money always attract attention, and my guess is they'd assume you were a drug dealer and put you in prison. Nothing adds up, Uncle Frank. Nothing! You'd never get away with it. And why, all of a sudden, do you want to go to Montana? You've had all your life to go there. You could have gone there years ago.'

'I've never had the money, lad. I've got the house and my pension, but that's about it. I'm not a rich man. I just want a change. Can't you understand that?'

'Since when have you liked change? For God's sake, Uncle Frank, you went on holiday to Llandudno for twenty-seven years running!'

'That was change,' Uncle Frank countered. 'Llandudno's in a different country and it's on the coast, too. I can't remember the last time I saw the sea. Anyway, I've had enough of this country. The people here don't like me and neither does the government. I want to go to a country where people will leave me alone and I can watch television in peace. I want to go to the country where General Custer made his Last Stand. That's the country I want to end my days in.'

Greg saw the look of dejection on his uncle's face and felt wretched, despised himself for being the person to prick the man's one remaining bubble of hope. There was no going back, though. Whether he liked it or not, he had to extinguish his uncle's crazy dream once and for all – for his sake.

'I'm hoping that what I've said has given you reason to change your mind, Uncle Frank, but if it hasn't, and you're still determined to go through with this madness,' he said, a nervousness creeping into his voice for the first time, 'I'm afraid I'll have to go to the police and tell them what you're planning to do. I'm not having my favourite uncle locked up in jail for the rest of his life. I owe it to you, and I owe it to my father.'

Greg held his uncle's stare for as long as he could, but had to turn away. He hated himself at that moment. Was this the burden of responsibility people talked about? No wonder he'd avoided it his whole life.

'What am I going to do now then?' Uncle Frank asked, his voice quiet and forlorn.

'You're going to go to Montana, Uncle Frank.'

'You promised him what?' Lyle asked.

'I told him I'd take him on holiday to Montana. I'm more than happy to do this, Dad. It's always been his dream to see the Wild West.'

Aware that his uncle had just swallowed the bitterest of pills, Greg had also promised him other things: they'd drive to the coast and stay overnight in a swanky hotel overlooking the sea; go shopping for a DVD player that would play the classic westerns they'd buy; and Billy would take a look at his television that picked up only static and his upstairs radio that picked up everything but Planet Rock. His life, he promised him, would change: it would get better.

Greg had also given him some advice: 'Roll with the punches, Uncle Frank. Once down, stay down: don't climb back on your feet just to get knocked down again. And try being nice to people. You don't have to like them; just let them think you do. It avoids conflict, and life runs all the smoother for it. Try it out on Betty. See if I'm not right.'

'And he's definitely shelved his plans to rob a bank?' Lyle asked.

Greg nodded.

'The crazy old coot,' Lyle said sadly. 'I knew he was lonely – most people are when they get to our age – but maybe Frank's lonelier than most. He'll never admit to it though, and he'll never tell you he misses having friends, either. He'll lead you to believe he's fine, but he's not fine. He regrets not having people around him.

'They always say that growing old isn't for the faint-hearted, and it isn't – especially when you live alone. It's hard to adjust to nothingness. I know it as well as anyone. Some days I used to look at the clock on the mantelpiece and feel disappointed when I saw that the hands had hardly moved since the last time I'd looked. Time ticks away too slowly when the days have nothing to offer.

'You bump into furniture and apologise out loud to it, and you do the same thing when you drop a plate or break a glass. It's a sorry state of affairs when objects become your day-to-day friends, but that's what happens, and talking to them gives you an excuse to hear a voice, even if it is only your own. All you have to look forward to is food and a good night's sleep, and sleep doesn't come easy for most old people. Frank's been waking up at 5:30am for years now.'

'I know. Just in time for *Bells on Sunday*, on a Sunday,' Greg said. 'He's posted a letter to the BBC complaining about it.'

Lyle laughed. 'I'll give Frank his due. He's always been prepared to take the world on. He'd do better banging his head against a brick wall for all the good it does him, but at least he gives it a shot. That's more than I ever did. You'll look after him, won't you, Greg? Make sure he's okay? And ask Billy to do the same. He lives closer to Frank than you do.'

'Of course I will, Dad. You know I love him.' He paused for a moment. 'Do you mind if I ask you something? Something about your father?'

'What do you want to know?'

'Did you love him?'

The question surprised Lyle and he took his time replying.

'It was my duty to love him, Greg, but I didn't like him – if that's what you mean. I never wanted to grow up and be him. None of us did. He was a stern parent, believed in discipline rather than love. He was always generous with the strap, but he was miserly when it came to showing affection. He never once kissed me or gave me a hug. He was the same with Eric, worse with Frank. Irene was the exception. She got off light when she was young, but she paid dearly for it later. His selfishness – and my mother's too – robbed her of a life.

'Eric left as soon as he could. I don't think you ever met my older brother, but he was the one with the smarts. He abandoned ship and never came back, ended up living in Surrey. I can understand why he cut his ties to my parents, but not why he cut them with Irene, Frank and me. We'd done nothing to him.

'Your mother didn't like my father either. The first time she met him, he more or less told her she was a gold-digger out for my money. He always looked upon himself as middle class, largely I suspect because we had a barometer on the wall – we were lower-middle class at best – and he resented the fact that Mary was from a working class family. He thought she was trying to better herself through me, believe it or not.'

'What was Mum's dad like?' Greg asked.

'He was the salt of the earth, Greg. My guess is that he had more goodness in his little finger than my father had in his entire body.'

He fell silent, remembering times gone by, and then asked Greg a question.

'I'm not about to ask you if you love me, Greg, but why did you ask me if I loved him?'

'I'm not really sure, Dad. I thought about him for the first time in years when I was waiting for Uncle Frank to get ready this morning. I barely remember him, but some stories Mum told me came back.'

'This is your Mum's stole, by the way. I bet you've never seen it before, have you?'

'No, I haven't. Where did you find it?'

'It was in a box under the wardrobe. It was the most expensive thing I ever bought her. I got a good deal on it though. We used to buy the fur we put on coat collars from a man called Joe Swerling and he got it for me. He'd spend six months of the year travelling around Russia buying furs and the other six months selling them to customers like us. We were one of his biggest and every Christmas he gave me a box of Cuban cigars.

'The damnedest thing though was that about a month after I gave it to your mother the anti-fur campaign started up and she stopped wearing it. She was afraid someone would throw paint on her. The places we went dancing that was unlikely, but she prized it too much to take the chance and so she hid it under the wardrobe.'

'What do you want me and Billy to do with Mum's clothes when you're gone, Dad? Give them to a charity?'

'No, I think I'd like you to burn them, Greg. I wouldn't want anyone else wearing them.'

'What about yours?'

'You can take mine to the dump. I only had one good suit and we both know what happened to that.'

They sat and chatted for a while, and Greg told his father about the village he'd taken Uncle Frank to that day, the cheese and onion pies they'd eaten for lunch and the journey back to the car.

Uncle Frank hadn't been up for the steep climb back and Greg had been forced to give the old man a piggyback ride. They'd only gone about ten yards when his uncle announced that he had to go to the toilet again. Greg had bent down; Uncle Frank had slid to the ground and emptied his bladder on a tussock of matgrass and then remounted. The sun by now had broken through the clouds and Greg started to sweat as he continued the sharp climb. Uncle Frank had nattered on about rabbits and moles for a time and then fallen asleep; snoring gently in Greg's left ear and drooling saliva on to his collar.

'I'd been hoping to wear this shirt for another day,' Greg complained to his father. 'I'm running out of clean clothes and I don't know how to use the washing machine. I don't suppose you could show me how it works, could you?'

Lyle led his son into the kitchen and explained the machine's simple mechanism. 'Go easy on the powder though. The water's soft here and if you're not careful you'll end up with suds all over the place.'

His father then told him he was going to turn in. 'Don't forget to lock the door, Greg. There was a burglary two doors down the other month, and I doubt it was your Uncle Frank on a practice run.'

'You know that question you said you wouldn't ask me, Dad?' Lyle nodded. 'The answer's yes. I do love you.'

Lyle smiled. 'I know you do, son. See you tomorrow.'

Love

That night was the first time Greg had told his father he loved him. He wondered why, wondered in fact why he never told anyone this. It was a word that discomfited him, a word that evoked feelings of obligation and committal, and a word he avoided using if at all possible. It was true he'd expressed love to several of his girlfriends over the years, but it was an insincere form of love and usually a means to an end, and in no way equated to their own understanding of the word.

Love within the family had always been unspoken and taken for granted, and expressions of such feeling would have been interpreted as an indication that something was wrong, that something bad was about to happen. His mother used the word occasionally, but his father never. It was as if the word didn't exist.

He recalled the time he'd left home for America to study at the University of Arizona. It was one o'clock in the morning and his father had driven him to the bus station to catch the overnight coach to London. He'd parked the car in a nearby street and walked with Greg to the station, and stayed with him until the coach arrived.

Both had been apprehensive, Greg wondering if his decision to study in Arizona was the right one, and his father silently debating what kinds of trouble his son would likely get into over there. Conversation between them had been intermittent and largely occasioned by his father asking him at different times if he'd packed his socks, handkerchiefs and underwear.

He remembered the bus drawing up and taking his father's hand, and his father telling him to take good care of himself. And then, unexpectedly, Greg had kissed him on the cheek. It was difficult to know who had been the more surprised. For a moment they'd stared disbelievingly at each other and then looked away embarrassed.

Greg had lined up with the other passengers, handed his ticket to the driver and found a window seat. His father had then walked to the outside of the window and stood there, seemingly undecided whether to fold his arms or put his hands in his pockets. They smiled awkwardly at each other until the bus pulled away and then waved farewell.

As the coach was about to turn the corner and disappear from sight, Greg glanced back and saw his father still standing there, still waving.

This was Bowman love, Greg surmised: silent, embarrassed, but always there.

He wondered if he should tell Uncle Frank and Billy that he loved them. He accepted that such news would puzzle them and no doubt leave them thinking he was about to die, but what the hell. Someone had to start the ball rolling. The family needed to change, needed to be more open with each other.

He looked at the clock on the bedside table and saw that it was time to get up. He wouldn't break the news to Uncle Frank and Billy today, he decided, or even tomorrow for that matter, but sometime before he returned to Texas and the moment felt right, he'd tell them both that he loved them.

He also decided that he'd give Jean a miss.

Greg spent the day preparing the downstairs rooms for painting: filling in cracks and then sanding them down. He'd never done work like this before and it proved more difficult than he'd expected, certainly more difficult than the directions on the tub of filler had led him to believe. Despite his hours of effort, the cracks – although now filled – stood proud on walls that were no longer flush, and a thin coat of white dust covered the furniture and carpets. After Billy had phoned to tell him he'd be there with Jean in the morning, he'd had no choice but to vacuum and dust the rooms all over again.

He ate his evening meal at the Brown Cow and wondered why Billy was bringing Jean with him tomorrow. He couldn't believe she'd be there to help, and her presence would only delay the conversation they needed to have. He reported this to his father that evening, who reminded him – as if he didn't already know – that he only had fourteen days of his furlough left. 'You've got to engineer some time alone with him, Greg. Get him to talk to you.'

Easier said than done, Greg thought over breakfast the following morning, sipping coffee and staring at the uneven walls. He realised he was more concerned about his brother's reaction to his handiwork at this moment than he was about the state of his brother's well-being. Why on earth was he bothered by what Billy might think? It had never troubled him before.

He supposed it was because he didn't like being judged – by anyone. And this is what concerned him most about his father's strange reappearance – the possibility of being brought to account and judged *after* he was dead. Greg wasn't sure if he'd ever believed in God. Certainly he'd never thought of shaking his fist at the heavens on the day his mother died, and neither had he accepted the notion that she was now in a better place and that her disappearance was no more sinister than a rowing boat being called back to shore: 'Come in Boat Number Three, your time is up!'

All he knew was that her death had left *him* in a worse place.

He'd never wasted time considering divine plans or mysterious ways, the purpose of life or existential exploration. The world was as it was; a place without rhyme or reason where good things happened and bad things happened. He was content to live with the way things were and happy to believe in oblivion.

The reappearance of his father, however, had indicated that there *was* life after death – even if only in the form of golf balls and pigeonholes. His father had admitted that he had no idea what awaited him once he passed through the transit camp, but what if there was a God? Was he to be called to account for his ways and given another carpeting? His father had certainly given him a mouthful.

His reverie was disturbed by a knock on the door and Billy calling his name.

'I'm in the back room, Billy. Come on through.'

Katy came bounding into the room first. 'Hi, Uncle Greg,' she said, giving him a big noisy kiss on the cheek. 'What're you doing?'

'I'm sitting here being kissed by you,' Greg smiled. 'What are you doing?'

'I'm talking to you, silly! Honestly, Uncle Greg, sometimes I wonder if you're stupid.'

'You're not the first person to wonder that,' Jean said. 'What in God's name have you done to the walls, Greg? They're all… wobbly.'

'Come on, Jean, they're not that bad,' Billy said, stepping to his brother's defence. 'The cracks are all filled in, and that's the fiddly bit. All they need is a good sanding down, and that's not easy if you don't have an electric sander.'

'Why don't woodpeckers get brain damage, Uncle Greg?' Katy asked.

'I don't know,' Greg said. 'Why don't woodpeckers get brain damage?'

'It's not a joke, Uncle Greg, it's a proper question! We've got a woodpecker in the garden and it's always banging its head against a tree. Mummy says that if I did that I'd never be able to walk again, let alone dance.'

'You and your questions,' Jean sighed.

'Can I make you coffee?' Greg asked. 'There's a coke in the fridge if Katy would like that.'

'Maybe another time, Greg,' Billy said. 'This is a flying visit I'm afraid. Jean just wants to look over the furniture and ornaments and see if there's anything she'd like for the house.'

'Billy says your mother used to have a mink stole, Greg. You don't know where your father used to keep it, do you?'

'I'm afraid I don't,' Greg said.

'Come on, Katy, we'll make a start upstairs and leave your Daddy and Uncle to talk.'

They left the room, and Billy took out a small notebook and wrote down the word 'sander'.

'How was Denmark?'

'Same old same old,' Billy replied. 'Bacon and herrings.'

'When did you get back?'

'Yesterday – just before I called you. The flight was a bit delayed, I'm afraid.'

It appeared that Billy was determined to tough out the conversation. He made notes while he talked and looked around the room, described the universities of Aalborg and Aarhus in too much detail and named the imaginary professors he'd met.

'What was the weather like?' Greg asked.

'The weather? I'd say it was fair to middling. Mostly sun, some rain. The usual.'

He knows, Billy thought. He knows I wasn't there. But if I keep pretending I was, I'll be okay. All I have to do is tough it out and stare him down. He can't prove anything. It's my word against Uncle Frank's. If only I could look him in the eyes. Thank goodness I brought my notebook. He'll think I'm busy writing notes and that's why I can't look at him. He won't know I'm filling pages with the word 'sander'. It's the same thing I do when I talk to professors. I can fool anybody.

'Is it okay if Uncle Frank has Dad's handkerchiefs?' Greg asked.

'Yes. He's already asked...' Oh flipping heck! Now I've gone and done it!

He looked up and saw Greg smiling at him, not the triumphant smile he'd been expecting but a sympathetic smile, a smile that surprisingly showed no pleasure.

'We don't have to talk about this now do we – with Jean and Katy in the house?'

'Of course we don't – and sorry for tricking you like that. It's just that Dad's been worried about you. Tell me in your own time. I'm here to help and not point the finger – if you can believe that.'

They were interrupted by Katy.

'Daddy, Mummy wants to talk to you upstairs about something.'

Billy left the room and Katy sat down in the chair he'd vacated. 'Can I have that coke, Uncle Greg?' she whispered. 'And if my parents come back into the room and I haven't finished it, can you pretend it's yours? I'm not supposed to drink coca-cola.'

Greg brought the can and opened it for her.

'Thanks, Uncle Greg. Do you want to know a secret?'

'Sure.'

'Mummy thinks the house should go to Daddy and not you. That's what she's talking to him about now. She says that Daddy was the one who changed Grandpa's light bulbs and unscrewed his marmalade lids and sorted his pills into containers. She said that he was always doing odd jobs for him around the house and reading small print for him. She says that you didn't do a thing except make his life a living hell and make him lose his hair. Is that true, Uncle Greg? Did you really do those things?'

'I hope I didn't. I think your Mum's exaggerating a bit, Katy. I couldn't do the things your Dad did for him because I lived too far away. But if I'd lived closer I'd have done them. I never abandoned your Grandpa, you know. We used to talk on the phone every week, and he used to tell me all about you.'

'What did he say?'

'That you were a bright girl and very pretty. He was very proud of you, Katy. Glad you were his granddaughter.'

'Quick, Uncle Greg: they're coming! Take the can, will you? And don't tell them anything about what I said. It's a secret, remember.'

When Jean and Billy came into the room, it was clear they'd had some kind of argument. Billy stared out of the window, while Jean opened and closed drawers in the sideboard and then moved to the lounge.

'The only thing I want is the mink stole, Billy,' she finally announced. 'The rest of it's junk. Come on, we need to go. I still have some ironing to do.'

Jean had arranged to spend the next few days with a friend in the Lake District and was taking Katy with her. She'd given

Billy permission to stay with Greg and help decorate the house in her absence, on the understanding that the sooner the house was sold the sooner she'd get her new bathroom suite.

'It's all arranged then, Greg. I'll be back tomorrow morning about ten. Kiss your Uncle goodbye, Katy,' Billy said.

This time Katy kissed Greg on both cheeks.

'There's no need to overdo things, Katy,' Jean said, who walked past Greg without so much as touching him.

Greg walked them to the gate and returned to the house smiling. He'd had qualms about burning his mother's clothes but now looked forward to the day, and imagined the conversation he'd have with Jean. 'Jean, you know that mink stole you wanted? Yes, that's the one. Well guess what? I found it. Perfect condition. I'm afraid not. Why? I burned it! Ha!'

Confession

Mrs Turton was standing under her veranda when Billy drew up outside the house. She was wearing her Sunday best and waiting for Barry to collect her in his state-of-the-art Skoda – 'German engineering at half the price!' he'd told his mother.

She called out and beckoned him. 'Have you got a minute, Billy?' she asked.

Billy put down his tools and joined her under the veranda. 'Hello, Mrs Turton. You're looking very smart. Off to church?'

'Thank you, Billy. Yes, I'm expecting Barry any moment now. Did you get my card?'

'Yes and thank you. It was very considerate.'

'It was a nice cross on the front, wasn't it? I liked the way the roses curled around it.'

'Yes it was,' Billy agreed. (He'd received a lot of cards with crosses on the front and couldn't immediately recall Mrs Turton's.)

'I don't want to worry you, Billy – and you know I'm not one for interfering – but I think Gregory's taking drugs again. I invited him round for coffee the other day and he burst out laughing and couldn't stop. I've seen programmes on television about drug takers and that's what addicts do – they stare at their feet and laugh all the time. And Gregory was saying some very strange things. If only I could remember what they were…'

'I'm sure he isn't, Mrs Turton. I think he's just got a different sense of humour to us. Come to think of it, I don't think I've ever understood his jokes.'

'It's not just the laughter, Billy,' Mrs Turton continued. 'He's started talking to himself at night. I can't make out what he's saying, but if I put a glass to the wall I can hear his voice as plain as day. That's not normal behaviour, is it?'

'Putting a glass to the wall?'

'No, talking to yourself!'

'You're sure it's not the radio?'

'Unless he's got a job as a presenter on Radio 4, Billy, I'm certain of it! I know your father always worried about him, and it's only because of your father that I'm mentioning this to you now. Mr Bowman was a good friend to me and it's out of respect for him that I'm telling you this. Most people would look the other way, but as a Christian I can't do that.'

'Well thank you, Mrs Turton. I think you're worrying unnecessarily, but I'll certainly have a word with him.'

'Don't tell him it was me who told you!' Mrs Turton said, panicked by the idea. 'I don't want him coming round here when he's high on drugs. I live alone, remember, and I haven't got an alarm, and – oh, here's Barry. He doesn't like to be kept waiting, Billy, so I'd better be going. It's communion Sunday today and Barry wants to get there early and box Diane into one of the back pews before they bring out the wafers. That girl! I quake to think how much toast she's had for breakfast.'

Billy waited while Mrs Turton climbed into Barry's car and then picked up his toolbox and entered his father's house. 'Greg!' he called out. 'Mrs Turton thinks you're on drugs again and talking to yourself at night. You're not, are you?'

'Of course I'm not,' Greg called out from the top of the stairs. 'But if I lived next door to Mrs Turton for any length of time I probably would be. It wouldn't surprise me if Dad didn't throw himself under that bus just to get away from her.'

Billy laughed guiltily. 'You shouldn't say things like that about Dad when he's dead.'

'I'm pretty sure he won't mind. Now, where do you want to start?'

They covered the furniture and floors of the dining room and lounge with old bed sheets, and Billy plugged in his electric sander. 'This thing makes a lot of noise, so I'll sand down the walls while Mrs Turton's at church. We don't want her calling the police and telling them we're disturbing her Day of Rest.'

Greg watched as Billy put a paper mask over his mouth and nose and started to smooth down the walls. He worked confidently and efficiently, and moved quickly from one filled crack to the next. By the time Mrs Turton returned from church the walls were ready for painting.

Billy showed Greg how to use the roller and then broke off from his own painting to change the lock on the back door. When, eventually, they'd knocked off for the day, the walls and ceiling of the dining room were covered in fresh magnolia and the room transformed.

'It should only take us a morning to do the hallway,' Billy said, 'and then we'll start on the woodwork. We should be able to get away with one coat, but we'll have to be careful not to leave any runs. There's nothing worse than a door that looks like it burst into tears.'

Billy brought his suitcase into the house and took it to

Greg's old bedroom – the small one. 'I see you've got my room at long last,' Billy smiled.

'I did, and you're not having it back,' Greg said. 'I'll tell you what I'll do though: as a quid pro quo, I'll treat you to a meal in the Brown Cow tonight. I can't say fairer than that.'

The pub was about half full when they arrived. They ordered from the menu and stood at the bar until one of the alcoves became free. 'Quick. Get the table over there before someone beats us to it, Billy, and I'll tell the barmaid where we've gone.'

The alcoves were private spaces intended more for lovers than brothers, but were ideal for tête-à-têtes. They'd worked well together that day and Greg hoped that with a few pints inside him, his brother would open up and explain his situation. (He didn't look forward to meeting his father that night and again telling him there was nothing to report. 'I only have twelve days left, Greg!' his father would no doubt point out.)

Greg waited until they'd finished eating and fresh pints were on the table before engaging his brother in more serious conversation.

'I'm afraid I haven't been much of a brother to you over the years, Billy, and I'm sorry for that.'

Billy looked at him surprised.

'There was something you once said to me, something that stuck with me. It's looped around in my mind for years, but it's only since I've been back here that it's started to make any sense.'

'What did I say?' Billy asked, amazed that something he'd said had stuck in anyone's mind.

'You told me that I always had to know best, always had to take things a step too far. And you were right. I behaved like an asshole when I was a kid, lorded it over you like a real shit. You shouldn't have taken it, Billy. You should have punched me in the face or stuck my head down the toilet. That's what I'd have done to you.'

'You never did though, did you? You just kept offering me your friendship, and every time you did I just slapped it away. I once told you I was embarrassed to have you as a brother. Remember that? It was a lie. You never embarrassed me. It was me that was the embarrassment.'

Billy was slightly off-balanced by Greg's remarks but generous in his response. 'You weren't that bad a brother, Greg,' he said. 'We – that's Dad and me – just thought you were more affected by Mum's death and so we made allowances.'

'She was your mother too, Billy. You didn't go off the rails. But one thing I never did understand is why you and Dad never cried at her funeral. Apart from the day we got the news I don't remember you or Dad ever crying.'

'We cried all right, Greg – just not around you. Dad thought it would only make things harder for you if you saw us crying. He told me I was the elder brother and had to stay strong for your sake. That's the only reason I didn't cry at the funeral. Lord knows I wanted to. I almost bit my lip off that day. I still miss Mum and I always will… but why are you telling me this now?'

'Because Dad's dead and I never got the chance to tell him the things I always meant to. I led him a right dance when I was growing up. I'd get into scrapes, he'd get me out of them, and I never once thanked him. I just took everything for granted. And I got to thinking, what if I was killed or you were killed and we'd never made up. I don't want that to happen, do you? I guess what I'm trying to say, Billy, is that I love you. You need to know that.'

'There's nothing wrong, is there, Greg? I mean you're alright, aren't you. Nothing you want to talk about?'

Greg smiled. 'No, there's nothing wrong, Billy. I just wanted to make sure you knew.'

'Well, I, I love you too, Greg,' Billy said, peeling the top layer off his beer mat. 'I hope no one can hear us,' he whispered.

'Men telling each other they love each other. It's a bit weird, isn't it? What if people think we're gay?'

Greg burst out laughing. 'Well, if they do, they'll be thinking you're punching a bit above your weight. I'm far too good-looking for you.'

'I'm not that bad looking,' Billy said. 'And I married Jean too. She thinks you've always been jealous of me for beating you to her.'

'She thinks what? Jesus Christ, Billy, you're welcome to Jean! Don't get me wrong, she's a good-looking woman, but there's no way I'd want to marry her. We'd end up killing each other. I can't believe she said that!'

'Well, don't tell her I told you.'

'Of course I won't. Another pint?'

'Why not? It's not as if I have work tomorrow – apart from painting.'

'You're pretty good at DIY, aren't you?' Greg said, back at the table.

'I think I am,' Billy replied. 'I wouldn't mind doing it for a living if I'm honest, but Jean says she'd never be able to show her face in public if I became a tradesman. She thinks that would be worse than sales.'

'How come you ended up in sales, anyway?'

'The mills closed down and I was no good at accountancy. The only qualification they asked for was a degree and, as I'd always liked reading, I thought publishing would be fun. The books we publish though are unintelligible. I haven't read one of them.'

He took another drink from his glass and picked up another beer mat.

'In an ideal world I'd still be working in the textile industry,' he continued. 'That's what my degree and training were in. Sometimes I feel like one of those actors who's gone to RADA and spent years touring the provincial theatres in the hope that one day he'll be playing Hamlet in Stratford-upon-Avon, and then finds himself working as an extra in a Steven Seagal film. That's what I feel about my job in publishing – I feel like I'm playing an extra in a bad film that I wouldn't pay money to see. Don't get me wrong, Greg, I don't hate my job, but I think I'd prefer to be a painter and decorator or someone who makes their living by doing odd jobs for people.'

'Why don't you do that then? Do something that makes *you* happy. Life's too short to fuck around.' Greg said.

'I might well have to,' Billy said gloomily. 'I think I'm about to be fired.'

He then found himself telling his younger brother everything: his abiding fear of feet, his infatuation with Polly, his suspension from work and his visits to Dr Haffenden. 'And Jean knows nothing about this, Greg. She thinks I'm still working, still going to the office and going on business trips. I have to lie to her and hide away from her, and that's the hardest part. I'm no good at deception. It makes me nervous at the best of times and when I saw Uncle Frank sitting in the tearoom I nearly had a heart attack! Don't tell Jean any of this, will you? Please, you have to promise me.'

'Of course I'm not going to tell her.'

Billy's story had been stranger than Uncle Frank's. Frightened of feet. Falling in love with a woman with no feet. Suspended from work. Seeing a therapist. What the fucking hell!

Greg had bitten the inside of his cheek when Billy first mentioned his fear of feet. He wanted to laugh out loud, but in the circumstances couldn't. He had to look concerned, empathise with his brother and put himself in his shoes – so to speak.

'So does this doctor of yours think he'll be able to cure you?'

'Yes, and he says I'm making good progress. You don't know what a relief it's going to be when I'm free of this phobia. I'll be able to lead a normal life again. And he thinks my obsession with Polly is just a symptom of the underlying cause, so that once I'm no longer afraid of feet I won't be infatuated with her either. And it's working. I've already stopped dreaming about her.'

'So once you're okay, you'll be able to go back to work for the company?'

'In theory, but the more I think about it, the less I want to. It would be too demeaning. HR is supposed to keep matters like this confidential but news always gets out, and I'd be surprised if the whole office doesn't know about it by now. If I went back, people would be looking at me and talking about me behind my back. Probably laughing. I don't think I could take that.'

'How long have you got before the six months is up?'

'About another two, I think. What would you do if you were me?'

'I wouldn't go back. I'd angle for some kind of settlement and use the money to start up a business.'

'But what about Jean? Jean's not going to like that one bit.'

'Fuck Jean! And whatever you do, don't tell her about Polly. It doesn't matter that you didn't sleep with her because Jean's always going to think that you did. There's no point getting divorced over this.'

The bell rang for last orders. 'One for the road?' Greg asked.

'No, not for me thanks,' Billy said. 'But when we get back to the house, is it alright if I touch your feet? Dr Haffenden said I had to practise.'

'I heard that as well!' a man's voice called out from the adjacent booth. 'If you want my opinion, there's something wrong with you two!'

Greg and Billy decided to give the Brown Cow a miss after that.

8

Freeview

Lyle watched as Billy climbed into bed and closed his eyes. His lips were pursed and deep creases furrowed his brow. Even at rest his elder son looked worried. He yearned to talk to him, ask the boy the cause of his disquiet, but couldn't. He could only find this out by talking to his younger son.

He moved downstairs and found Greg sitting in the dining room, his socks neatly folded and placed next to his shoes.

'Why are you barefooted, lad? I know it's summer, but it's not that warm.'

Greg told him.

'Well I'll be,' Lyle said, after his son finished the story. 'Why did he never tell me this? Why did he keep it a secret? It must have eaten the poor boy up.'

'I think he was ashamed, Dad. I think he thought he was the only person in the world suffering from podophobia. If it's any consolation, he never told me either.'

'It's not,' Lyle said. 'You'd have been the last person he'd have confided in.'

'Hmm, you're probably right there,' Greg admitted. 'I've apologised for the way I treated him when we were growing up, though. Your words weren't wasted on me.'

'I'm glad to hear that, Greg. And you're doing what you can to help him through this?'

'Yes, and it's weirding me out, if you want the truth. He played with my feet for forty minutes tonight – and he wants to do the same tomorrow!'

Greg told him how Billy had removed his shoes and hesitantly clasped his socked feet that evening; how he'd gently squeezed and caressed them and then paused, closed his eyes and taken a series of deep breaths. He described how his brother had pulled the socks from his feet, cautiously taken hold of his right foot and then traced the bones connecting the talus to his toes: the cuboids, naviculars, cuneiforms and metatarsals.

'He was clinical, Dad, almost detached – a bit like a pathologist performing an autopsy and recording his findings into a microphone. He remarked on the grain of the shoe leather and the craftsmanship of the stitching; the fine weave of my cotton socks and their colour. He told me I had twenty-six bones in each foot, thirty-three joints and over a hundred muscles. He talked like a zombie.'

'A zombie?' Lyle mused. 'I wonder if that's what I am now. Do I talk like a zombie?'

'No. Apart from an American accent you talk the same way you always did,' Greg reassured him, and then continued.

'When he started to massage my bare feet his manner changed and he got a bit too involved for my liking. He began talking to them as if they were long lost friends or something. Told them he respected them and meant them no harm. Hoped they respected him too and meant him no harm either. Said how they needed to see more of each other and learn to understand one another better. Maybe it's just his way of getting through all this, Dad, but it was creepy. I half expected him to give them a goodnight kiss.'

'What happened then?' Lyle asked. 'Was Billy okay?'

'I'm not sure, Dad. He just crumpled. Sat cross-legged on the floor and hung his head. It was obvious the ordeal had exhausted him, but when he looked up he was smiling. He looked almost happy. He said he couldn't believe he'd done it; couldn't believe he was making such good progress. And he told me he couldn't have done it without me – and he couldn't when you think about it, because it was my feet he'd been fondling. And he ended by saying he was glad you were dead, because your death had brought the two of us together again.'

'He said what! He really said he was glad I was dead?'

'No, I was just joking when I said that,' Greg laughed. 'But he did say that bit about togetherness.'

Lyle looked at his son and then smiled grudgingly.

'And once this doctor of his has cured him, he'll be able to go back to work?'

'That's the theory, but Billy's toying with the idea of setting up his own business and becoming a painter and decorator.'

Lyle mulled the idea over. 'Good,' he said eventually. 'He'll be happy doing that. I've always admired his DIY – and good tradesmen are hard to find these days.'

Greg was in bed reading a paperback he'd bought at the airport when his father appeared the following night.

'You've left the windows open downstairs.'

'I know. We're trying to get rid of the paint fumes.'

'What if someone breaks in?' Lyle said. 'I never left windows open when I was alive.'

'You never opened windows period, Dad. And unless there's a marauding band of midgets in the area, I can't see anyone climbing through them. Besides we left them on their latches.'

Lyle shook his head. 'You can never be too careful, Greg. The neighbourhood's changed since you lived here. At one time I knew everyone who lived on the Grove and we all used to look out for each other. It's different now. I'd be hard pressed to name any of the neighbours apart from Mrs Turton and the Collards. There are too many renters for my liking.'

'Why are you so late tonight?' Greg asked. 'I waited downstairs for long enough and then gave up. I thought you weren't coming.'

'I think I must have slept in, son – or something like that. I like it in the loft. It's easy to forget about your troubles up there. I don't know why I never thought of living up there when I was alive.'

Unlike previous evenings, there was little of interest to tell his father. He and Billy had finished painting the house that day, eaten fish and chips for dinner and made a start on sifting through the papers in their father's cardboard file. Tomorrow morning they were planning to visit Uncle Frank and in the afternoon the Probate Office. On Wednesday, Billy would drive down to London to meet with Dr Haffenden, and return to the house on Thursday.

'Where did you get your fish and chips from?' Lyle asked.

'The chip shop opposite the Brown Cow.'

'You should have gone to the one on the top road, Greg. They give you scraps there without having to ask for them – and they're cheaper.'

'I'll remember that for next time,' Greg said. He paused for a moment. 'I don't suppose you left a will, did you, Dad? We couldn't find one in the file.'

'There's a letter in the front room bureau,' Lyle said. 'It says that everything's to be divided equally between you and Billy and that Katy is to get £1,000. And make sure you tell Billy that it's not for dancing lessons.'

Greg couldn't remember if he'd fallen asleep during the conversation or after his father had disappeared, but he awoke the next morning to find Billy kneeling at the foot of his bed massaging his feet.

'What the hell are you doing?' he asked, more sharply than he intended.

'I'm practising. You don't mind, do you?'

'No… No… It's just that you caught me by surprise. How long is this going to take?'

'About ten minutes,' Billy replied. 'By the way, I know why Mrs Turton thinks you talk to yourself.' Greg looked at him for an explanation. 'You talk in your sleep. I heard you last night.'

'Really? Come to think of it, a girlfriend once told me the same thing,' Greg lied. 'Do you think I need to see Dr Haffenden?'

'He just takes the big cases,' Billy smiled. 'Sleep talking would be too run-of-the-mill for him.'

Billy finished kneading his brother's feet and after washing his hands thoroughly went downstairs to prepare breakfast. Greg joined him ten minutes later, and once the plates were cleared called Uncle Frank.

The phone rang and rang and then his uncle answered.

'If you're calling from India you can forget it because I'm not interested!' Uncle Frank bellowed into the phone. 'And if you think you fool anyone by calling yourself Thomas or Simon you're mistaken because no one bloody-well believes you! Hello… Hello?'

'It's me, Uncle Frank – Greg. I'm bringing Billy to look at your television. Is it okay if we come in about twenty minutes?'

'Sorry, lad, I thought you were one of those salesmen who tell you they're not trying to sell you anything. They're about the only calls I get these days, and nine times out of ten there's no bugger at the other end of the line when I pick the phone up. Bloody nuisance! I'll leave the side door open. Just knock and come in… Hello… Hello?'

'Okay, Uncle Frank. We'll be there soon.'

Billy looked through his toolbox and picked out two small

screwdrivers and a wire cutter. Being an irregular visitor to Uncle Frank's house, he'd been completely unaware that his uncle's television wasn't working, but he was confident that the problem would be a simple one, and one he could fix easily.

They drove to Uncle Frank's house, knocked on the door and walked in. The radio was turned up loud and, as usual, tuned to Planet Rock.

'This is the station he can't get on his upstairs radio,' Greg explained, turning down the volume.

'I didn't know Uncle Frank liked rock music,' Billy said. 'There again, I didn't know he was planning to rob a bank, either.'

Determined that the family now be open with each other, Greg had confided Uncle Frank's intention to Billy on the strict understanding that he didn't tell Jean or Betty. It was also his way of letting Billy know that there were other people in the world with problems as strange as his own.

'Where is he?' Billy asked.

'Probably upstairs. I'll give him a call.'

Greg went to the bottom of the stairs and called up: 'Uncle Frank! Uncle Frank!'

'I'm having a shit, Greg!' his uncle shouted through the bathroom door. 'Make us a cup of coffee, will you?'

Greg boiled the kettle and put coffee powder in three mugs. He was taking the cups through to the back room when Uncle Frank appeared in the hallway.

'Remind me to get some haemorrhoid cream, will you, Greg? My piles are playing up something rotten.'

'Hello, Uncle Frank,' Billy said. 'It's good to see you again.'

'You didn't seem too pleased to see me the other day,' Uncle Frank tackled him. 'You bolted right out of the tearoom.'

'That was you?'

'Of course it was me – who did you think it was? Santa Claus? And why did you run off like that?'

Billy shifted in his chair wondering what to say, and looked to Greg for help.

'Billy's a podophobe, Uncle Frank.'

'Good God in Heaven!' Uncle Frank cried out. 'A child molester? Bloody Nora! What the hell are you thinking of, Billy? You've got a child of your own, for God's sake!'

Greg burst out laughing.

'What are you laughing at?' Uncle Frank challenged him. 'There's nothing funny about child molestation!'

'He's not a child molester, Uncle – he's afraid of feet!'

'How can anyone in their right mind be afraid of feet?' Uncle Frank said. 'I've never heard anything so daft!'

'I don't know, Uncle Frank, but Billy's managed it.'

'Well, thanks a lot,' Billy said to Greg, before turning to face his uncle. 'At least I'm not planning to rob a bank. Podophobia's a condition – not a criminal offence!'

'Why did you tell him that?' Uncle Frank asked Greg. 'It was supposed to be a secret!'

'And my podophobia was supposed to be a secret too!' Billy said.

'Look,' Greg said, now on the defensive. 'We shouldn't have secrets from each other – we're family. If we can't trust each other, who can we trust?'

'Okay, you tell us one of your secrets then,' Uncle Frank dared him.

'I don't have any,' Greg replied honestly. 'I did all my screwing up in public. Remember?'

The three of them stared at each other and then Billy spoke.

'Okay, but we're all agreed that these matters stay with us – they don't leave this room? Jean doesn't get to hear about it and neither does Betty.'

Uncle Frank and Greg nodded, but Billy wanted further confirmation.

'And you two aren't going to start making stupid cracks in

front of them about me *putting my best foot forward* or *falling on my feet*? You're not going to say things like *I wouldn't want to be in Billy's shoes*, or tell them *I never put a foot wrong*?'

'Of course not,' Greg said. 'Why would we say anything like that?'

'Because that's the type of thing you used to say in front of Jean. You were forever making horse jokes.'

'You knew we were doing that?' Greg asked, surprised that his brother had picked up on their joke.

'Of course I did. I'm not stupid, Greg. You're just lucky that Jean didn't twig what you were up to.'

'Greg started it,' Uncle Frank said. 'It was his idea – not mine.'

'Jesus Christ, Uncle Frank!' Greg protested.

'I don't care who started it,' Billy said. 'You were both as bad as each other. Now, do I have your words on this?'

Uncle Frank and Greg gave Billy their assurances, and then the eyes of Uncle Frank and Billy fell on Greg; remained there and silently accused him of betrayal.

'Why don't we take a look at the television?' Greg suggested casually.

Billy went to the television, put the plug in the socket and turned on the set. Static! He played with the controls. Nothing! He opened the doors of the cabinet below the television and looked inside.

'Where's your Freeview Box, Uncle Frank?'

'What did he say, Greg? I can't hear him from here.'

Greg turned the radio down. 'He asked you where your Freeview Box was.'

'What's a Freeview Box?'

'I don't know,' Greg shrugged. 'What's a Freeview Box, Billy?'

'Something you need to pick up digital transmissions. The old analogue signal was turned off and you need a box to decode the new signal. New televisions have them built in, but old sets like this won't work without a box.'

'Whose idea was it to change the signal?' Uncle Frank asked.

'Well, the government's I suppose,' Billy said.

'I knew it! I damn well knew it!' Uncle Frank said triumphantly. 'People laughed at me when I said the government had turned off my television, but I was right, wasn't I? I've been right all along!'

'It was the same for everyone,' Billy said. 'They sent leaflets to every household explaining what they were doing and what people needed to do; and because of your age, they'd have sent someone to your house to connect everything. You did get a leaflet, didn't you?'

'Anything pushed through the letterbox without my name on it goes straight in the bin,' Uncle Frank said. 'You wouldn't believe the junk I get. And I'm about sick to death of those plastic bags. I got *four* last week asking for my clothes! Who do these charities think I am – Donald Trump?

'Anyway, I don't want any government officials coming into my house and poking their noses around. They'd start suggesting I get Home Help or Meals on Wheels, and before you knew it they'd have me in a home. I'm never going into a home! I'd rather be shot! And Frank Bowman doesn't need anyone's charity, either. He pays his own way. He doesn't need a *free* View Box. He'll pay for it himself.'

'They're not free, Uncle Frank,' Billy said. 'You *have* to pay for them.'

'You mean the government's going to charge me for what used to be free? That's not right. What's the damn licence fee for?'

There were times, Greg thought, when a pneumatic drill was required to get either sense into Uncle Frank's head or oddball ideas out of it. He looked at his watch. 'We need to get moving, Billy. We have to be at the Probate Office in an hour.'

'One more question, Uncle Frank,' Billy said. 'Is the upstairs radio a digital radio?'

'I don't know,' Uncle Frank said. 'It used to be your Auntie Irene's.'

Probate

They parked at the edge of the city centre on a piece of land that had once been the site of Billy's old grammar school. The school had burned down some fifteen years earlier, but by then the school had moved to a new location and the building had been taken over by the Department for Work and Pensions. Billy had gone to sign on there after the mill closed down, and the irony of the situation hadn't been lost on him.

In the days when few students went to university, the school had mounted ornate wooden boards in the assembly hall to honour those of its students who had. Their names were written in gold-coloured paint and listed in alphabetical order and by year of graduation. When the school relocated to another part of the city the boards were left behind, and as the Department for Work and Pensions was there only on a temporary basis, it too left the boards in situ and simply partitioned the assembly hall into small offices.

The honour boards now provided the backdrop to the offices and when Billy first visited the repurposed building to sign on for the dole, he'd found himself sitting in an office staring at a board with his name on it. He recognised then that life didn't always run to plan.

'You know this was the original site of your school too, don't you?' Billy asked.

Greg didn't.

'Well it was. Your school moved to where it is now in 1920 and the building here was supposed to have been torn down.

But in that year my school went up in flames and everyone had to be moved here. It was only supposed to be for a short time because the building had already been condemned. There were large wooden buttresses propping it up at the back.

'I can still remember the stone steps inside the school. They were grooved on both sides, worn down over the years by thousands of feet. We were supposed to always walk to the left and in single file, and a prefect stood at the top of the staircase to make sure we did. If you came up two at a time you got sent back down to the bottom again, and if you overtook someone you'd be given an order mark. Three order marks in one week and you were on detention.'

'I was always being placed on detention,' Greg said. 'How about you? Did you ever get it?'

'No, but a prefect once gave me two order marks for just leaning against one of the buttresses. That struck me as being a bit unfair, but you could never appeal their decisions. I've never understood why schooldays are supposed to be the happiest days of your life. They weren't mine. I hated gym and I hated exams. I can still remember walking to school one exam week and passing an old bloke up a ladder cleaning windows. He was whistling away to himself as happy as Larry. I'd have done anything to trade places with him that day.'

At Greg's suggestion, they left the car park and school day reminiscences behind them and set off for the Probate Office.

What was most noticeable about the city centre Greg walked through was how unnoticeable it was. Most of the buildings were still there but the bustle was gone, and there was no evidence of any commerce worthy of the name. The shopping areas were decimated and countless premises abandoned. The large stores and familiar names he remembered had all but disappeared and only the bargain shops remained to compete with the thrift stores that now dotted the streets of whitewashed windows.

He glanced at Billy, and Billy read his thoughts.

'I know. Depressing, isn't it?'

It wasn't just depressing, Greg thought, it was heartbreaking – like going to visit a loved one in the hospital and realising for the first time that they were going to die. The centre was no longer the thriving nucleus of a proud city, but the residue of a city that had missed out on the nation's booms and shared in all its busts. The few people they passed were lumpen and bedraggled, joyless and ragamuffin and walked without purpose: the remnant of an army defeated in economic battle whose only recourse was now to appear on *The Jeremy Kyle Show*.

'Try not to make eye contact with anyone,' Billy advised. 'People carry knives these days.'

They walked past their fourth Romanian accordionist of the day and entered a building at the rear of the city hall and took the lift to the fourth floor. They gave their names to the receptionist at the desk and took seats opposite an elderly Asian couple dressed in traditional salwar kameez. The woman was wearing a headscarf and the man a Sindhi cap.

'Hey, what's happening?' Greg said.

'My wife's father died,' the man said, mistaking Greg's greeting for a question.

'My brother wasn't meaning to pry,' Billy apologised. 'It's just that he lives in America and that's the way they greet each other there.'

He then fell silent and hoped Greg would do the same.

'I like the hat,' Greg said. 'Where did you get the hat from?'

'From a shop,' the man replied.

'Does the hat have a name?' Greg persisted.

'It's called a Sindhi cap,' the man said.

'Well, I'll be,' Greg said. 'I've got a girlfriend called Cyndi. I ought to buy her one.'

Billy wondered if his brother was as cheery and talkative

as this in a doctor's surgery. There were places where conversation was neither welcomed nor appropriate, and to his way of thinking the Probate Office was one such place. There was, however, something familiar about the old man sitting opposite him and it slowly dawned on him who he was.

'Mr Aziz?' he asked.

The man looked surprised and nodded warily.

'I don't know if you remember me, Mr Aziz, but I'm Billy Bowman. We worked at the mill together.'

Mr Aziz broke into a broad grin and stood to shake Billy's proffered hand. 'Mr Billy,' he said. 'How are you my old friend?'

'I'm well, thank you. And you – how are you?'

'Old as the mountain I can no longer climb,' Mr Aziz laughed. 'But I'm well enough. My health remains and I draw a pension.'

'Mr Aziz was one of the foremen in the mill,' Billy explained to Greg. 'He was one of our best workers… this is my brother Greg, by the way, Mr Aziz.'

Greg and Mr Aziz shook hands, and Mr Aziz then introduced them to his wife.

'It was a sad day when the mill closed down, wasn't it, Mr Aziz? What did you do after that?'

'I drove a taxi, Mr Billy. The money wasn't good, but at least it paid for my daughter and son to go to university. They have good jobs now, but live far away. No work for them in this city. What you do now?'

'Well, I got married, and I have a daughter called Katy who's seven. I sell textbooks for a living – travel to universities and talk to lecturers. What I'd really like to do though…'

One of the office doors opened and the names of Mr and Mrs Aziz were called.

'Nice people,' Greg said, once the Aziz's had entered the office and the door closed behind them. 'Why was he calling you *Mr* Billy? Was the mill you worked in a leftover from the Empire or something?'

'It was his idea,' Billy said. 'I told him to call me Billy, but he insisted on calling me Mr Billy. I think he felt more comfortable doing that, and it was his way of showing respect. I wish the other workers in the mill had been as well-mannered. They could have taken a leaf out of Mr Aziz's book.'

'Why, what did they call you?'

'Billy Bonkers, if you must know,' Billy said. 'I once found some graffiti in the men's toilet that said "Billy Bonkers has no Conkers". Can you believe that?'

Greg smiled. He found it very easy to believe.

The probate hearing was straightforward. Their father's estate was small and uncomplicated, and as Lyle had died intestate – his letter of intent having no legal standing – it passed directly to Billy and Greg. They were named as co-executors and told that the certificates of probate would arrive early the following week.

Greg and Billy walked back to the car and drove to a small retail park at the edge of the city to buy a Freeview Box, a digital radio and a DVD player for Uncle Frank. Billy chose them and Greg paid for them. They packed the boxes into the large boot of Billy's car and returned to their uncle's house.

Greg and Uncle Frank watched as Billy connected the box and the DVD player to the television and tuned in the stations.

'How many channels did you say, lad?'

'About sixty, Uncle Frank,' Billy said. 'But most of them aren't worth watching.'

'By heck, did you hear that, Greg? Sixty! There'll be no point in me going to bed at night.'

Billy carefully stuck labels to the remote controls (TV, FV, and DVD) and then demonstrated the functions of each arrow and every button. His explanations were clear and unhurried, and very soon Uncle Frank was handling the clickers with the adeptness of a professional gunslinger playing with his revolver. Greg and Billy watched for a time as he surfed through the channels and then left him in the capable hands of *Judge Judy*.

The next day, Billy left for London to meet with Dr Haffenden and Greg started to clear the house. He looked through drawers, cupboards and wardrobes, and filled cardboard boxes and plastic bags with the detritus of his father's life. He loaded his car, drove to the tip and dumped them all into the same skip. If the practice had been good enough for his father and was still good enough for Syd Butterfield, it was certainly good enough for him. The country of his birth was no longer his responsibility, he decided. It could sort itself and its rubbish out. His hands were already full with Billy and Uncle Frank, and besides, he now lived in America – though as a non-voter, he didn't feel any responsibility for that country either!

He was woken the next morning by a loud knocking on the front door. He quickly pulled on his jeans and T-shirt and went downstairs to investigate. He found two men standing there and a large lorry parked on the road.

The men greeted him cheerily – far too cheerily for eight o'clock in the morning. 'I think you're expecting us, Mr Bowman. We're here to fix the wall-ties.'

Greg had completely forgotten.

'I'll warn you now, Mr Bowman, it's going to get noisy,' one of them said. 'You might want to leave the house for a while.'

Greg made the men coffee and told them he'd play it by ear. 'A wise choice of words, Mr Bowman,' the man smiled.

Greg washed and changed, and then poured himself coffee. He'd planned to finish clearing the house that day but, as the lorry was now blocking his car in the drive, decided instead to sort through his father's papers. He took the brown manila file from the sideboard cupboard and went to the front room.

He'd just spread the documents from the first section on to the settee when the drilling started. The noise was relentless and ear-splitting, and the house vibrated. It was as if the man with the drill was standing right next to him. Greg decided to take the workman's advice and leave the house for a few hours. But where to go? Uncle Frank's was the obvious choice, but he opted instead for the local park. The day was warm and windless and, unlike Uncle Frank's house, the park would be peaceful. He needed to concentrate, and listening to birdsong would be a lot more conducive to thought than Planet Rock.

He quickly put the documents back into the file and went outside to tell the workmen of his decision. He told them the back door was unlocked and that they were welcome to use the downstairs toilet and help themselves to tea or coffee. He then set off for the park, the manila file under his arm and his ears ringing.

The park was at the top of a long tree-lined avenue about a mile from the house and close to the junior school he'd attended. It had been there for over a hundred years. The large iron gates, which were locked shut at night, had already been swung open and Greg took the path that led down to the lake. He passed the bowling greens and tennis courts and chose a bench by the lakeside that was shaded by a large oak tree. There were no rowing boats now but the ducks were still there. At night they nestled on a small island in the middle of the lake, but during the day splashed and quacked closer to shore.

Greg opened the file and started to work through the papers. His father, he soon realised, had organised the documents alphabetically rather than in subject order. Consequently, he found gas and telephone bills in the 'B' compartment (British Gas, BT), electric bills in the 'N' compartment (npower), and water bills in the 'Y' compartment (Yorkshire Water). Bank statements, however, which he'd expected to find under 'B' for **B**arclays, were in the 'M' compartment – presumably for Money, and because the 'B' compartment was already jammed to capacity.

He kept only the most recent statements from the utility companies and placed the backlog on the growing pile of paper next to him: old receipts, details of car repairs, out-of-date television licences and MOT certificates. He was about to do the same with the bank statements (seven years' worth) when he noticed something odd. There was a monthly standing order for £200 that didn't appear to relate to anything he'd found in the file. It was simply marked GD.

Greg looked again through the few documents that remained in the 'G' and 'D' sections, but found only an insurance policy – already accounted for by one of the standing orders – and the name and address of his father's gardener. He didn't know why, but the thought crossed his mind that maybe it had something to do with the woman who'd been at the funeral, the woman who'd slipped in and quietly slipped out without introducing herself.

It was difficult to believe that his father had been the victim of blackmail. And what blackmailer would turn up to a funeral service to pay their respects? But if it wasn't blackmail, then what was it? Some sort of responsibility? But what responsibility demanded a payment of £200 every month?

There was only one that Greg could think of.

Child support!

Hospital

Billy returned from London just after nine o'clock that evening. He looked exhausted and immediately slumped into a chair.

'You look like you could use a drink,' Greg said.

'I could use two,' Billy said. His voice was weak and he spoke almost in a whisper.

Greg opened a bottle of wine and poured two glasses.

'How did you get on with Dr Haffenden?' he asked, handing Billy the glass with the larger measure.

'It was all a bit traumatic,' Billy confessed. 'It was okay when I was touching his feet, but when he touched mine I… I panicked. I completely lost it, Greg. I started screaming and kicking out and we had to stop. He gave me a couple of sedatives and we tried again half an hour later, but even with the drugs we never managed to get past my shoes. Dr Haffenden told me he'd half expected my reaction, but said that he was surprised by how hard I kicked and suggested that next time I wore slippers.'

'Do you want me to touch your feet?' Greg asked, hoping the answer would be no.

'Please, but not tonight. Let's try tomorrow. I think I need some time to recover.'

Greg readily agreed and started to tell Billy about the men who'd arrived that day to put in the new wall-ties, fix the crack in the back wall and replace the windowsill. He then told him about his visit to the park.

'You're telling me that we might have a half-brother or half-sister?' Billy asked incredulously. 'I can't believe that, Greg. It's… it's just not possible. Dad wasn't like that. There's got to be another reason.'

'Well, I'd like to know what it is then, because I can't think of one.'

'No, Greg, you're wrong. You're jumping the gun. There has to be another explanation. Wait until we get the letter of administration and then go to the bank and find out what the standing order's all about. I bet you anything you've got the wrong end of the stick.'

'I hope I have, Billy, but think about it. This family's full of secrets. I didn't know you had a foot thing until last week, and I certainly didn't know Uncle Frank was planning to rob a bank. Why should Dad be any different? Why wouldn't he have a secret?'

Billy was about to answer when his mobile rang.

'Hi, Jean... Dear God... not Betty... I will... I'll be right over... '

'You're supposed to be at the office,' Greg whispered.

'... in about five hours... no, there's no need to wait up... I'll phone them tomorrow... they'll understand... I love you too, Jean.'

'What's wrong?' Greg asked.

'It's Betty. She's been rushed to hospital and they're going to operate tomorrow – triple bypass!'

'I didn't know she had anything wrong with her heart,' Greg said.

'She's suffered from angina for years,' Billy explained. 'She takes pills for it and we thought it was under control. But when Jean got back from the Lake District yesterday, Betty was in bed complaining of chest pains. Thank goodness for private health insurance. If Betty was reliant on the NHS, she'd be dead.'

Billy looked at his watch. 'I'd better not have anything more to drink, Greg. I'll have to leave here at 2.30am. Do you have an alarm clock?'

The operation was a success. Betty ended up having a quadruple bypass, the surgeon throwing in the fourth for free. It was now Tuesday and she was feeling well enough to receive visitors.

Greg picked up Uncle Frank just after lunch.

'I'm surprised you want to visit her, Uncle Frank. I thought you didn't like her.'

'I don't,' Uncle Frank said, 'but I'm taking your advice and being nice to people. I'm starting with Betty and I've bought her a present.'

'That's very thoughtful of you. What did you buy her?'

'It's a surprise. I'm pretty sure she'll like it though.'

Greg noticed a strange smile cross his uncle's face, but presumed it was the Bell's palsy playing up, as it sometimes did.

He parked the car in the wooded grounds of the hospital and walked with Uncle Frank to the reception. 'We're here to visit Betty Halliwell,' Greg said. 'Can you tell us what room she's in?'

'By heck, lad,' Uncle Frank said, as they walked through the lobby to the lift. 'This place is like a bloody hotel! I wouldn't mind being ill more often if they brought me to a place like this. It's like being on holiday.'

They took the lift and climbed out at the second floor and turned left as directed. They saw Katy tap-dancing in the corridor, practising a new routine.

'Hi, Uncle Greg. Hi, Uncle Frank,' Katy shouted. 'Granny's in this room here and she's a lot better now. She's watching television with Mummy and Daddy.'

'By heck, television!' Uncle Frank said.

They entered the room and found Betty propped up on pillows and Jean and Billy sitting in armchairs. It wasn't as if Greg and Uncle Frank were her most favourite people, but Betty did her best to smile.

'You're not dead then, Betty,' Uncle Frank said.

'Fortunately not, Frank, but do you mind if we talk after the programme's finished? I haven't seen this episode.'

'What are we watching?'

'*Diagnosis Murder*,' Betty replied. 'It's got Dick Van Dyke in it – and seemingly most of his family. That one there's his son and the younger man is his grandson.'

Uncle Frank sat down and perched at the end of the bed.

'I can't see with you sitting there, Frank,' Betty said. 'You're blocking my view.'

'Where am I supposed to sit then? Tell you what, Betty: budge up a bit and I'll climb into bed with you. I've been gardening all morning and I could do with a lie down.'

'Sit here, Uncle Frank,' Billy intervened. 'I need to talk to Greg anyway.'

Billy and Greg stepped outside the room and Uncle Frank sat down in Billy's chair. 'Can you turn it up a bit, Betty? I can't hear what they're saying.'

'We're in a hospital, Uncle Frank,' Jean said. 'You'll have to turn up your hearing aid.'

He fiddled with the volume control and the hearing aid gave a sharp whistle. Betty glanced at Jean and then looked up to Heaven, just as Dr Mark Sloan – the Dick Van Dyke character – looked down on the body of a man and pronounced him dead.

'It's a bit rubbish this, isn't it?' Uncle Frank said after a time. 'Why would a grown man want to live with his father?'

'You tell me, Frank,' Betty said. 'You lived with your father for long enough.'

'I had no choice in the matter, Betty. He wouldn't let me leave!'

The door opened at that moment and a nurse ushered Katy into the room. 'I'm afraid Katy's tap-dancing is disturbing some of the patients, Mrs Halliwell,' she said. 'She can dance in here but not in the corridor.'

'Come and lie down next to me, Katy,' Betty said.

'How come she can lie down with you and I can't?' Uncle Frank asked. 'That's nepotism, that is – just like the casting of this stupid programme!'

Eventually, the crime drama ended and Betty turned off the television.

'I've brought you a present, Betty,' Uncle Frank said. 'It's in this shoe box with a ribbon tied round it.'

'That's very kind of you, Frank. Shall I open it now?'

'No, wait till I've gone. It'll give you something to do when everyone's left. Did I tell you my television's working again? I was right, you know, the government had turned it off, but Billy's fixed it and I can get sixty channels now. I could only get five before. You wouldn't believe some of the stuff that's on, Betty. I've been watching this one programme called *The Orange Women of America*. It's about these women who blow up their knockers with bicycle pumps and go out drinking together. They act nice as pie to each other when they're together, but when they get home they slag each other off like fishwives. I'm not saying it's as good as *Judge Judy* – she's a woman after my own heart she is, tells it like it is – but I can't seem to stop watching it.'

'What on earth are you talking about, Frank?'

'He's talking about *The Real Housewives of Orange County*, Granny,' Katy said. 'It's good. Who's your favourite housewife, Uncle Frank?'

'The one with the big lips that looks like a fish,' Uncle Frank said.

'What are you doing letting Katy watch programmes like this, Jean? It doesn't sound suitable for a girl of seven.'

'It's on in the afternoon, Mummy – well before the watershed. Uncle Frank's making it sound a lot worse than it is.'

There was a knock on the door and The Reverend Tinkler popped his head into the room. 'And how's my favourite parishioner today?' he asked.

'There's nothing wrong with me, Bill,' Uncle Frank replied.

'I forgot to mention,' Greg said. 'The grant of administration came through this morning. I'll go to the bank in the morning and ask about the standing order. Do you want to come with me?'

'I can't,' Billy said. 'I'm supposed to be going to Scotland next week and I promised Jean I'd spend this week with her.'

'Why are you going to Scotland?'

'I'm not. But it's the week I normally go there and Jean would get suspicious if I didn't. I'll stay at the house with you, if it's okay.'

'I was planning to take Uncle Frank to the coast on Monday and stay overnight. Why don't you come with us?'

Billy thought for a moment. 'I could do that. It would make a nice change. Which part of the coast are you going to?'

'The east coast, but I haven't decided just where yet.'

'Why don't we go to The Gap?' Billy suggested. 'We had some good holidays there with Mum and Dad when we were kids. It's one of the memories I focus on when I'm having my foot therapy. You remember it, don't you? We used to stay in a bungalow halfway down the cliff and walk to a farm for milk every morning. There were poppies everywhere.'

'I remember it,' Greg said. 'But there aren't any hotels there, are there? I promised Uncle Frank we'd stay in a nice hotel overnight.'

'There are plenty of resorts up the coast. We could drive to one of them after we've been to The Gap and stay in a hotel there.'

It was decided.

'When are you going back, by the way?' Billy asked.

'Two days later. I booked a flight yesterday.'

'That's a pity. Katy will miss you.'

'How about you? Will you miss me?' Greg smiled.

'Of course I will. That goes without saying. It also goes without saying that Jean won't. I hope you can live with that.'

Greg laughed. 'I guess I'll have to.'

'Have to what?' Uncle Frank demanded.

'Nothing important. Where are you off to?'

'I'm going for a coffee with Bill. We're going to talk about the Bible.'

For a man of the cloth, The Reverend Tinkler couldn't have looked less enthusiastic about the prospect.

'Come on, Bill. We haven't got all day.'

He then took The Reverend Tinkler's sleeve and pulled him towards the lift.

'Poor old sod,' Greg said.

'Uncle Frank?' Billy asked.

'No, The Reverend Tinkler,' Greg replied. 'The man doesn't stand a chance.'

The man who didn't stand a chance bought two coffees at the servery and took them to the table where Uncle Frank was sitting. He sat down and nervously asked what it was he wanted to talk to him about.

'Jesus, Bill. I want to talk about Jesus. You see the way I see it, Jesus wasn't as special as everyone makes Him out to be. I know He healed people, but lots of people in those days did the same thing. The disciples did it, and it says in the Bible that Jesus appointed another seventy people to go around curing people. How come we never hear about them in church?'

'I don't think we're trying to hide anything, Frank. And you have to bear in mind that it was Jesus who gave these people their power to heal. Israel was a big country, you know, too big for one man to travel its length and breadth and minister to all its people.'

'But what gets me, Bill, is the miracles. When I was growing up I was led to believe that only Jesus performed miracles, but that's wrong, isn't it? Miracles weren't new. Both Elijah and Elisha raised people from the dead, and Elisha's down as curing leprosy and blindness as well. He even made iron float. So what makes Jesus so special is my question?'

The Reverend Tinkler sipped his cup of coffee wishing it was a glass of whisky – preferably a single malt with two ice cubes. Why, he wondered, had Betty suggested he talk to Frank in the cafeteria?

'Jesus is special, Frank, because He's the Son of God. He's the only Son of God there's been and He's the only Son of God there ever will be. Elijah and Elisha were *men* of God. God worked miracles through them while Jesus did them off His own bat. There's a major difference.'

'So tell me this then. Why didn't Jesus like pigeons?'

The Reverend Tinkler was completely taken aback by the question and the coffee in his mouth spluttered back into the cup. 'I didn't know that he didn't,' he said, wiping his mouth on a paper napkin.

'You *have* read the Bible, haven't you, Bill?'

'Of course I have, Frank, but I don't remember anything about Jesus not liking pigeons.'

'It's part of the Palm Sunday story, Bill – only one of Jesus' biggest days! He walks into the Holy Temple and once He's finished overturning the tables of the money changers He turns on the pigeon sellers and tips over their seats. Why did He do that? What beef did He have with pigeons?'

'Oh, I see what you mean, Frank. Jesus didn't do that because He didn't like pigeons. He did it because He didn't like the idea of people *selling* pigeons in the temple. He believed the House of God was a place for prayer and not commerce.'

Uncle Frank saw Greg and Billy coming into the cafeteria. 'Greg and Billy are here for me now, Bill, so I'll have to be going. What I'd like you to consider before our next meeting though, is what a girl of fourteen was doing marrying a man closer to ninety. You'd get locked up for something like that these days.'

'Who in particular do you have in mind, Frank?' The

Reverend Tinkler asked, determined there would be no next meeting.

'Jesus' mother and father, of course: Mary and Joseph!'

Uncle Frank got up from the table and walked with Greg and Billy to the car. The Reverend Tinkler remained sitting in stunned silence, gently rubbing his cheek. He wondered what his ex-wife Joan was doing at this moment, wondered if she too was wondering what he was doing at this moment.

'You're not still trying to recruit The Reverend Tinkler into your gang, are you?' Greg asked.

'No, I'm just messing with him,' Uncle Frank laughed. 'He didn't answer my question though, did he?'

'You never gave him a chance. You just stood up and punched him in the face.'

'That was an accident, Greg. I meant to punch him on the arm. You know, one of those punches buddies give each other.'

They reached the car and Greg opened the door for his uncle. 'What did Betty think of your gift?' he asked.

'I don't know. I told her to open it after I'd gone.'

'So, what was it?'

'Two pounds of tripe,' Uncle Frank said, bursting into laughter.

Billy was horrified. 'What in Heaven's name have you done, Uncle Frank? Betty's just had a quadruple bypass. The shock could kill her!'

'I doubt we'll be that lucky,' Uncle Frank said.

Billy wasn't so sure and went running back into the hospital.

'So what happened to being nice?' Greg sighed.

'To tell you the truth, lad, I don't think it rightly suits me.'

9

Lyles

Greg and his father continued to meet in the evenings. Conscious that his days were now numbered, Lyle was determined to spend as much time with his younger son as possible. He would appear at eight o'clock and stay for about three hours – the maximum his batteries allowed – and at eleven, start to flicker and then disappear. For much of the time they would sit in companionable silence or listen to his father's recordings of Gilbert & Sullivan operas. Neither was discomfited by the fact they were running out of things to say to each other. It was sufficient simply to be together.

There was one thing, of course, that Greg did want to talk to his father about: the standing order. The subject, however, was a potentially delicate one, and he saw no point in broaching it before the facts were established. Time, however, was against him: it was now Tuesday, and in little more than three days his father would disappear for good.

Wednesday morning dawned and Greg climbed out of bed early. He took a quick bath, shaved and dressed formally; ate a bowl of cereal, drank two cups of coffee and left the plates in the sink. He put his father's death certificate and letter of administration in a large brown envelope, checked his passport was still in his wallet and then drove to the branch where his father had banked. He arrived early, and waited in the car until the bank opened for business.

Once the door was unlocked, he entered the premises and explained his business to one of the cashiers. He was shown to a small office and met there by the assistant manager, a woman in her late forties. She remembered Lyle and offered Greg her condolences. He thanked her and then asked about the standing order – how long had it been in place and the name and address of the recipient. She left him, and returned five minutes later with the details he'd requested. His father, she told him, had set up the standing order fifteen years ago for a Ms Gillian Diamanti.

Greg thanked her, returned to the car and phoned Billy. He asked if he recognised the name Gillian Diamanti or the address where she resided. Billy didn't recall the name but was familiar with the street, which was about a half mile from their father's house and just off the top road.

It took Greg less than ten minutes to drive there. Rather than park on Bateson Street, he decided to leave the car on the top road and walk to number 15. The houses were a mixture of old terraces and newer semi-detached and number 15, he discovered, was a small hairdresser's shop.

He glanced through the window and saw a woman of about his age putting curlers into the hair of a woman about twice his age. He was debating whether to wait until the customer left the shop before entering, when the door opened and his father stepped out – or, at least, a fifteen-year-old version of his father.

Greg gasped. The boy looked at him questioningly for a moment and then climbed on a mountain bike and pedalled away.

Greg braced himself and walked into the shop.

The hairdresser looked up from her work and gave him a half smile. 'It's Greg, isn't it?' she said. 'I was wondering if you'd turn up.'

'There's no doubt about it, Billy. He's the spitting image of Dad.'

'But has she actually said that Dad's his father?'

'No, but she couldn't talk. She had some old biddy in the chair with her and she said she had appointments booked for the rest of the day. I'm supposed to go back at four.'

'What was she like? Is she nice?'

'I don't know if she's nice or not, but she looks to be about our age. Mid-to-late thirties, at a guess. She's attractive though – I'll say that for her.'

Billy did some quick calculations in his head. 'Dad must have been about sixty-eight when he met her then, and if she's in her late thirties now she must have been only in her early twenties when they had their affair. It doesn't make any sense. Why would an attractive younger woman go out with someone like Dad?'

'Mum did,' Greg said. 'She was nearly twenty years younger than him. Maybe he had got a thing for younger women and this hairdresser's got a thing for older men. Maybe she was looking for a father figure.'

'Dad was old enough to have been a *grandfather* figure,' Billy said. 'The only women you read about going after men that age are gold diggers. Dad wasn't rich. She could have done a lot better than him... oh that sounds bad, doesn't it? I didn't mean it like that.'

'I know what you mean: the same thought crossed my mind, too. Are you sure you don't want to join me when I go back?'

'I'd like to, Greg, but I'm taking Jean and Katy to the outdoor swimming pool today. I can't really get out of it. What did the boy look like – apart from like Dad I mean? Did he look a decent sort?'

Greg shrugged. 'He seemed pleasant enough. He didn't spit

at me or try to run me down with his bicycle, if that's what you mean.'

'Hang on a minute, Greg…'

Greg heard Jean's voice in the background and Billy telling her he'd be with her in a minute.

'I have to go, Greg. Call me on my mobile as soon as you know anything. I don't know how I'm going to break this news to Jean. She already thinks my side of the family's a dead loss.'

And that's without her knowing the half of it, Greg thought.

He walked to the front room and lay down on the settee. He had five hours to kill before returning to the hairdresser's – five long hours. While Gillian Diamanti washed, cut, and styled hair of varying lengths, age and gender; Greg remained on the couch prostrate and motionless. He closed his eyes and thought about what he'd say to Gillian Diamanti, thought about what she might say to him, and wondered about the boy whose name he didn't know: the half-brother his father had failed to mention. His father, he calculated, had made an expensive mistake: £200 a month for fifteen years amounted to £36,000!

He considered the circumstances of their meeting and tried to imagine how two people from such opposite ends of the spectrum had been drawn to each other. He blenched when he thought of the consummation that had led to the birth of the boy on the bicycle, the boy who hadn't spat at him or tried to run him down. Would his father expect him to take responsibility for his half-brother as well as Billy and Uncle Frank? Was he supposed to assume the burden of the standing order and embrace the child as a Bowman?

If his father did want these things, he was going to be disappointed. As far as Greg was concerned his responsibilities ended with Billy and Uncle Frank. They were his family. He had no use for a half-brother. The boy was Gillian Diamanti's responsibility, not his. What Billy decided to do was a matter for him.

He drifted in and out of sleep and rose from the settee with a crick in his neck. He did stretching exercises and then went to the bathroom and splashed water on his face. The day was warm and he decided to walk to the hairdresser's shop. He sauntered slowly and deliberated his opening words. He wanted something short and to the point, something that would put her on the defensive and not him.

But why was he so nervous? He never felt nervous. He walked into lecture halls every day of his working life and felt no more intimidated than if he'd gone to a 7-Eleven for a loaf of bread. He was known for not being nervous. After further reflection, he decided that it was probably because he was going to visit a hairdresser. Hairdressers always made him nervous.

He arrived at the shop and noticed two bicycles propped outside, the one belonging to the boy and the other, presumably, to an adult. The sign said CLOSED, but the door was unlocked and Greg walked in. A bell rang.

Inside, the shop was empty, but he could hear voices from above and then footsteps of people descending stairs. Gillian appeared, followed by the boy and a man of about her age clad in tight-fitting Lycra.

'I'll be with you in a minute, Greg,' she said, and then turned to talk to the man.

'Make sure he wears his helmet, Ben, and don't take him on any busy roads.'

'You worry too much, Gill. Lyle's not a child. He knows what he's doing.'

Lyle! Wasn't it sufficient for his father to have sired the child without her flaunting the boy's parentage to all and sundry? What had possessed the woman to give the boy his father's name? Was she stupid, lacking in tact, or simply without imagination?

The boy recognised Greg from the morning and smiled at

him when he passed. At least he has manners, Greg thought. At least there's something positive about him I can tell Billy.

'You're sure you don't want me to stick around?' Ben said to Gillian, looking at Greg.

'I'll be fine, Ben. Now scram. And don't bother coming back if Lyle isn't still in one piece.'

Ben smiled and the two of them kissed on the lips.

Lips! How brazen was this woman? His father had been dead for barely a month and she was already involved with another man. Gillian Diamanti certainly didn't let the grass grow under her feet.

Lyle (the boy) was already outside the door sitting on his bike, resting an arm against the wall. 'Come on, Ben!' he called.

Ben walked past Greg but didn't smile. Instead he gave him a look, a hard look if Greg read it right. What the hell was with this man? What reason did he have to be so high and mighty?

Greg waited until the two of them had disappeared, and then turned to face Gillian.

'I believe you're the mother of my father's child,' he said, in a voice more sonorous than he'd intended.

She stared at him incredulously and then burst out laughing, as if Greg had just told her the funniest joke in the world.

He waited while she composed herself, surprised by her reaction. Had she no shame?

'You really don't know, do you?' Gillian said eventually.

Greg said nothing. He was used to power plays from attending departmental meetings and knew when to remain silent.

She spoke again.

'I'm not the mother of your father's child, Greg. I'm the mother of *your* child!'

The colour drained from Greg's face and he gazed at her

dumbfounded. How in the name of God could he be the father of a child whose mother he'd only met that morning? The idea was preposterous – far too preposterous to be true. The woman was trying to con him, trick him into paying her the money his father no longer could. The charlatan! He was about to call her bluff when another and altogether more uneasy thought nagged him: the notion was also too ludicrous to be a lie. Why, in times of DNA testing, when parentage could be proved or disproved in a matter of hours, would anyone make such a claim if not true?

'You don't even remember me, do you?' Gillian said, in a voice more hurt than angry.

The sad truth was that Greg didn't. He couldn't place her name and neither could he find any familiar contours when he searched her face. He was unable to say with any certainty, however, that he had neither met nor slept with her, and this realisation troubled him. His younger years, he was aware, had been hedonistic – fuelled as often as not by drugs and alcohol – and his memory of them was worryingly cloudy. For all he knew, there could be a platoon of Gillian Diamantis lurking in these shadows. But what was he to say? How was he to explain this to Gillian without devaluing both her and himself? In the event, he did what any decent person placed in similar circumstances would have done, and lied through his teeth.

'I don't know if my father mentioned this to you, Gillian, but I had a serious motorcycle accident last year and suffered some brain damage. It's not irreversible, I'm glad to say, but my memory's temporarily impaired and there are gaps in my life that I still know nothing about. You couldn't help me out here, could you?'

'Oddly enough, I don't think your father ever did mention this,' Gillian replied somewhat sarcastically. 'Perhaps the incident slipped his mind.'

'Well, he was getting on in years,' Greg volunteered.

'He was old, Greg, not senile! Anyway, I'm always happy to assist those less fortunate than myself – especially the brain-damaged – so, if it's of any help, you knew me as Sudge and we met in The Cat.'

The name Sudge did ring a faint bell in Greg's mind – how could a name like Sudge not? It tinkled at first, dinged for a while and then started to clang loudly. Of course, Sudge! No wonder he hadn't recognised Gillian. Gillian was... well, just plain normal by comparison, another person entirely. And yes, she was right: they had met in The Cat – or to give the club its full name, The Little Fat Black Pussycat.

The events of the evening Gillian spoke of, events that had occurred approximately two weeks before he'd left for America, slowly fell into place. He remembered meeting up with friends in The Continental Coffee Bar, popping some pills and then moving on to The Coffin, another of the city's underworld clubs. They'd stayed for a couple of hours and then moved on to The Little Fat Black Pussycat to listen to some live music, and it was here that he'd met Sudge, a strange-looking girl with short pink hair, green lips and coal-black eyes.

They'd fallen into conversation at the bar and then, after what passed as a respectable length of time for two people as high as kites, into each other's arms. They'd spent the evening dancing together, sweating, gyrating, and then, during a break in the band's performance, gone outside and smoked a joint. And then what had they done? As far as Greg could remember they'd gone back inside and danced some more. So when had they slept together? When had they made love? Surely not in the street!

And then it dawned on him... Little Lyle had been conceived in Big Lyle's bed after all.

'Sudge!' Greg said, holding out his hand and smiling. 'It's good to see you again.'

'*Fuck* you, Greg!' Gillian replied.

Cafetière

The meeting with Gillian Diamanti – mother of his child and *friend* of his father – had been a sobering experience that left Greg in need of a stiff drink. Rather than return home after leaving the shop, he headed instead for the nearest pub and ordered a large whisky.

The sun had long since set on the fortunes of The Rising Moon, and though the hostelry was still open for business it was now for sale. A large sign invited potential purchasers to make a difference to the local community by restoring the inn to its former glory – which, so far as Greg could determine, would have entailed not only gutting the premises, but single-handedly reversing the economy, overturning the smoking ban and securing permission from the brewery to buy alcohol from supermarkets.

He avoided the possibility of being dragged into conversation with any of the regulars hovering at the bar, and took his drink to a table at the far end of the room. The air in the pub was stale, the carpet worn and sticky and the upholstered benches torn and in need of repair. The Rising Moon, he decided, was highly suited for a man who'd just had the stuffing knocked out of him.

Once Greg had acknowledged their relationship, Gillian had led him to the upstairs flat and left him in the lounge while she made coffee. The room was neat and tastefully decorated; the furniture distressed and framed posters on the walls. A large yucca plant stood in one corner, a large flat-screened television in another and, on every available surface, photographs of Lyle Jr – or Bicycle Boy, as Greg preferred to call his son.

He'd been lost in thought when Gillian returned to the room, silently rueing the day he'd taken it upon himself to investigate the standing order instead of leaving Billy to tie up the loose ends of his father's estate. If he'd done that, he'd have never called at the shop that morning and come face to face with the consequences of his past. He'd have been happy simply not to have known. Ignorance, as people so often said, would indeed have been bliss.

Instead of doing this, however, he'd opened the lid of a Pandora's Box and now had to deal with the repercussions. What was wanted of him? Was he supposed to renew his relationship with Gillian and become an actual father to the boy he'd unknowingly sired, or was he simply expected to take on the mantle of his father and carry the financial burden?

In the event, Gillian expected neither. She simply depressed the plunger of the cafetière and poured out a story: what had been and what would be.

They'd made love just the one time, maybe twice, but on the same occasion. The moment, as Greg had surmised, had been his leaving party, though at the time, she pointed out to him, he'd failed to mention either the small matter of it being a *leaving* party or the fact that he was decamping for America. As far as she'd been concerned, it was the first of many parties they'd attend together. She'd given him her number… he'd promised to call… nothing!

Had she fallen in love with Greg that evening, fallen apart when he hadn't called and locked herself away in a dark room? No. She'd chalked it up to experience, a drunken fuck, and was annoyed with herself for having been so easily sweet-talked into spreading her legs for a boy she'd only just met. She got on with her life – something she always did – and forgot all about him until she missed her period and bought a self-testing kit. Then she remembered him – remembered him in spades!

She'd been nineteen at the time and he'd been her second partner – yes, second! If he'd been under the impression that she was 'easy' and slept around, then he'd be wrong. She wasn't that kind of girl – still wasn't. Convincing her parents of this, however, had been a different matter. They were old-fashioned Italians, set in their ways and strict Catholic. Sex before marriage was a taboo in their eyes, and as far as they were concerned she'd brought shame on the family. She'd made her bed and now she had to lie in it, her father told her – making it clear that it wouldn't be a bed in his house. It was then that she'd moved into the flat above the hairdresser's shop.

Gillian had been training in the salon for two years by then, and had become friendly with the middle-aged woman who owned the shop. A kind and nurturing person, Elsie Barraclough had empathised with her trainee's plight and invited her to move into the upstairs rooms, which at the time had been unoccupied. Even though Elsie charged only half the rent she normally asked for, Gillian had still struggled. On top of the rent, she had gas and electricity bills to pay and food to buy, and on a trainee's salary this proved difficult. It was then that she'd reluctantly decided to track down Greg.

By now, she held her erstwhile lover in low regard, and was of the opinion that she and her unborn child would be better off without him. Although she was aware that it had taken the two of them to tango that night, she blamed him more than she did herself for her predicament. He'd promised to pull out before ejaculating, but in the event had stayed put and come inside her. And then, after this act of selfishness, he'd simply discarded her with as little thought as the tissues he'd flushed down the toilet that night. And this, no doubt, is what he'd want her to do with the foetus – discard it, abort the complication.

Abortion for Gillian, however, was off the table. If not a good Catholic girl, she was still of the Catholic faith and believed abortion to be a sin. She'd already decided to carry the baby for the full term and then have it adopted. She'd knocked on Greg's door, therefore, not in the hope of love or a proposal of marriage, but for financial and possibly emotional support.

She hadn't known Greg's telephone number or even his last name for that matter, but at least she'd known where he lived. She'd walked there from work one evening and nervously rung the bell. His father had come to the door holding a can of paint and a small paintbrush. He'd been wearing a collar and tie and a flat corduroy cap, and had given her the most wonderful of toothless smiles.

'When he told me you'd gone to live in America, I burst into tears. I think it was the hormones as much as anything – certainly not the thought of never seeing *you* again! He told me to come in and gave me one of his handkerchiefs to dry my eyes on. I still have it. He asked me if I'd eaten tea yet and offered to make me a sandwich. He said he'd opened a can of Spam only that morning and could easily get some cherry tomatoes from the greenhouse. I thanked him but said no, and told him that I'd settle for a cup of tea if he didn't mind. He boiled the kettle, mashed real leaves and then poured the tea into two of his best china cups. I was touched by that. Someone making that kind of effort for a person they didn't even know.

'When I told him I was pregnant, he didn't seem all that surprised. He just gave a big sigh – he used to sigh a lot, if you remember – and said that he'd been half-expecting some girl or other to show up at his door with this news for years. You can imagine how special that made me feel!

'Anyway, he apologised to me on your behalf. He said your heart was in the right place, but was unsure if your head was. If he was honest, he said that he didn't think you had much common sense and wondered how reliable a husband you'd be. When I told him I had no intention of marrying you and had just hoped for your support, he brightened up a bit and said that if it was okay with me he'd be happy to help in any way he could. Not many fathers would have done that, Greg. He was head and shoulders over mine.'

Lyle had become Gillian's friend and father figure, a constant in her life. He'd helped out with her living expenses, driven her to the hospital for appointments and had been sitting in the waiting room when she'd given birth to a child bearing a striking resemblance to himself.

The moment she held the baby in her arms was the moment she'd given up any idea of having the child adopted. The beautiful newborn – or Bicycle Boy, as Greg transposed in his head – would be hers forever. And no one had been more pleased to hear this news than Lyle, who had immediately gone to the bank and arranged the standing order – at his, rather than her, suggestion. It had been her idea, however, to name Bicycle Boy in his honour.

Gillian had gone to Lyle's house only the one time – the day she'd been looking for Greg. The woman next door, his father had told her, was a Nosey Parker and a dreadful tattle-tale, and suggested it would be better if he visited her which, at least once a week for the next fifteen years, he did. He'd gone there for meals, for company, for haircuts and to babysit for Gillian when she went out with friends, or on the rare occasions she had a date.

Lyle had got on famously with his grandson who'd known him only as a family friend. He'd bought him birthday and Christmas presents, played games with him, and taken him for walks and to the swings in the park. In return, Bicycle Boy had drawn pictures for him, written him cards and presented him with bits of stone and pebbles. The most precious gift of all, however, and the one Lyle prized most, was the small boy's love.

There was a time in his early life when Bicycle Boy had asked about his father, who he was and where he lived, but eventually he stopped asking and came to accept that his family comprised only him and his mother and, for this, was all the more special. He was a fine boy, Gillian had said, the finest boy in the whole wide world. He was doing well at school and had lots of friends. He was happy and considered others, and would grow up to be a man who treated women with respect and not as a random pin cushion for his prick!

Gillian said that she'd never fully understood the reason for Lyle not telling Greg about the child, but as she herself had no intention of telling him, hadn't been unduly concerned by this particular nor by Lyle's insistence that their 'arrangement' remain secret, something for only them to know about. The bank, of course, got to know about it when they approved Gillian's mortgage for the salon she now owned, and so too did Ben, after Gillian accepted his proposal.

'We're getting married in November and your father was to have given me away...'

At this point, her voice had wavered and she'd looked away.

'He was just the most wonderful man, Greg. You don't know how lucky you are to have had him as a father. I miss him terribly. I still can't believe he's gone. Every time the bell rings and someone walks through the door, I keep expecting it to be him...

'He was supposed to come for Sunday lunch. I'd made Yorkshire pudding with sage and onion stuffing, the way he liked it, and we'd waited and waited. I phoned his house but there was no answer, and I thought he must have forgotten and gone out somewhere. I called again the next day and when he still didn't answer, I knew then that something was wrong. I called the police – I didn't know who else to call. I told them a friend of mine might have had an accident and gave them his details, my details, and then waited on the phone for what seemed like an eternity. A different person came on the phone, a woman, and she told me that she was very sorry but a man by that name and description had been knocked down and killed the previous Friday... he'd got years left in him, Greg. Good years. It's just so unfair.'

She'd bought the local newspaper every day after that – something she normally refused to do on the grounds that it was fit only for fish and chips – and scanned the death notices for details of Lyle's funeral. She'd read the editorial that painted him as a pathetic old man who'd sat at home and drunk himself to death, and afterwards called the newspaper and angrily told them to get their fucking facts straight before they printed such shit!

She'd decided not to take Bicycle Boy to the funeral – in part to spare her son the ordeal of the service, and in part to forestall any chance meeting with Greg. He'd been distraught when she'd broken the news of Lyle's death to him, completely heartbroken.

Ben would have gone with her – he'd liked Lyle – but had to be in Nigeria on business that week. Going to the crematorium alone, however, had made it easier for her to slip in and out without drawing attention to herself and having to explain her connection to Lyle. When Greg had splish-sploshed his way into the chapel wearing only flip-flops, shorts and a Hawaiian shirt, she'd known for certain then that she and his father had made the right decision: Bicycle Boy was better off not knowing his father.

'And now comes the difficult bit. I think it's best if you return to America and forget all about Lyle. There's no role for you to play in his life. He's started to look to Ben as a father now and I want to keep it that way. Ben wants to adopt him.

'And I don't want your money, either, if that's what you're thinking. I wouldn't have been able to manage in the early days without your father's generosity, but I don't need the money now. Ben and Lyle had already agreed that his contribution would end on the day he married me.'

Although Greg had pretended to be hurt by the idea and accept Gillian's suggestion only reluctantly, he'd felt an overwhelming sense of relief. The entire proposition was music to his ears. Of course, he'd apologised to her, admitted that his past behaviour was inexcusable, but had also tried to mitigate his guilt by telling her he hadn't known anything. If his father *had* told him, he would have returned home and stepped up to the plate.

Needless to say, he was lying. If not honest with Gillian, he was at least honest enough with himself to know that without an extradition order he would never have returned to England. He was glad his father had kept him in the dark about Bicycle Boy and assumed the responsibility that should have been his; forever grateful that his father had allowed him to forge a life in America unencumbered.

He looked at his watch and realised he'd forgotten to call Billy. He kept the conversation short, gave his brother only the barest bones of the story and told him he'd explain the full situation later.

He took another sip of the whisky and thought of Gillian. He was glad they'd left on amicable terms. She'd even suggested he return to the salon for a trim before he went back to America. 'It will be on the house,' she'd smiled. 'We can't have you going back to America with all those split ends!'

He'd forgotten just how striking a girl Sudge Diamanti had been and realised he was still attracted to her. She was, however, unattainable – she'd made this more than clear to him – and this, no doubt, was a part of the attraction. But what if he did manage to attain her affection and walk back into her life, how long would it be before he'd tire of the relationship and walk out of it again? He had no idea. There were no guarantees in life. It was a chance he could never afford to take, and a chance that Gillian would never give him.

He thought of Cyndi. What would he do if she told him *she*

was pregnant? Would he marry her, settle down and become a family man at long last? Without having to think too hard about it, he quickly realised he wouldn't. He'd suggest she have an abortion, stand by her during the ordeal and then...

And then... after a suitable period of time, he'd move on.

It was what he always did.

Fire

Greg was surprised to find his father already in the dining room when he returned to the house. 'You're a bit early, aren't you, Dad?' he said.

'I think you'll find it's you that's late,' Lyle said, looking at his wrist.

There was no watch there. It was strange, he thought, how old habits didn't die with a person. He shifted his view to the carriage clock on the mantelpiece.

'Four minutes past eight,' he said. 'You're four minutes late.'

'I'm sorry, Dad, I didn't realise the time. I stopped off for a curry on the way home.'

'On the way home from where?'

'Gillian Diamanti's house,' he replied nonchalantly, and then watched as his father looked away and repositioned himself in the chair.

'You know then?' Lyle said. 'You know about the boy?'

'I do now, but I went there thinking he was *your* son.'

'My son?' Lyle chuckled. 'I'm flattered you thought that, lad, but why my son?'

'Because of the standing order you paid Gillian, because of the way you pretended not to know it was her at your funeral, and because... well, because the boy looks just like you.'

'He also looks like you, if you hadn't noticed. And the boy's got a name, Greg. You should call him by it.'

'That's the other thing – he has your name!'

Lyle beamed. 'I was cock-a-hoop when Gillian called him that. It really made my day. I could have died happy that night.'

'And £36,000 the richer,' Greg said. 'Why did you never tell me I had a son?'

'Do you want the truth?'

'Of course, I want the truth, Dad. Why did you keep him a secret from me?'

Lyle adjusted the dress around his groin and then spoke to his son matter-of-factly.

'I thought there was a good chance you'd screw his life up, Greg – screw up Gillian's life too while you were at it. I didn't want to take that risk. You weren't a nurturing person in those days and you did daft things. I was forever having to get you out of trouble. I just did what I always did and cleared up the mess after you. It was force of habit as much as anything.

'But I'll tell you one thing: it was the best mess of yours I ever did have to clear up. My life changed for the better when Gillian and Lyle came into it. She's a lovely girl and that boy of hers – my grandson – well: he's just the nicest kid you're ever likely to meet. I was glad to help them.'

'You didn't think that was my responsibility?' Greg asked.

'Of course I thought it was your responsibility!' Lyle snapped. 'But I also knew that you'd do everything possible to side-step it. Apart from that, you'd just gone to live in America. How would it have helped anything if I'd dragged you back here? It would have ruined your life as well as Gillian's, and it was easier for me to fix just the one life. Besides, I thought I owed it your mother.'

'My mother? Why did you think that?'

'Because she always had high hopes for you, Greg. Always thought you'd do something special with your life. She loved both you and Billy, but she loved you in a different way. If a parent can have favourites, then you were hers. I did it for your mother as much as I did it for you – if you can understand that. I didn't want her to be disappointed… anyway, did you see the boy? And how did you and Gillian get along?'

'I saw Bi… Lyle, but we never spoke or anything. He smiled at me though, and I think I left Gillian on good terms. She's promised to cut my hair before I go back.'

'She'll probably shave your head!' Lyle laughed.

'You really think so?' Greg said, alarmed by the idea.

'No, but she's got some fire in her, lad. It's probably that Italian blood running through her veins. Are the two of you going to keep in touch?'

'I don't know, Dad. I'm not sure there's much point. Gillian doesn't want me to play any role in Bi… Lyle's life, and she said that Ben was hoping to adopt him.'

'He's a good one, is Ben. Solid as a rock. I liked him the first time I clapped eyes on him. I was supposed to give her away at their wedding, did she tell you that?'

'Yes, she told me. She got upset just talking about you. She loved you a lot, Dad – thought of you as a father as well as a friend.'

Lyle smiled sadly. 'Are you mad at me, son? Annoyed with me for not telling you about them?'

Greg was silent for a moment, thinking.

'No, I'm not mad at you, Dad. I should be, but I'm not. A decent person would be mad at you, but I'm not that person. You know that as well as I do. The truth is I'm thankful to you for what you did. I'm glad you didn't tell me. But I'm going to do something for Gillian and Lyle now – if Gillian will let me, that is.

'I figure it this way. You've given Gillian £36,000, and this is money I should have given her. When we sell the house, I'm going to deduct that amount from my share of the proceeds and give it to Billy. In the circumstances I think that's only fair, and it will help him if he decides to start his own business. The rest of the money I'll give to Gillian to keep in trust for

Lyle. I'll probably ask Billy to arrange things so it looks as though you've left him the money and that way she won't be able to refuse it. What do you think of the idea?'

'I like it, Greg. I like it a lot. Thank you.'

'It's me that should be thanking you, Dad. Thanks for taking care of them… thanks… well, thanks for everything.'

The day of Lyle's last night on earth dawned. The sky was overcast, rain threatened and Greg was unsure what to do. There was, in fact, little for him to do. The house was now decorated and ready for market, and the problems that had brought his father back to earth were in hand. This time next week, Greg reflected, he would be back in Texas.

The day passed slowly. He made breakfast, washed plates, read a book, lay on the settee, made lunch, washed plates, tidied the house, fell asleep, listened to the radio, made dinner, washed plates, and then kicked his heels until his father appeared.

Lyle had pulled out all the stops that evening and was wearing a midnight blue ruched ball gown. The mink stole was again draped over his shoulders and his old corduroy cap perched on his head.

'This is it then, lad. The big night. I'm a bit nervous, to tell you the truth. That Big Dipper all over again. And then what? It's the not knowing. I'm going to miss the loft. What did you have for your dinner?'

'I just boiled some eggs, Dad. I wasn't all that hungry.'

'I used to like eggs,' Lyle said. 'Liked them runny though and not hard. I liked dipping pieces of bread into them. We called the bread "soldiers".'

'I remember, Dad. That's what Billy and I still call them. Katy calls them that, too. Would you like to listen to some music?'

'I don't think so, but thanks for asking, lad. I know Gilbert

& Sullivan isn't to your taste. I wish you liked good music, though.'

Greg remembered the times his father had knocked on his bedroom door and told him to turn his music down: 'It's just noise, Greg. There's no melody to it. You'll have Mrs Turton banging on the wall.'

'I'm glad we got to see each other again, Greg. Glad we had the chance to talk. When you're alive you think you have all the time in the world to talk, but you don't. You put off things you should say and then all of a sudden it's too late to say any of them. I'm not sure I ever told you this when I was alive, son, but I love you – and make sure you let Billy know how much I loved him too.'

Greg swallowed hard, smiled at his father and then silently nodded his head. Nodding was easier than talking at this moment.

'And thanks for taking care of Billy and Uncle Frank's problems,' Lyle continued. 'At least I can return to wherever it is I'm returning to feeling a little easier about things. Banks, feet – who'd have thought it? What an odd family we are.

'What is it they say: you can choose your friends but not your family? Well, I wouldn't have traded any of you. I married the best woman in the world and had two of the finest sons. And I got to have Gillian as a daughter and Lyle as a grandson. I've been a lucky man, Greg. The only regret I have is that I never had more time with your mother.

'I knew people who travelled the world and took in its wonders, saw things I never saw – but I didn't envy one of them. As far as I was concerned, there was no greater wonder than coming home from work at night and finding your mother in the house. She always took my breath away.

'When she was thinking of marrying me her friends advised against it. They told her the age difference was too great. They said it wouldn't matter in the early years of the marriage but that later it would, and that by the time she was fifty I'd be almost seventy and we'd be living in different worlds. I always thanked God she ignored them.

'The funny thing though, is that no one advised me one way or the other. No one said: "Look Lyle, what happens if Mary dies when you're fifty-four and leaves you to bring up two children on your own?" If they had, I'd have ignored them too and still married your mother. We only had thirteen years together, but they were the best thirteen years of my life. I hope you get to marry a woman like Mary, Greg, settle down and have a couple of kids like you and Billy. There's no joy to life in growing old alone.'

'I'm not sure I'd want a son like me, Dad,' Greg said. 'If I did, I'd probably tie him to a chair until it was time for him to leave home. Anyway, I'm not alone. I've never been alone.'

'You might have people around you, Greg, but it's not the same thing as I'm talking about. What do they say about a person being alone in a crowded room, and then there's that story of the grasshopper and the ant...'

'Jesus, Dad, what have you been doing in the loft? Reading a book of clichés?'

Lyle smiled. 'There's truth in clichés, lad. People underrate them. Anyway, let's change the subject. I don't want to argue with you on my last night. What are you going to do with your time before you go back to America?'

'I'm taking Uncle Frank and Billy to the seaside. We're planning on going to The Gap – you know, where we went for holidays when we were small – and staying overnight in one of the resorts.'

'I don't know about the resorts, but I think you'll find The Gap will have changed. The coast there was always unstable, and from what I've heard the bungalow we stayed in disappeared over the cliff...'

Lyle suddenly started to flicker and Greg glanced at the

clock. It was eight-fifteen. And then he remembered – that had been the time his father had first appeared to him twenty days ago.

'I'm going, lad. I can feel it,' Lyle said, slightly panicked. 'I love you, Greg. Always did. One… one last thing…'

The flickering intensified and Lyle's voice grew weaker. Greg sprang to his feet and moved closer to his father.

'What is it, Dad? What are you trying to say?'

He strained to hear the words.

'Be careful how you cross the roa…'

And then Lyle was gone. All that remained in the chair was the crumpled dress, the stole and the flat corduroy cap. Greg took the cap in his hand and clenched it, stroked the worn corduroy and started to wail.

'That boy!' Mrs Turton muttered, the glass to her ear. 'Thank goodness Barry doesn't do drugs.'

For the first time since returning home, Greg woke up in the house alone Saturday morning. He felt sad, indescribably sad, sadder even than the day he'd first heard of his father's death. It had all happened so quickly. There had been no time to say goodbye. His father had just disappeared. But his father knew – knew that he loved him. He was pleased he'd told him this.

He made coffee and then went to the garage for the stepladders and a torch. He carried both back to the house and positioned the ladders on the landing underneath the loft hatch. He pushed the square piece of wood upwards, slipped it to the side and then hauled himself into the void. He shone the torch and saw his mother's dresses folded neatly in a corner. Mindful to keep his weight on the joists, he carefully retrieved them and dropped them to the floor below.

He then returned to the garage for a can of petrol and took the container and dresses to the bottom of the garden. He put the first of the dresses in the old metal dustbin his father had used for burning twigs, doused it with petrol and struck a match. There was a whoosh as the petrol ignited and the material burst into flames. He waited until the dress burned away and then threw in another, and then another and another until all his mother's dresses had been consumed by the fire.

He went back to the house for the mink stole and carried it down the garden. It was soft to the touch, luxuriant and in many ways too good to burn. It had, however, been his father's wish that the stole be destroyed and Greg was now the dutiful son. It cheered him to know, however, that Jean would never have the pleasure of wearing it.

He slowly lowered the garment into the dustbin and waited for it to catch fire. Instead of burning, however, the fur only smouldered and thick smoke started to fill the garden. He carefully added more petrol, poked the stole with a stick and then stretched out on the lawn and closed his eyes.

He fell asleep and dreamt his arm was being shaken by someone calling his name: Mr Bowman, Mr Bowman. He woke up and was astonished to find a policeman doing the exact same thing: 'Mr Bowman, Mr Bowman.'

'Well I'll be damned,' Greg said. 'I was just dreaming of you.'

There were two policemen in the garden: one standing over Greg and one peering into the dustbin.

'Are you Gregory Bowman?' the one standing over him asked.

'Yes, is there a problem? Has something happened?'

'It appears so, Mr Bowman. We're in receipt of information that leads us to believe you're illegally burning a dog.'

Greg turned to Mrs Turton's house and saw the curtains twitch.

10

Journey

Sunday passed, as Sundays always do: a day of meaning for some, a day of no meaning for others.

While Barry, Diane and Mrs Turton went to church and congratulated themselves on being Christians, the Collards drove to a country pub and ordered Toad in the Hole.

While The Reverend Tinkler spoke of Jesus' Sermon on the Mount and the Beatitudes, Uncle Frank listened to Planet Rock and detached a company of soldiers to Indian Territory.

While Jean and Katy sang hymns and bowed their heads in prayer, Billy – supposedly catching up on a backlog of paperwork – visited DIY stores and compared the prices of paint, brushes and rollers.

While Betty Halliwell sat in a private hospital room reading verses from the Bible, Syd Butterfield tinkered with the engine of an old Wolsey 680 – fourteenth hand and a collector's item – in the garage now heated by Lyle's electric fire.

And while Gillian Diamanti prepared lunch for the cyclists in her life, Greg Bowman stayed in bed and read the newspaper.

It was his first day of rest since returning home, a respite that lasted until seven the following morning when the doorbell unexpectedly rang.

'Sorry to wake you up so early,' Billy apologised, 'but I had to leave the house at six.'

'Six? Why six?' Greg asked, slightly disgruntled that Billy had woken him so early. 'Uncle Frank isn't expecting us until ten.'

It was, Billy explained, because Jean was under the impression he was spending the week in Scotland, and whenever he made a business trip to Scotland he always left the house at six in the morning. He was a man of habit and his wife was aware of this; to have changed routine would have aroused suspicion and his situation was already complicated enough without Jean getting wind of it.

'Anyway, go back to bed and I'll make breakfast. Toast and coffee okay?'

'There's no bread left,' Greg said wearily. 'There's some cereal in the cupboard, but I'm not sure there's enough milk for two.'

'I've already eaten, Greg. All I want is a cup of coffee and I can drink that black.'

At 8:30am, Greg was woken for the second time that morning by his brother. He propped himself against a pillow and accepted the bowl of cereal Billy handed him.

'Is it okay if I massage your feet while you eat? I'm seeing Dr Haffenden on Wednesday and I need to get some practice in.'

Greg nodded, consoling himself that only three more days of this weirdness remained.

'I don't know how you can eat that stuff,' Billy commented as he watched Greg spoon the cereal into his mouth.

'I like it. It keeps me regular,' Greg replied.

'I don't need anything to keep me regular,' Billy sighed. 'Life does that. It makes me nervous.'

'It'll be different once you get this foot thing sorted out,' Greg assured him, uncertain if he was telling him the truth or not. 'Who knows, you might even end up having to order All-Bran by the truck-load.'

'I doubt it. It's not just the podophobia, Greg: I worry about everything. I always have done. I'm looking forward to getting old and retiring, getting to the stage of life where no one expects anything of me anymore and I can just sit in an armchair and watch television all day. I don't know how you manage to be so laid-back the whole time. You don't even seem fazed knowing you have a son.'

'What would be the point? It happened. I can't do anything about it now. Besides, Dad took care of it.'

'But wouldn't you like to know Lyle? You know… now that you know he's your own flesh and blood and everything. If it was me, I'd feel… well… sort of obliged to do that.'

Greg thought for a moment. 'No. What would be gained? I think the boy's happy not knowing who I am – and Gillian certainly is. And, if I'm honest, I'm happy with that situation too. I don't want to become a father, not yet anyway – maybe never. I'll make sure he's okay financially, but that's where my involvement… ouch! That hurt! I've got a blister on that toe.'

Billy apologised and stared at the blister unflinching. No doubt about it: he was definitely making progress.

'Do you mind if I say something?' Greg said, not waiting for Billy to reply before saying it. 'I think you want people to like you too much. You're always trying to please others instead of yourself. You shouldn't give a shit what people think of you, whether they like you or not. Worry about yourself and leave others to worry about themselves. The world takes care of itself, Billy. It always has and it always will. Live by those rules and you'll be constipated in no time. Ha!'

Billy smiled but said nothing. Somehow he couldn't imagine living with his brother's trail of wreckage on his conscience. He wished, however, that he could.

He finished massaging Greg's feet and waited downstairs

while his brother washed and dressed. He checked the windows to make sure they were latched, tried the handle of the backdoor to make sure it was locked and retied his shoelaces. Eventually Greg appeared carrying a small holdall that had belonged to their father and indicated he was ready to leave. Billy watched to make sure Greg locked the front door properly and then climbed into his car.

'What kind of mood do you think Uncle Frank will be in knowing he's going on holiday?' Billy asked.

'His usual one,' Greg smiled. 'We could be calling to tell him he'd just won a million pounds on the Premium Bonds and he'd still find something to grumble about. He'd tell us that the money he'd spent on Premium Bonds over the years would have earned him more interest in the bank and that we were short-changing him.'

Uncle Frank was already waiting for them by the gate when they arrived, a plastic grocery bag in his hand.

'What have you got in the Sainsbury's bag?' Billy asked.

Uncle Frank checked the contents carefully: 'Pac a Mac, pyjamas, toothbrush, tube of Euthymol.'

'You're going on holiday and you're taking your things in a Sainsbury's bag?'

'Of course I am. You don't think I'm going to walk into a hotel carrying a plastic bag from the Co-op, do you? First impressions are important, Billy. You should know that: you're a commercial traveller.'

'I'm a Senior Academic Sales Executive, Uncle Frank,' Billy corrected him.

'It's the same thing,' Uncle Frank rejoined, 'just fancier words. Anyway, what do you think the receptionist's going to think if I walk into the hotel holding a bag from the Co-operative Society?'

Probably the same thing she'll think when she sees you holding a Sainsbury's bag, Greg thought, but saw little point in telling his uncle this. Instead, he took the plastic bag from him and put it in the boot of the car alongside his and Billy's overnight cases.

'What's in that other plastic bag?' Uncle Frank asked.

'Dad's handkerchiefs. You still want them, don't you?'

It was as if Christmas had arrived early. Uncle Frank's eyes lit up and he broke into a broad lopsided smile. 'You bet I do, Greg. I'll look through them while we're driving. It will give me something to do. I presume it's me that's sitting in the back?'

Billy nodded, and Uncle Frank climbed into the back seat muttering something about second-class citizenship.

Rather than drive through the city and cut across country, Billy decided to make for the motorway and connect with a large arterial road that headed north. It was a more circuitous route but faster, and less demanding on the driver. Uncle Frank opened the plastic bag and took out Lyle's handkerchiefs: fifteen white, seven blue, four tartan, one bearing a printed map of London on one side, and another twelve that were still in their original boxes and embroidered with the initial L. He carefully counted them, and then recounted them: thirty-nine.

'I've got sixty-three handkerchiefs now,' he announced proudly.

He replaced them in the bag and shortly closed his eyes. Billy turned up the volume on the radio to drown out his snoring and manoeuvred expertly through the morning traffic. He'd just turned on to the road leading to the coast when his uncle regained consciousness.

'What are you listening to?' he asked.

'Some dumb phone-in programme,' Greg said dismissively.

'It's not dumb: it's interesting,' Billy said. 'I listen to this station all the time when I'm driving. It helps pass the time... they're asking people about their favourite sandwich, Uncle

Frank. The last caller suggested avocado and grape.'

'Avocado and grape? What person in their right mind would put muck like that on their bread? I make sandwiches all the time and I bet no one's mentioned my favourite sandwich. It's a right bobby-dazzler.'

'Why don't you call them, then? You can use my phone, but just make sure you don't mention my name on the air – Jean listens to this station.'

Billy handed his mobile to Greg and Greg, though doubting the wisdom of letting their uncle talk live to the nation, punched in the station's number and handed the phone to Uncle Frank.

'Hello… hello… Frank… how long… well quick as you can then… seventy-nine…

'They've got me on hold,' Uncle Frank whispered. 'I'm on next.'

Two minutes later, the presenter of the programme announced that they had Frank, a senior citizen, on line two. 'Hi, Frank, you're through to Pete on the nation's favourite talk radio station. Good to talk to you, old buddy. Tell me: where are you calling from and what's your favourite sandwich?'

'I've no idea where I'm calling from, Pete: I've just woken up. I'm in a car somewhere and I can see some cows… and we've just passed a big tree…'

'You haven't been kidnapped, have you, Frank?' the presenter chortled. 'Do I need to call the police?'

'Stop talking daft, Pete. Of course I haven't been kidnapped. Do you think a kidnapper would let me use his phone and call a radio station? Now, do you want to hear about my sandwich, or not?'

'I'd love to, Frank. I'm sitting here with bated breath and salivating at the very thought. So tell me, old buddy, what *is* your favourite sandwich?'

'Cheese!' Uncle Frank said exultantly.

There was a short silence as the presenter absorbed the import of Frank's submission. 'Cheese? Cheese and *what*, Frank?' he asked eventually.

'What do you mean cheese and *what*? You don't need to put anything with cheese. That's the whole point of a cheese sandwich – it's made from cheese!'

The presenter made some remark about having tapped into a rare vein of imagination in Frank, and then asked his old buddy if he had any other nuggets he'd like to share with the nation.

The presenter's sarcasm hadn't escaped Uncle Frank and the old man bristled: 'Yes I do, Pete: you're a bloody pillock and with very little effort you...'

At this point, Greg grabbed the phone and Billy changed the station.

'I hadn't finished talking!' Uncle Frank protested. 'And I don't like this music, either. I want to listen to something else.'

'Tough!' Greg and Billy said in unison.

They drove through countryside that Greg identified with home: neatly trimmed hawthorn hedges, verdant fields and stands of tall sycamore trees; ancient stone market towns, picturesque villages, castles and duck ponds. His memory was selective, rose-tinted and as accurate as the painting on a chocolate box. He forgot about the chimneys and factories, the rows of back-to-back terraced houses and the littered streets.

Billy seemed to read his thoughts. 'It's beautiful here, isn't it? I don't think I'd ever want to live in another county, never mind another country. Don't you miss not being here?'

'Sometimes, but not often. I've lived in America for almost as long as I lived in England and I feel more at home there now. I like Texas – or at least the part of Texas where I live. The climate's a hell of a lot better and there's a beauty to the arid landscape. You ought to come out and visit sometime?'

'I'd like to – and I know Katy would. But I think I'd have a hard time getting it past Jean.'

'Don't tell her then and just come on your own. Tell her you're going on a business trip to Scotland or Denmark. You've had plenty of practice at that.'

'Very funny, Greg. Remind me to laugh, will you?'

'Uncle Frank's coming out next year. We're going to Montana. You could come with him and tell Jean I've asked you to escort him. He'll need someone to keep a rein on him if he wants to get through immigration. What do you think, Uncle Frank?'

'I think I'd like to have been a dog,' Uncle Frank said absent-mindedly.

Greg and Billy looked at each other.

'Why a dog?' Greg asked.

'Because if I was a dog I could eat meat everyday and sleep in front of the fire. And I could bite people and run off and piss in the street whenever I wanted to and not worry about being caught short.'

'I don't think you'd want to be a dog, Uncle Frank,' Billy said. 'There's a good chance someone would have you put down, especially if you bit people. I know Betty certainly would.'

'She'd be the first person I'd bite,' Uncle Frank said. 'She and her... oh, bloody hell fire! All this talk about pissing's made me want to go to the toilet. Stop the car will you, Billy? Soon as you can, lad.'

'You'll have to wait a minute, Uncle Frank. There's a car right behind me and there's no hard shoulder. I'll pull over as soon as I can.'

Uncle Frank started to fidget and drum on the back of Greg's headrest. 'Blood and sand, Billy, I can't hold off much longer and these are my only trousers. You've got to stop... now!'

Billy turned on the indicator and started to slow down. The car behind honked its horn and then overtook him, the driver's middle finger raised. Billy eased the vehicle on to the verge, careful to avoid the potholes, and then stopped. Uncle Frank fumbled with the door handle and scrambled out. It took less than a minute to relieve himself.

'And that's another thing about dogs,' Uncle Frank said, once he was back in the car. 'They don't have to wear trousers!'

Revelation

They arrived at the small village close to The Gap and looked for a sign posting the cliffs. After a couple of false starts, they drove down a narrow lane and parked on an area of rough ground where the track ended, close to the entrance to a large holiday village crammed with caravans and chalets.

Neither Greg nor Billy was sure of their surroundings. Certainly there'd been no caravan park in the area when they'd stayed at The Gap, and now there appeared to be no clear descent to the beach. Greg climbed out of the car and walked to the far end of the uneven land, and then disappeared from sight. He returned after about five minutes.

'We're at the right place,' he confirmed, 'but we'll have to be careful. It looks like there's been an earthquake down there.'

Greg hadn't been exaggerating. The concrete slipway that led to the beach – built more for the purposes of gravel extraction than tourism – had been ripped apart and torn into two foot thick slabs. The wall that had retained the slipway had all but disappeared and huge blocks of concrete and masonry now littered the beach. The soft boulder clay of the reddish-brown cliffs had eroded dramatically and the structures that had depended on its stability crumbled: the ramp, the WWII military defensive positions and the holiday bungalows.

They made their way slowly, Uncle Frank sandwiched between his two nephews. Sometimes Greg took his arm, other times Billy his hand and, on occasion, both held on to him. It took them fifteen minutes to descend to the shore, but they arrived safely.

The beach was as magnificent as both Greg and Billy remembered. The tide was out and the sands of the crescent-shaped bay reached far into the distance. They walked past children paddling in pools, playing games and clambering over eared and lozenge pillboxes that had fallen from the cliff. They passed grown-ups sitting in chairs, sunbathing on large beach towels and scouring the clay for fossils: ammonites, belemnites, corals and molluscs.

The sky was azure and cloudless, the sun smiled brightly and knighted them with its warmth, and a gentle breeze carried the scent of the waves to their nostrils. It was a day made to order, a day saved up from yesteryear for a special occasion, a day when no terms and conditions applied, a day…

'It's not exactly Llandudno, is it?' Uncle Frank commented.

'It's not meant to be,' Greg said. 'Just enjoy it.'

'What I can't figure out is where the bungalow we stayed in was,' Billy said. 'And that farm – the one we used to go to for milk in the morning – where's that gone to?'

'The farm will be up there somewhere,' Greg said, pointing to the bluffs. 'It was inland from the bungalow and won't have been affected by the erosion. But the bungalow's probably gone. Dad was under the impression it already had.'

'When did he tell you that?' Billy asked surprised.

'A long time ago,' Greg said. 'In one of his phone calls.'

Billy was about to question him more on the subject when his brother's phone rang and Greg walked a short distance away from him and Uncle Frank.

When Greg rejoined them he looked serious. 'Is anything wrong?' Billy asked.

'Not wrong as such – just strange,' Greg replied. 'That was Cyndi. Ever since she decided to have a boob job she's gone all religious. I just don't get it. She goes against God's nature by having implants in the first place, and now she seems to be trying to get back into His good books by preaching at *me*. Do you know what her last words were? "Don't let the Devil lead you astray." Can you believe that?'

'What did you say?' Billy asked.

'I said that unless the Devil was a keen caravaner, he wouldn't even know this place existed!'

'What did she say to that?'

'I don't know: I hung up.'

'She sounds to me like one of those Orange Women,' Uncle Frank said. 'Every one of them has false breasts and they're all either crossing themselves or talking about their special relationship with God. Check her lips when you get back, Greg, and see if she looks like a fish. That's what the symbol for Christianity is – a fish. Orange Women tend to wear religion on their lips rather than their sleeves.'

'I'll do that,' Greg laughed, and then noticed that his brother was trembling. 'You okay, Billy?'

'Something weird's happening, Greg,' Billy gasped. 'I'm having a sort of flashback to when we were kids, seeing things that were here then but aren't here now. There's Mum sitting in a striped deckchair and Dad leaning against a boulder with his trouser legs rolled up and smoking a pipe. And I'm lying on my back and you're playing near a large pipe with water coming out of it.'

'You mean that pipe over there?' Greg asked, pointing to an old rusted pipe jutting from the cliff.

Billy looked at it and made a strange noise. He groaned, fell to his knees and started to hyperventilate. 'This is… this is where it happened… it was you… you're the one that made me the way I am.'

Billy's eyes rolled and then closed, and he toppled face forward into the sand.

'What's wrong with him?' Uncle Frank asked.

'I think he's fainted,' Greg said, carefully turning his brother on to his back and cradling his head.

'He's a bit of a Nancy that brother of yours, isn't he? First it's feet and now it's sewage pipes. That boy needs to toughen up, Greg. He wouldn't have lasted two minutes in the Wild West.'

'He's been living in the Wild West for most of his life, Uncle Frank. He's tougher than you think.'

Of all the places and events in life that Billy might have chosen, it was odd that he'd decided upon childhood memories of The Gap as a focal point for therapeutic relaxation, especially when the location proved to be the very source of the fear that Dr Haffenden was treating him for.

When Billy came round, and after the small crowd of gawkers and well-wishers had dispersed, he sat cross-legged on the sand and told Greg and Uncle Frank about the day that changed his life...

The family, as usual, had gone to The Gap for two weeks of summer holiday. Billy had been seven at the time and Greg three. For much of the first week it had rained and they'd spent the time either making daytrips to nearby resorts or staying in the bungalow and playing games. The second week, however, had been one of glorious sunshine and wiled away on the beach. It was on the last full day of the holiday – the day before they returned home – that the incident occurred.

Billy had been lying on his back sunbathing, his mother sitting in a deckchair reading a magazine and his father leaning against a boulder smoking a bowl of Phillips' Grand Cut. Greg, however, had wandered off and was splashing in water spilling from a large pipe – something both boys had been forbidden to do. (It appeared that even at this age Greg was unwilling to take direction from others.)

The pipe conducted sewage and wastewater from the bungalows to the sea and at high tide was hidden from sight. When the tide ebbed, however, the pipe was exposed and waste matter pooled beneath it. Greg was already ankle deep in the mire when Lyle spotted him, and had then ignored his father's exhortations to leave the ooze and wash his feet in the sea. It was only after Lyle had made a beeline for him that Greg had skipped out of the sludge and zigzagged his way to where his brother was sunbathing. 'Don't go near Billy! Don't even touch him!' Lyle had shouted. 'Mary, get Greg! Quick as you can, love.'

Getting out of a deckchair quickly, however, had never been on the cards, and Lyle's entreaties not to do something only put an idea into Greg's head that previously hadn't been there. He'd stood by Billy and stared tauntingly at his approaching father and then, just as Lyle reached to grab him, raised his foot and wiped it slowly and deliberately over his brother's face. Everything that had lodged on Greg's foot – smell, secretions and excrement – now rested on Billy's face: in his mouth, in his nostrils, in his eyes and in his hair.

Billy, unable to breathe through his clogged nose and with an unpleasant taste in his mouth, had pushed his brother away and jumped to his feet. He'd snatched the nearest towel and blown vigorously, and then spat the contents of his mouth on to the sand. All he could smell was shit and all he could taste was shit.

Lyle had quickly washed Billy's face with Coca-Cola – the only liquid to hand – and then tried to console his sobbing son. But Billy was as deaf to his words as he was oblivious to the wasps now buzzing round his head: he heard only the voice and words of his mother as she remonstrated with Greg: germs, feet, diseases, feet, suffocation, feet, blindness, feet, hospital, feet, tetanus shots and feet. Feet, feet, feet!

And so, the seeds of Billy's podophobia were planted.

'This would never have happened if you'd gone to Llandudno for your holidays like I did,' Uncle Frank said.

'Will you stop going on about fucking Llandudno, Uncle Frank? You're not helping!'

'It's not my job to help,' Uncle Frank countered. 'You caused the problem, not me! It strikes me you have a lot to answer for, lad.'

'He does, Uncle Frank,' Billy said unhelpfully. 'It's not just my life he's ruined. He got a girl pregnant before he went to America and he's got a fifteen-year-old son. And he wasn't three when that happened!'

It took them almost thirty minutes to climb the cliff, and it was left to Greg to manage their ascent. Uncle Frank was naturally infirm and now, as a consequence of reliving *the day that changed his life*, so too was Billy. Uncovering the cause of his phobia would benefit him enormously in the long term, but its immediate effect had been to drain him of all physical power and, judging from the occasional sob, also a fair amount of emotional strength.

It was also left to Greg to drive the car to their overnight destination, Billy deciding it would be safer if he rested on the backseat. Uncle Frank, now promoted to the front passenger seat – or shotgun position, as he called it – was given responsibility for reading road signs, a duty he performed conscientiously for five minutes before falling asleep.

The hotel Greg had chosen was close to the harbour and in the shadow of a large rocky promontory topped by the ruins of an old castle. He parked in a bay reserved for guests and then unceremoniously roused his sleeping passengers, whose snores had been irritating him for most of the journey.

He and Billy walked into the hotel carrying overnight

bags and Uncle Frank his plastic carrier bag. They signed the register, took their keys and climbed the stairs to the second floor. The rooms were sea-facing and pleasantly spacious, en suite with baths *and* showers, but sadly, as far as Greg was concerned, no air conditioning.

Greg looked at his watch and suggested a stroll before dinner. Uncle Frank licked his lips and agreed: he wanted an ice cream; to his way of thinking there was no point going to the coast if they didn't eat ice cream. Billy, however, demurred and said they should go without him: he needed to rest and regain composure. Despite the tough-love urgings of his uncle to *pull himself together* and *not be a wet lettuce*, Billy stood his ground, and Greg and Uncle Frank – a person who would never be invited by the Samaritans to man a phone line – left without him.

The resort bustled with holidaymakers and was a lot more pleasing to Uncle Frank than The Gap, which he now likened to a deserted quarry. They walked down to the harbour and looked at the boats – fishing trawlers, privately owned yachts and pleasure steamers – and then moved to the promenade. They passed deckchair renters, seaside rock vendors, bought large cornets of soft ice cream and descended to the crowded beach. They took off their shoes and socks and paddled in the sea for a time, and then found an empty space and sat down. Seagulls hovered, scavenged and screeched, and Uncle Frank considered adding them to the Tombstone List – the world, he told Greg, would be a better place without them. He asked Greg about what Billy had said: had he got a girl pregnant and was it true he had a child? Greg told him the story.

'And how old were you when this happened, lad? Twenty-one? You were having sex with girls when you were only twenty-one? Is that normal these days? By heck! I'm seventy-nine, Greg, and I still haven't had sex. If I'm not careful I'm going to die a virgin.'

He fell silent, suddenly saddened by the thought, and Greg felt for the old man. He squeezed his uncle's puny arm, told him there was still time and that he should never give up hope, even though he himself was now of the opinion that sex was overrated. Uncle Frank continued to look rueful, doubting his nephew's words and thinking of the life he'd never lived. Greg suggested they dust the dried sand from their feet and put their socks and shoes back on. He then helped his uncle to his feet and they continued on their way.

'Donkeys!' Uncle Frank suddenly exclaimed, pointing to a small drove tethered close to the esplanade, and instantly brightening. 'I haven't had a donkey ride in years. Come on, lad: let's get some practice in before we go to Montana.'

'We can't, Uncle Frank: the donkeys are off limits to us. Look, read the sign: "No Adults. Riders must not exceed 7st or 12 years of age".'

'That's not going to stop me,' Uncle Frank said, continuing his approach to the donkey master. 'If he asks you who I am, just tell him I'm your son.'

Despite Uncle Frank's assertion that he was an eleven-year-old boy suffering from progeria, the donkey master declined his money. Unsurprisingly, the man had never heard of the ageing disease but was savvy enough to know an old man when he saw one. 'Health & Safety, mate,' he shrugged.

'There'd better not be any of that Health & Safety cobblers in Montana, Greg. I'm not going all that way and *not* riding a horse.'

They crossed the road separating the promenade from the commercial strip and walked back to the hotel past shops selling beach balls, buckets and spades, paper flags and novelties; past restaurants selling fish and chips, pizzas, and more fish and chips; past ice cream parlours and more rock vendors; and past noisy amusement arcades with slot machines and funfair claws that never picked up prizes. Uncle

Frank stopped outside a cinema and read the notice.

'We ought to bring Billy to see this,' he said. 'It might cheer him up. It says it's *The Feel Good Movie of the Summer* and *Laugh-out-loud Funny*. It sounds good, doesn't it?'

'That's just shorthand for crap,' Greg said. 'They describe all bad movies that way.'

Farewells

After a brief stop at an old-fashioned sweetshop, where Uncle Frank bought six packets of Fisherman's Friends – good for sore throats and colds, he told Greg – they reached the hotel and Greg went to get Billy. Uncle Frank could see no point in climbing stairs unnecessarily and gave the lozenges to Greg for safekeeping and arranged to meet him in the pub next door to the hotel.

Greg knocked on Billy's door and Billy invited him in. He was relieved to see his brother looking more like his old self and, when asked how he was, Billy remarked that he was feeling remarkably chipper – all things considered.

'It was an exhausting business, Greg, but at least I know now why I'm the way I am – and that it's your fault.'

'For God's sake, Billy, I was three! How many more times do I have to tell you that? I didn't do it on purpose.'

'Oh, I know that, Greg,' Billy said brightly. 'I'm not expecting you to feel guilty about it. What I meant is that, subconsciously, I think I've always known it was your fault and that's why I resented you.'

'I didn't know you did resent me.'

'Maybe *resent*'s too strong a word. I mean, I never begrudged you your success or anything like that. Just the opposite in fact: I was proud of you. But there were times when I felt anger towards you and I could never explain why. It used to worry me. But I understand it now – just like I understand why I'm podophobic. And I'd never have discovered any of this if we hadn't gone to The Gap together. I think it was being there with you that caused the flashback.'

'It's on the house, Billy. No need to thank me.'

'I wasn't aware I was thanking you,' Billy said. 'It was more of an observation. But an odd thought struck me while I was lying on the bed: pipes, which are supposed to connect things, have always driven us apart. I wonder why that is? First it was the sewage pipe, then the drainpipe, and I also remember you smashing my copy of *Mull of Kintyre* into smithereens because you didn't like bagpipes – you still owe me for that, by the way.'

Greg smiled. 'I remember. Oddly enough, it was the only time Dad didn't tell me off for doing something. I wonder what that tells us. Anyway, we need to get moving. Uncle Frank's waiting for us in the pub next door and God knows how many people he's upset by now.'

Uncle Frank had in fact upset no one. Indeed, when Greg and Billy arrived there it appeared that their uncle had made a friend: a strange-looking man with a swastika tattooed on his forehead. 'God in Heaven!' Greg muttered.

He bought drinks and, after letting his uncle know that he and Billy had arrived in the pub, took them to the table where Billy had taken a seat. 'I'll be right with you,' Uncle Frank told him.

'He looks a bit of a rum character, doesn't he?' Billy said. 'Do you think he's a Hell's Angel or something?'

'I've no idea,' Greg said. 'I didn't wait to be introduced.'

Uncle Frank sidled over to the table and sat down. Billy was just about to ask him who the person he'd been talking to was when the man passed them.

'Nice meeting you, Frank,' he squeaked, in a voice that sounded as if it had broken upwards.

'You too, Killer,' Uncle Frank replied.

'Who the hell's Killer?' Greg asked, once the man had left the pub.

'Killer Kilshaw,' Uncle Frank said. 'He's the local rat catcher.'

'How on earth did you fall into conversation with him?' Billy asked. 'You know he's got a swastika tattooed on his forehead, don't you?'

'I'm not blind, Billy, but when I started talking to him he was facing forward and I could only see his profile. I thought he was suffering from Bell's palsy to tell you the truth – that's the reason I started talking to him. I told him not to despair and that his face would sort itself out in a few weeks, but when he turned to look at me the other side of his face was exactly the same. He was all right about me saying it though: I think he thought I was making a joke. Anyway, we got to talking and found we had a lot in common.'

'You haven't got a tattoo of a swastika on your forehead,' Billy pointed out.

'I'm aware of that, you daft hap'orth, but I was in pest control all my life, wasn't I – and that's what he's in. And don't think I didn't tell him about that tattoo of his either. I told him it didn't do him any favours and that a lot of his countrymen had given their lives fighting Hitler and his...'

'Were you in the war, Uncle Frank?' Billy asked. 'I know you never talk about it, but...'

'I was bloody six at the time! How could I have been? None of the Bowmans fought in the war: we were all either too young or too old. Even if I had been old enough though, I doubt the government would have let me go.'

'Why, because you were too small?' Billy suggested.

Uncle Frank looked at his eldest nephew scornfully. 'No, you dimwit – because they'd have classified me as a key worker! How would the government have looked if the troops had come home and found their houses overrun with rats? Anyway, do you want to hear about Killer, or not?'

Billy apologised for his interruptions and Uncle Frank continued.

'He very much regrets having the tattoo on his forehead, if you must know. He said he was impetuous in his youth and ran with the wrong crowd – actually, he used the words *fucking stupid*, but I'm cleaning his conversation up for your benefit, Billy. Anyway, to cut a long story short, he told me that the swastika no longer reflects his political views and hasn't done for some time. He votes UKIP these days and he's saving up to have it removed. He might look the rough sort, but deep down, if you dig deep enough, he's okay. You can't always go by appearances.'

Billy ordered another round of drinks, and by the time they reached the Italian restaurant Uncle Frank was quite squiffy. A waiter brought them menus and Greg ordered a bottle of Chianti. When it came to ordering, Billy and Greg placed theirs straightaway.

'And you, sir: what would you care for?' the waiter asked Uncle Frank.

'I want the world and I want it now!' Uncle Frank replied playfully, quoting a line from a Doors song.

'I'm sure we'd all like that, sir,' the waiter replied straight-faced, 'but in the meantime is there anything more specific you'd care to order – like food, for instance?'

'Egg and chips then,' Uncle Frank replied, without bothering to look at the menu.

'Make that the Cotoletta alla Milanese, will you?' Greg said to the waiter. 'You'll like that, Uncle Frank. It's what I'm having.'

The food was good and the wine drank easily. They ordered another bottle and made toasts – to Lyle's memory, to the Wild West, to Billy's feet, to Montana and to themselves – the Last of the Bowmans.

It was their Last Supper. In the morning, they would drive

home and go their separate ways: Billy would drive to London for his Wednesday morning appointment with Dr Haffenden; Greg would gather his belongings and leave for Heathrow the following day; and Uncle Frank would return to the planet of Rock and the worlds of *Judge Judy* and *The Real Housewives of Orange County*.

Billy waited in the car while Greg went inside the house. Greg asked his uncle to check he hadn't left anything in the car and Uncle Frank emptied the contents of his plastic bag on to the table: Pac a Mac, pyjamas, toothpaste and brush, hotel soaps and shampoos, Lyle's handkerchiefs and the Fisherman's Friends. All was in order.

Greg then put his arms around the small man and drew him close. Rather than shy away – as Greg feared he might – Uncle Frank welcomed his embrace and hugged him back. It was the human touch he'd longed for – the touch that had been denied him through life.

'Thanks for taking me to the coast, lad,' Uncle Frank said. 'Maybe next time we could go to Llandudno for a visit. You'll like Llandudno. And we're still going to Montana next year, aren't we?'

Greg told him they were: they'd ride the range together, buy cowboy boots and cowboy hats, drink in saloons with swinging doors and visit the scene of Custer's Last Stand. It would be the holiday of a lifetime – for both of them.

He kissed his uncle on the top of his head and told him he loved him.

Deep in the folds of Greg's shirt, Uncle Frank raised an eyebrow. Love? What was the boy trying to tell him? That something was wrong? That there was something he wanted to get off his chest? The cogs in his mind started to turn: a diamond stud in his nephew's ear; his preference for tissues rather than handkerchiefs; his unusually white teeth…

He pulled away from Greg and looked up.

'You're not trying to tell me you like musicals, are you, lad?'

There was a For Sale sign outside the house when they returned. While Billy inspected the rooms and made a note of the furniture, Greg boiled the kettle and made coffee. Billy came into the kitchen and told him he'd phone the British Heart Foundation when he got back from London/Scotland and arrange for the house to be cleared. They did it for free, he explained, and it would save them the expense of hiring a professional clearer who would only tell them the furniture was worthless, charge them £400 for its removal 'as a favour to them', and then sell it for twice that amount.

They took their coffees into the back garden.

'They've done a good job,' Billy commented. 'You can see where the crack's been filled, but at least they pebble-dashed over the new cement. With time and a bit of weathering, you won't even know there was a crack. I wonder if Dad knew it was there.'

'I don't know,' Greg said. 'His eyes were bad, but I can't believe he wasn't aware of it. He'd have known it wasn't structural, though. He'd lived in the house long enough to know that. He probably thought we could take care of the superficial stuff – and we have.'

'We have, haven't we?' Billy smiled. 'We worked well together.' He paused for a moment. 'And we're okay now, aren't we? I mean the two of us?'

'I was always okay,' Greg replied. 'You were the problem.'

Billy looked at him with a wounded expression, and Greg started to laugh. 'Of course we're okay, you big lug!' He pulled Billy towards him and hugged him. 'We're more than okay, Billy – we're brothers.'

'Mrs Turton's watching us,' Billy whispered. 'What if she gets the wrong idea?'

'Fuck Mrs Turton,' Greg said. 'She always gets the wrong idea.'

'Just one other thing, Greg: It's no big deal, but you're standing on my foot.'

Greg rose early the following morning. He ran a bath and lazed in the warmth of the water for half an hour and then towelled himself dry. He dressed in his travelling clothes – Bermuda shorts and Hawaiian shirt – and slipped the flip-flops on his feet. He carried his suitcase to the car and returned to the house for one last look, one last smell.

He locked the front door behind him and placed the key under a large stone for Billy to retrieve. He walked up the garden path and released the catch on the wrought-iron gate. He saw Mrs Turton standing at the next-door window and ignored her. She ignored him back.

He left the house with a framed photograph of his mother, and keepsakes that would remind him of his father: Lyle's flat corduroy cap, his mangled toothbrush and the hardened paintbrush. And, at the bottom of his suitcase, wrapped in thick newspaper, the helmet and gasmask his father had retrieved from the loft.

Greg would never see the house again, but he returned to England four months later.

MONTANA

On a hot July morning, a year to the day after Lyle had been laid to rest, a black sedan left the car park of a hotel in downtown Billings and travelled east through the dry sloping prairies of south-eastern Montana. Behind the wheel was Billy, and beside him his now eight-year-old daughter Katy. Greg was sitting in the back, directly behind Billy, and on the seat next to him rested an old leather saddlebag.

Lives had changed over the year.

Billy and Jean, though still living under the same roof, were now separated by a wall: Billy banished to the flat once occupied by Betty, and Betty back in the main house living with Jean and Katy. It was an arrangement borne of convenience and the complicated ownership of Spinney Cottage rather than any desire on Jean's part to remain physically close to Billy. The separation, after all, had been her idea, instigated not because of the circumstances of Billy's resignation from the company – which she still knew nothing about – but because Billy, against her expressed wishes, had set himself up as a painter and decorator.

Although Jean had always looked down on Billy's career in sales, his position had always been masked by the cachet afforded by the word 'publishing'. If asked what her husband did for a living, she would simply reply 'publishing' and leave them to presume whatever they liked, which was usually along the lines of Billy being a commissioner of literary masterpieces. She'd noticed that people were always impressed by her answer and it was obvious, even to her, a person who never read books, that publishing was a profession that carried status.

If she could have described her husband as an artist or a painter – which at one social gathering she had – and be allowed to live behind yet another mask, then their relationship might have survived. But Billy could never be relied upon to give traction to such subterfuge, and she still remembered the above soirée with horror.

That evening, over pre-dinner drinks, she'd explained to one of the guests that her husband was a painter and left the man with the impression – as she'd intended to – that Billy was an artist. Over the dinner that followed, the same man – who was interested in commissioning a portrait of his wife – asked Billy what medium he preferred to work in, an answer he expected to be either oil or watercolour. When Billy had replied emulsion and gloss, the man had stared strangely at him for a moment and then, in a somewhat querulous voice, asked if he *was* or *wasn't* a painter.

'I don't like to blow my own trumpet, Pete – it is Pete, isn't it,' Billy had replied, 'but I like to think of myself as being slightly more upmarket than that: I'm a painter *and* decorator. I also wallpaper.'

That evening Jean died, and so too did their marriage.

For Jean, there was no status whatsoever in being attached to a tradesman, certainly not one who dressed in brown overalls and drove around in a second-hand van, and she decided that life for her would be easier and more pleasant if she just told people that she and her husband, who *had worked in publishing*, were now separated and likely to divorce. She was comforted that these two words – *separated* and *divorce* – had the same effect on people as telling them she had cancer, a condition she'd once read about in *Reader's Digest* and afterwards eaten a four course meal to ease the plight of those suffering from the disease. It was the evening she'd met Billy.

Billy adapted to the situation quickly – too quickly for Jean's liking. His conversations with Dr Haffenden had been wide-ranging and he'd already come to the conclusion that he and Jean had fallen in love with a set of circumstances rather than each other, and that love built on circumstance was no more solid than a bungalow built on the cliffs of The Gap. And Billy's changed circumstances pleased him. He was a free man. He no longer feared feet! He was his own boss doing a job he enjoyed and a job he was good at. He slept in his own bed at night instead of in characterless hotels and saw his daughter every day. He'd made new acquaintances and rekindled old friendships. And he was now free to talk on the phone to the friend he valued more than any other: his younger brother.

Greg, though still single, was surprisingly unattached. He'd broken up with Cyndi shortly after returning from England – two miles from the airport, to be exact. She'd met him at the gate and they'd hugged silently, pecking each other on the lips. But then, in the car, Cyndi had unwisely asked if he'd missed her while he'd been away, and when he'd told her no, had even more unwisely pressed him on the point of love: did he still love her? And his answer was again no. At this point, Cyndi had stopped the car on the hard shoulder of the interstate and told him to get his sorry ass out of her car and walk home.

It would have been better if she'd asked him these questions back at his apartment, Greg later told Billy, who in turn suggested that it might have been better if he'd just lied until they'd arrived there. Certainly, the journey home would have been more comfortable in her air-conditioned car than it had been in the back of the pickup truck that had stopped to give him a lift. 'Live and learn,' Greg had said. 'Preferable to living and not learning,' Billy had replied.

Since then, Greg had dated no one seriously. Without intention he'd found himself thinking of Gillian Diamanti, thinking of Bicycle Boy, and wondering if he was only thinking of Bicycle Boy because he was thinking of Gillian and not because Bicycle Boy was his son. But there'd also been occasions when he'd found himself thinking not of Gillian or Bicycle Boy, but of Lyle Jr: his son, his father's grandson, and the boy who was living testament to his father's love for both of them. But as suddenly as these thoughts came he as quickly brushed them aside. They disquieted him and filled him with feelings safer not to pinpoint. As he'd once forced himself not to think of his mother after she died, he now trained himself not to think of Lyle Jr. It was easier to cope by thinking only of Bicycle Boy and keeping his son at arm's length.

There were times when he was tempted to call Gillian, but every time he picked up the phone he wisely replaced the receiver. He thought of asking Billy to discover her situation: had she married Ben, or had Ben fallen off his bicycle and sustained injuries that had left him with no desire to marry a hairdresser. Billy, he knew, would have willingly obliged him. His brother would have parked his van outside her shop and studiously taken notes of who went in and who came out; he would have observed her movements through night vision binoculars and gone through her rubbish bins while she slept; and, if she'd gone anywhere on foot, he would have followed. Greg didn't doubt that his brother would have executed the task wholeheartedly, but did worry about his brother's discretion. Billy had already proved himself inept as a stalker, so how capable would he be as a detective? And what if he was stopped by the police – how would that pan out? It was safer for both of them, he decided, if Billy wasn't involved.

To rid himself of such a complicated and futile infatuation, Greg threw himself into writing a book on black trade unionists, a subject he'd chosen as much to piss Mrs Turton off, as advance his career – though advance his career it undoubtedly would. It also pissed him off that Barry and Diane had bought their father's house, even though their offer had been closer to the asking price than any other. The Grove, if the other residents weren't careful, was in danger of becoming a Turtondom, where the Law of Barry would prevail: hands chopped off for littering, legs broken for building walls and public lashings for those found guilty of trafficking in scented candles.

Of all the lives that had changed over the year, however, Uncle Frank's had changed the most. It wasn't his expectation of old age or disease that killed him, but an unfortunate alignment of Planet Rock with a Fisherman's Friend.

It happened in early November when Uncle Frank had come down with a cold. The cold ran for three days and three nights and filled thirty of his sixty-three handkerchiefs. On the fourth day it started to dry and Uncle Frank decided to stay in bed until lunchtime. His neighbours were out and he used the opportunity to unplug his hearing aid and listen to Planet Rock with the volume turned up.

When the Anorak Quiz came on that morning – when a listener had sixty seconds to answer rock trivia questions that might win him or her (usually a him) a Planet Rock anorak – Uncle Frank popped a Fisherman's Friend into his mouth and waited for the questions. (In the years he'd been listening to the station, his own top score had been three – and one of those answers had been a complete guess.)

The morning DJ always asked the contestant where he was and what he was doing, and usually the answer was the name of an industrial city and some kind of trade beginning with a P: either plastering, painting or plumbing. On this particular morning, however, the aspirant had answered: 'I'm in the back garden burying a dog, Rob,' and had then burst into tears. It was the funniest thing Uncle Frank had ever heard on the radio and he started to laugh uncontrollably. It was then that the lozenge slipped from his tongue and lodged in his throat. Three minutes later he was dead, forever unaware that the person playing the quiz had scored eight points.

He died a virgin.

Although it had taken Uncle Frank only three minutes to choke to death, it took a further three days for his body to be discovered, and then only because his neighbours had got sick to death of listening to rock music all night. For the first two nights, they'd thought Uncle Frank was just being his usual bloody-minded self, trying to torment them and purposely ignoring their knocks on his door when they went round to complain. After the third night of sleep deprivation, however, they started to wonder if something might have happened to their ornery neighbour and telephoned the police. The door was broken down, the radio turned off and Uncle Frank's body removed to the mortuary.

Against all expectations, there were as many people at his funeral as there had been at Lyle's. The Reverend Tinkler performed the eulogy (one index card) to a congregation of eleven: Greg and Billy; Jean and Katy; Betty (there to confirm Frank's death rather than to mourn his passing); Syd Butterfield, Lyle's best friend and Uncle Frank's intended wheelsman; Uncle Frank's neighbours (there out of guilt rather than sadness); and three members of the police force Uncle Frank had befriended in the days of turning himself in.

It was Greg's idea to have his uncle cremated and the remains shipped to Texas. He'd promised Uncle Frank he'd go to Montana and go to Montana he would. Once the ashes arrived, he transferred Uncle Frank's cinerary remains to the pouches of an old cowboy saddlebag he'd found at an antique shop, and then placed the bag in a wardrobe. There the ashes remained until Billy and Katy arrived that summer, and now, in the back seat of a large black sedan, they approached their final resting place: the Little Bighorn Battlefield National Monument, the place where the Sioux and Cheyenne had wiped out the 7th Regiment of the US Army.

Greg, Billy and Katy, wearing cowboy hats and cowboy boots in honour of Uncle Frank, and taking it in turns to carry the saddlebag, toured the battlefield and memorials for over an hour and then drove to a quiet bluff overlooking the Little Bighorn River. It was here they scattered the remains of their dear departed uncle.

'You're sure Uncle Frank's going to be happier here than in Llandudno?' Billy asked, somewhat late in the day for such a question to have any meaning.

'Uncle Frank's not likely to be happy anywhere,' Greg smiled, 'but the Wild West was always his spiritual home and this place is the nearest thing to it. Besides, he always talked about Custer's Last Stand and, when you think about it, his demise was as untimely as the General's. I think we're doing the right thing.'

When the last handful of ashes had been emptied from the saddlebag and released into the wilds, Greg went back to the car and slotted It's a Long Way to the Top by AC/DC into the CD player.

'Do you think Uncle Frank would prefer to hear Lady Gaga?' Katy asked. 'I'm sure he said he liked her music.'

'Nice try, Katy, but Uncle Frank hated pop music. He was a rock 'n' roller – and this was his favourite song.'

He then pressed the play button and turned up the volume. 'Okay, let's do it! Let's give Uncle Frank his send-off.'

The opening guitar chords split the silence like an axe. The riff was jagged and hypnotic, the cadence taunting. Drums pounded, symbols crashed and a voice honed on Jack Daniels and unfiltered cigarettes started to howl the valedictory words.

Greg flailed his arms, hopped from foot to foot and spun in circles; Katy followed suit, abandoning practised routine for abandoned self-expression; and Billy, the most self-conscious of the three, jumped up and down on the spot and clapped his hands together.

And then the bagpipes chimed in, raucous and sneering; pipes that would have led soldiers into battle and not be seen dead in a *Top of the Pops* studio. The three celebrants whooped and hollered, linked arms and swung each other in circles, wished their uncle was there to see them, wished he was there to dance with them.

The music faded and there was silence. The leather saddlebag was empty, the celebration of Uncle Frank's life over.

The younger brother started to cry and the older brother held him.

'What's Uncle Greg crying for, Daddy?' Katy asked. 'Uncle Frank was *old*, you know.'

From a distance, far far away, Lyle Bowman smiled.

About Us

In addition to No Exit Press, Oldcastle Books has a number
of other imprints, including Kamera Books, Creative Essentials,
Pulp! The Classics, Pocket Essentials and High Stakes Publishing
> oldcastlebooks.co.uk

For more information about Crime Books go to > crimetime.co.uk

Check out the kamera film salon for independent, arthouse and
world cinema > kamera.co.uk

For more information, media enquiries and review copies please
contact marketing@oldcastlebooks.com